PROTECTING HER

Book One in the *Summer Knights* Series

Tracey Gerrard

Copyright © 2024 Tracey Gerrard

All rights reserved.

First published in e-book format by self-publishing via Amazon (Kindle Direct Publishing) in 2024. Tracey Gerrard assets the moral right to be identified as the author of this novel. No part of this book may be reproduced, or stored in a retrieval system, or transmitted in any form or by any means, electronic, mechanical, photocopying, recording, or otherwise, without express written permission of the author, Tracey Gerrard. This book is a work of fiction. Names, characters, organisations, places and events are either the products of the author's imagination or used fictitiously. Any resemblance to any actual persons, living or dead, is purely coincidental.

Imprint: Independently published.

Cover design by Amanda Sheridan using images from Pexels as follows: Sky background – Vinicius Vieira; Couple – Anna Tarazevich; Chess piece – beytlik.

ISBN-13 : 979-8884650633

TABLE OF CONTENTS

    Acknowledgments

1	Meadow	1
2	Meadow	11
3	Meadow	18
4	Kane	23
5	Kane	27
6	Kane	36
7	Kane	44
8	Meadow	52
9	Meadow	65
10	Kane	73
11	Meadow	88
12	Kane	104
13	Meadow	113
14	Meadow	128
15	Meadow	136
16	Meadow	146
17	Kane	159
18	Meadow	167
19	Meadow	176
20	Kane	183
21	Meadow	190

22	Kane	197
23	Meadow	206
24	Kane	213
	About the Author	219
	Other Books	220

ACKNOWLEDGMENTS

I'm always grateful for any support I get so once again, I need to give a huge thanks to my family and friends for their continued support. I'm always blown away with your kind words and encouragement.

A special thank you to Charlie, Lisa, Millie, Little Charlie, Sharon, Sarah, Margaret, Catherine, Angela, Serena, and Vicky. You have all played an enormous part, no matter how big or small, and I couldn't have done it without you all.

I also need to give a special mention to two amazing authors for the support they have given me. Amanda Sheridan author of the *Rapid Eye Movement* Series and designer of this beautiful cover for *Protecting Her*. I can't thank you enough for your help with formatting and getting my manuscript ready to be published. Laura Lyndhurst, author of The *Criminal Conversation Series* for all your advice and support. Thank you, both so much.

And lastly, but by no means least, YOU, the reader. Thank you, I hope you have enjoyed reading this novel as much as I enjoyed writing it. Please leave a review before you go and look out for my next book.

CHAPTER 1

MEADOW

I inhale the sweet scent of jasmine and lavender as I step into the silence of the office. I love this time of day. A tranquil moment before this place becomes testosterone-heavy and the sound of booming voices bounces off the walls.

The room is dark, so I juggle the two trays of baked goods I made for today's meeting in one hand, my laptop case in the other and my bag over my shoulder as I struggle to reach for the light switch. Miraculously I don't drop anything, and once I can see one foot in front of the other, I close the door behind me, appreciating the cheery and welcoming room.

The warm mocha walls matched with the antique dark oak desk and the plush two-seater sofa, I find homely—especially with the sunflower paintings which hang on the wall across from my desk, and the various plants I have situated around this place. It feels warm and inviting, unlike the chrome, greys, and blacks, which in my opinion suggest cold. Just like the office next door and the man that resides there, ten hours a day. My boss. Kane Summer is the epitome of manliness but as cold as Antarctica. He's beauty personified, and he knows it. Women flock to him, surrounding him like seagulls on the seafront. For what? Just a few titbits he throws to them. They hang off his arm while he mingles at various events, hoping they'll be noticed. Some of the women are well and truly noticed. Legs up to their navel, pouty lips and silicon boobs—let's just say there's not a man that wouldn't want one of them in his bed, and if they're out with my boss then that's where they'll end up. Well, not his actual bed, a hotel room just for the night. Believe me, I know.

Not that I've been there myself. Nooooo. However, I have fought off many of them. Endless phone calls, trying to catch his attention but failing miserably in getting a second date—and because I'm the first port of call it's me who lets them down gently. They've even turned up at the office, demanding they have a meeting with him—and of course, because I deal with his day-to-day meetings, it's me who's left to turn them away. Oh, I'm polite and sisterly, informing them what an arse he is, and how they're so much better than the woman who's willing to look needy all because of a man who doesn't give a crap about her. Most of them turn on their stiletto heels and never return, but there is the odd one that does. In that case, I add that his wife is on the rampage, hunting for the floozy who he hooked up with for the night, while the heavily-pregnant Mrs Summer was at home.

The thing is, he's not married. There's no Mrs Summer, fiancée, or girlfriend in his life—but I think if there was then he'd be as faithful as a puppy. I don't know what makes me think that. Perhaps it's the warmth I see in his eyes when he's around his brothers. When he thinks no one is watching him. The way he protects them. Yeah, they fool around, arguing and fighting, that's understandable. With five brothers there's always going to be some sibling rivalry, but most of the time it's in jest. It's comical to witness. I think any man who stands in as a father figure to his four younger brothers from an early age—helping and caring for them with his mother—would make an awesome husband and father. I'd never tell him that though. He'd think I'd gone off my rocker. The only time we interact is when we're going through his calendar, while I'm setting up meetings for him, and sorting through his emails. Most of the time I prefer to deal with Callum or Mason.

I don't even know how it became part of my job to turn away Kane's endless string of one-night stands, because it certainly wasn't in my contract when I was employed at Summer Knights Security. I'm willing to do it though, even if he does blank me most of the time and complain about my fashion sense. He hates my taste in furnishings, but it'll be a cold day in hell before I change it.

The antique desk which he hates so much belonged to my grandfather, who died last year. It was passed down to him from his father, and he'd taken extremely good care of it while using it daily. When I was young, I was always intrigued by its many hidden compartments, and to this day I don't think I've found them all. One day I might have the time to try and discover all the secret little nobs and switches that open them. Who knows what I might find?

The paintings were my grandmother's. She passed away five years ago and left them to me along with the settee, which she kept in the conservatory to sit in there reading whenever she could. I've many fond memories of being curled up by her side, rapt at her gentle voice as she read to me. Her soothing tone would lull me, and I'd end up falling asleep.

When I landed this job two years ago my granddad asked if I'd be able to use his desk. Because Kane was away on holiday at the time I approached Callum, his younger brother who'd employed me—and who's much more approachable, I might add. He was accommodating, said yes to me making the office my own and told me to bring whatever I wanted. He even laughed, along with the other three brothers, Mason, Henry, and Connor. They were all only too aware of what their eldest brother would say about it. However, I'm not one to back down from an argument, so when Kane instructed me to remove the *old tat* from his building, I soon got on my soap box. As the *old pieces of tat* are still here, I won that battle—yet I've lost many too.

I place the lemon cupcakes, an already sliced chocolate fudge cake, and a mix of homemade biscuits in the space behind Vera and Rose. That's Aloe Vera and Rosemary, two more plants I like to keep around this place, hoping their mixed properties of triggering calmness, reducing anxiety levels and combating negativity—as well as their many more enhancing positive vibes—will rub off on the bad-tempered bugger. They don't. Even the ones I've placed around the lion's den haven't helped with his moods and grumpiness. No matter what I do, say or try, I'm still greeted with a grunt and a nod. It's been the same ever since he came back from his holidays and found that I'd been employed as his new secretary. If I didn't need this job, I'd tell him to stick it up his arse. However, I do need it, and I love working with the other brothers—so I put up with his moodiness.

When my grandma became ill, I was only too willing to cut back my hours at my old job so I could help my grandad take care of her. They'd been there for me my whole life, taking care of me since I was six years old after my mum died. Mum and I had lived at my grandparents' house from when I was born—so when she died of a brain tumour, it was inevitable that I'd stay with them. I never knew who my father was and, because I was so young when my mum died, I never found out the reason why, until my grandma told me when I was sixteen. According to her, Mum and Dad had a summer romance, and I was conceived in a meadow—hence the name. As they were both heading in different directions career-wise—my mum into nursing and my father off to the US—they agreed that's all their relationship would be, a two-month fling. Once my father took off, my mother didn't give him a second thought—until twelve weeks later, when she found she was expecting me. Grandma said she did try to contact him but was unsuccessful. The phone number she had no longer existed, and she'd never met any of his friends. It was always just the two of them. So that's the reason I grew up without a father.

As I said, Grandma and Grandad had taken care of me from a very young age. Extremely good care, nothing was too much trouble. They played the part of my mother and father, taking and picking me up from school, attending parents' evening and after-school activities. They made sure I had the best of everything and loved me dearly. That's why, when Grandma became ill, I cut back my work hours. After a short time, and her health worsening, I knew she was too much for Grandad to cope with on his own, so I asked for a long-term leave of absence from my employers. After she died, I gave up work altogether. Grandad never asked, but I hated leaving him alone throughout the day, so I made a conscious decision to hand in my notice. Spending time with him, returning the care and love he'd shown me all my life, felt important and right. It wasn't until the year before he died that I started looking for a new job, and then only because Grandad was sick and tired of me being under his feet. He'd always been a force to be reckoned with and prided himself on his independence—so when he made it clear that he was fine on his own, and that I needed to start looking out for myself, I agreed. I insisted on terms though, that he ate healthily while I was out, and that he'd still go for his daily walk. Our neighbour offered to walk with him, so we were both happy.

I miss my grandparents so much, which is why I'm still living in the home we shared, with happy memories plus all the gifts they bought for me and the possessions they passed on. I'd never sell or get rid of any of them, and if I can keep some at work and at home for as long as possible then all's right with the world.

Switching on my computer, I wait for it to load so I can check my emails. I scroll through hundreds, sieving out anything important and forwarding them to Mr Summer, then I send relevant ones to the departments his brothers head up. I drop a shit load in the recycling bin, then decide it's time to switch on the kettle and set up the office for this morning's meeting.

*

'Good morning sunflower.' Callum's greeting makes me jump, too lost in my thoughts to hear my boss's office door open. I'd come in to set up the room for our usual Monday meeting, to water the plants and make myself a drink. Once I'd finished, I opened the blinds and I've been standing here, taking in the early morning sky while sipping my first coffee of the day, lost in my own little sad world.

Living on my own, with only three real friends who are currently sunning themselves on some hot sandy beach, I get lonely. Louise and her boyfriend are touring Europe for six months. She's only been gone for four weeks, and I miss her like crazy. We Facetime a few times a week but it's not the same as having a girly night in or a Saturday night out clubbing, especially when her boyfriend interrupts us all the time. Then there are Henry and Connor, Mr Summer's two youngest brothers, twins I've known since school. We four hung around together, all through high school. Louise and I met in year seven, sat together and became inseparable. Then Henry and Connor became our good friends in year eight, and that's all it was just the best of friends. When we all went off to college, Louise and I stayed in touch, but we lost touch with the twins, and it wasn't until two years ago that we met up again in a nightclub. We arranged to meet for a catch-up, and that's when they told me about the vacancy, hearing I was looking for a new job. Mr Summer was away on holiday, so it was Callum who interviewed me. He remembered me from the times we'd hang out at their house with his two younger brothers. He offered me the job on the spot, and I've been happy here ever since.

'You grinning idiot,' I say, smiling as I take in the dimple on his left cheek. 'You scared the shit out of me.'

'I know,' he chuckles. 'I saw the light from under the door and I knew it wasn't Kane. I couldn't help myself.' He shrugs his shoulders and moves over to the conference table, where today's treats lie untouched.

'What do we have here?" I don't have time to stop him from reaching over and grabbing one of the cupcakes.

'Jesus, these are better than sex,' he moans around a mouthful. 'You know, if you ever get sick and tired of this place then a bakery shop would be perfect for you.'

'Well thank you for the compliment.' I reach over to cover them up, so they don't go stale and to stop him taking another one. Callum and Mason would wade through the lot in no time if I let them, and I like to save a treat for my boss. He says he doesn't have a sweet tooth, but I know when no one is around he'll indulge in a couple. 'But I can't see that happening anytime soon. I enjoy baking as a pastime when I'm bored. Plus, I know you and your brothers would be upset if I didn't bring in a few delights on a Monday morning.'

'You're too good to us.' He pops the last bite into his mouth. 'How was your weekend?' There's a softness in his voice. Both Callum and Mason are aware I have nobody in my life. No family, no boyfriend, and my only friends are away on holiday. Over the last few weeks, they've invited me out with them and their friends at the weekend and I've declined, because how sad would I look, tagging along with my bosses because I have no friends of my own. They've also asked me to join their regular midweek meet-up at Marlos, for ribs, wings, and drinks with their oldest brother. That sounds more appealing, but only if it were just Callum and Mason. I'm sure Mr Serious wouldn't want me there as much as I wouldn't want to be around him outside of working hours.

I play it cool. 'Oh, you know.' I turn, picking up the tiny silver watering can, pretending I haven't already watered my little gifts to my handsome boss, hoping they'd calm his somewhat temperamental mood. I try to hide my awkwardness and the truth that they all know that I'm a sad case. 'It was a nonstop party. Friday, I went on a blind date. We ended up at my place where we had wild dirty sex until the wee hours. Saturday'—I keep my back turned moving around the desk to the next plant— 'we were at it like rabbits again until midday. When we got hungry, we ordered takeaway, then I spent the evening with him drizzling chocolate on my intimate parts and letting him lick it off while he fed me strawberries.' I hear laughter and I join in, on my over-exaggeration. I'd be happy with just the blind date.

The smile on my face soon drops, hitting the floor with a huge bang when I turn around to see not just Callum but Mason too. He must have heard me explaining my fictional weekend activities because he's standing beside Callum, leaning on his brother's shoulder as he chortles loudly. No—not Callum's. He's leaning on my boss's shoulder. Mr Summer—and while his brothers might find my embellishment of the weekend somewhat amusing, he definitely does not. How do I know?

For one thing, his lips are set tightly in a thin line, and there's a little tick in his jaw. His arms are crossed over his chest, and I swear his nostrils flare. While his whole body language screams that he's not happy, his electric blue eyes shout something else. I'm not sure what it is and I'm not hanging around to find out, because I certainly don't want the wrath of his tongue on a Monday morning.

I avert my eyes, realising we've both been staring at each other way too long, and replace the watering can on the window ledge. I straighten my shoulders. 'Sorry, I was joking around,' I say as I try to move past the three huge men blocking the doorway. 'My weekend was just like me, sad and boring. Good morning, Mason. Good morning, Mr Summer.' I use my most professional voice as Callum steps to one side, giving me room to pass while he bites his lip to stop his laughter from spilling out.

I make it to my desk, letting out a puff of air, then drop into my chair and shut my eyes just as the door slams shut.

'That was hilarious, Meadow. I thought Kane was about to burst a blood vessel.' Mason laughs, standing at the other side of my desk with his hands in his pockets. 'Your face was a picture when you realised we were all there listening.'

'Oh, shut up.' I know that technically I'm employed by these two, and I shouldn't be speaking to any of them like that. But I get away with it because, like the twins, I have a good relationship with Callum and Mason. 'You know I was only joking around, right?'

'Of course,' Callum says. 'However, I don't think our big brother was at all happy hearing you speak that way. You know, you two need to get it on and get whatever it is out of your system before one of you explodes.'

'Excuse me?' Confused, I look from one to the other, both still laughing. 'What do you mean, get it on? Get what out of our system?'

'Jesus. Meadow, you're not that naïve. It's as clear as the sky's blue that you've got the hots for each other.'

'We do not.' I'm quick to answer. The shock of what he's just said must be written all over my face. Yes, I know I have a little crush on my boss. What woman wouldn't? He's got that whole sexy, macho thing about him. He smells of manliness, and his presence encompasses you when he's near. I might get a bit hot and fuzzy when he's close by or when I think of him, but it's only infatuation, something like a schoolgirl crush. I'm sure the feeling isn't reciprocated.

'You keep telling yourself that girl, but we know what we see and it's not just one way,' Callum adds, just as the buzzer sounds and my boss's voice infiltrates the air.

'Meadow, have you forgotten something?' His tone is authoritative, which sends a shiver through my core. Maybe I do fancy him more than I'm letting on, but let's face it, it's never going to happen with us. For one thing, he's a male slut, and I'm just not going there. He's also my boss and my two best friends' older brother. But the main thing is that I can't believe for one minute he sees me as anything but an annoying secretary.

'No, Mr Summer just getting it now.' I put to bed all thoughts of my boss being anything but that—my boss.

'I've forgotten his coffee.' Callum and Mason roll their eyes. 'I'm blaming you two if he gives me any trouble.'

'You do that.' Amusement flickers across Mason's face.

'I want to know why he gets called Mr Summer, and we're called by our first names?' Callum's eyes are wide, and he has that cheeky smirk.

'Because he'—I point at the closed door between our offices, hoping he isn't watching through the one-way glass—'is the authority figure around this place, and you two are not.' I smile sweetly at them, knowing I can get away with it.

'That's fair enough.' They agree, in unison., and then Callum makes to leave.

'I need to check my emails, but all things aside Meadow, don't sit at home bored. You're more than welcome to join us on Wednesday evening and Saturday night.'

'Definitely. We'll have a blast.' Mason agrees.

'We'll see,' I tell them although I know I won't be joining them.

'Okay, we'll be back at nine for the meeting. Make sure his Lordship doesn't eat all those delicious goodies.'

'I'll see what I can do.' They both take off to their office, leaving me with a lot to think about.

I can't see where they get the idea that Mr Summer has a thing for me. He rarely smiles at me, and when he does it's forced—which is a damned shame, because if it's anything like his younger brothers' then it would be a sight to see, and a beautiful one at that. All of them with their naturally straight white teeth and dimples could model any toothpaste advert.

Knowing it won't do me any good to ponder over what Callum said, I bury the thought and set about making his coffee.

He doesn't lift his head from the computer when I walk in, so I quietly place his cup down on the desk. There's no "thank you," and I don't bother to remind him of his manners because he doesn't have any. I make my way back to my desk, and just as I sit down his voice startles me.

'Meadow, can you make sure you have all the updated information ready for our meeting with the council.'

I hate this machine. A present from Callum for his Lordship. One day I'll throw it at him.

The local council's put out a tender for a new security company to cover all council-run events and social gatherings. Summer Knights are in the running for it, but we have competition from two other companies. Luckily for us, we know who they are and what they have to offer, which puts us at an advantage. Not that we need it. This company runs like a well-oiled machine and would probably get the contract without Connor's intervention. He's the only one in the family who doesn't work for the company—well, he does, sort of, when he's not apprehending criminals. He's worked in the police force since he finished his education. He wanted to follow in his eldest brother's footsteps, because he looked up to him so much, and Mr Summer had served as a firearms officer in an armed response team for ten years. He only gave it up when he was shot whilst attending a robbery at a supermarket, and the bullet fired by one of the assailants struck him in the shoulder, hitting the bone. It put an end to his career, as the bone was shattered and had to be rebuilt using pins—but Connor had joined the force anyway.

When he'd gone on a night out with his mates and ended up with some woman, it turned out she worked in the council department that would be interviewing and selecting candidate companies for the contract. How the topic came up I'm unsure, but by the time she realised what she'd divulged it was too late. Not that she can do anything about it—if she were to tell anybody she'd lose her job. It wasn't even Connor who informed his older brother of the conversation. Henry had been privy to it as well, and it was he who passed on the information. Connor wasn't happy, but he let it slide when Callum told him there was nothing wrong with getting a little inside intel on the competition.

'Already on it,' I answer when I hear Mr Summer tapping his pen. 'The files are on your desk, and everything's backed-up on your computer. Mason will have the numbers for our proposal with him.' I hear rustling, as he's probably looking for them. When everything goes quiet, I know he's found them, and ended our call. Rude.

CHAPTER 2

MEADOW

One minute I'm sitting at my desk minding my own business as I organise and file all the documents, I'd been tasked to do by my boss, which he needs for his meeting next week when my chair is spun round and I'm lifted out of it, spun in the air then sandwiched between two, six feet walls of solid muscle.

'Oh my God, you two. Put me down,' I shriek through my laughter. Henry and Connor place me on my feet both looking like bronze gods. 'I didn't hear you come in. When did you get back? Look how tanned you are. I'm jealous,' I tell them both, going in for another hug.

'We got back last night but were too knackered to come over to yours, so we thought we'd come in early to surprise you.' Henry hands me a package with a huge smile on his face.

'What is this?' I ask, knowing fine well what it is. Duty-Free perfume. Armani Because It's You. It's my favourite. 'Aw, you guys, thank you.'

'You're welcome.' He then brings his arm from behind his back and hands me a bunch of yellow carnations. 'Thought they'd brighten up your office.' He bends down and kisses my cheek.

'You didn't need to bring me flowers.' Inhaling their sweet smell, I then give them both another hug, thanking them.

'We missed you. And you missed one hell of a party, girl.' Connor wiggles his eyebrows at me. 'Two weeks of non-stop f**king…'

'Okay, enough,' I chuckle, putting my hand over his mouth. 'I don't need to know all the details.' These two are not just friends, I treat them like brothers, which means I don't need to know all the gory details of what they had gotten up to while they were in

Magaluf.

'I was going to say it was two weeks of nonstop f**king fun.'

'I'm sure you were. Come on I'll put the kettle on.'

'I can't stay long. I'm back at work today. My shift starts in an hour.' Connor gives me an asymmetric smile.

'We'll make it quick. I'm snowed under here, which is why I was in early.' I turn towards my desk and pick up the flowers, knowing that's a lie. Yeah, I have a lot of work to get through but I'm always the first in the building. Nothing or no one to keep me at home or in bed.

Finding a vase for the flowers I set them by the photo I have of my grandparents. Once the coffee is made, we sit at my desk, chatting about their two weeks' holiday.

'Sounds like you had a wild time,' I say, listening to all the shenanigans they got up to with a few of the lads from their old football club.

'We did, although Andrew was an arsehole the whole time.'

'Why doesn't that surprise me.' I had my fair share of that idiot when we all went out one night. Couldn't keep his hands to himself and needed to be taught a few manners.

'Yeah, well let's just say the next time we go on a lad's holiday he won't be joining us.'

'Look at the time, I need to shoot,' Connor says jumping to his feet. 'We'll catch up later when I've finished my shift, if that's, okay?'

'Of course, no problem. I have a lot to do anyway. Listen you're going to be tired this evening let's leave it until later in the week or the weekend. We can go out for a bite to eat and then for a few drinks.' I haven't been out in almost a month. Yeah, I was invited to join Callum and Mason last week, but I declined their invitation. Knowing Mr Summer might be with them, it didn't sit right with me. I struggled with him at work, I wasn't about to show myself up because I would. After a few drinks, I can get a bit—let me just say I wouldn't be able to hold my tongue and would probably give him a piece of my mind for being such a pain in the arse boss.

'Sounds good—Oh shit, no can do. I'm on duty this weekend.'

'Never mind. As I said, it's crazy here at the moment. Your brother's going to be riding my arse all week.'

'Wooh, too much info. Whatever you and Kane get up to in the privacy of your office, we don't need to know.' Henry's blue eyes dance with humour.

'You idiot.' I slap his arm. 'Do I look like your brother's type? I think not.' I don't let them answer because I know they will tell me I'm beautiful and the women Kane knocks around with aren't a patch on me. Plus, I'm still trying to comprehend what Callum said last week and I really don't need these two adding fuel to the fire. I say fire because every time I'm around my boss or he walks into the room, I heat up like a furnace. 'Get to work the pair of you, I'm sick of you already.' I smile, rolling my eyes at them.

'Yeah, I better go make myself useful before Mason comes in. I'm sure he will have left me all of this year's accounts to do.'

Henry and Connor are just about to leave when Callum and Mason stroll in, closely followed by the eldest of the Summer brothers. The office explodes into raucous laughter, male hugging, and a lot of foul language.

Sitting there mesmerized, I'm unable to peel my eyes off the man who normally in the office wouldn't crack a smile but today I get to witness it in full bloom. And it's magnificent.

I've worked with the five of these men for almost two years and although I have known the two youngest since school, and get along famously with Mason and Callum, I feel like I'm intruding on a family get-together. I know they are all close and worry endlessly about each other. I also know the twins were missed, not just by me but by their three older brothers so once I have gained the ability to remove my eyes from Mr Summer's stunning smile, I pick up my bag and sneak out without any of them noticing.

As I make my way across the foyer I see that Liz, who works at customer service, isn't at her desk. She wouldn't be at seven thirty in the morning, she has a life out of this place and doesn't start until nine when she's dropped her young children at school, unlike me who has no one and will arrive here anytime between six and six thirty. I make my way to the lift contemplating putting in the code for the penthouse, where Mr Summer resides, just so I can have five minutes to myself. It's not like I haven't been up there many times. Being the person who collects his Hugo Boss suits and shirts from the dry cleaners, I'm the one designated to hang them in his oversized wardrobe. I don't. I hit the button for the general lift and when it arrives, I press the button for the car park.

I'm on my own time, my hours are eight until five, that is unless I'm asked to come in early or stay late so it's not like I can't get into trouble for not being in the office. Once I'm sat inside my car, I decide to call Louise. I need some girl time, and this is the nearest I can get with her on her travels. If my calculations are right, then it should be after nine in the morning in Belgium, I think that's where she is this week. It rings and rings then goes to voice mail. I leave her a short message and then lean the back of my head on the seat.

At twenty-six years of age, you'd think I'd have a string of female friends whom I could call. Only I don't. At school, I had a bunch of them but once we left, the only ones I kept in touch with were Louise, Henry, and Connor. Then after a year or so I even lost touch with the twins for a good number of years. The colleagues from my last job were nice enough and we all went out on occasion but again once I left there, we didn't keep in touch. As for boyfriends, let's just say that's another lonely subject.

A tap on the window scares the shit out of me and I sit up too quickly, bagging my knee on the steering wheel. 'Ouch.' I rub at it as I peer out, noticing Connor standing there, hands in pockets, eyebrows knitted together.

'You, okay?' He asks when I roll my window down. 'Why did you take off?'

'Needed to make a personal call.' I wave my phone at him not wanting to get into a discussion about how I'm feeling.

'Oh. Okay then, as long as you're all right. Everyone was wondering where you had gone, I think they're ready to send out a search party.' His eyes widen and he steps back as I climb out of the car.

'I'm absolutely fine.' I fake smiling as I link his arm not giving him a choice but to walk me to the lift. 'Are you late for work?'

'Not yet. I have twenty minutes, so I better get moving. Listen, let's try and meet up in the week. I know something is bothering you, so don't lie. You have that little pulse under your eye, ticking away.' He points at it, and I bring my hand up, placing a finger on the soft skin under my left eye. 'When you are stressed or worried that makes an appearance.' He tilts his head at me a concerned look on his face.

'Honestly, nothing is wrong, but I'd love a night out, a catch-up when you and Henry have the time. Louise isn't back for five months, and I'll go crazy if I have to wait until she gets home to let my hair down.'

'Leave it with me, I'll see if I can swap Saturday then we can make a weekend of it.'

'Don't worry if you can't. I'll cope. I have a ton of work here to keep me busy,' I roll my eyes. He does too, adding a shake of his head. 'And I've neglected the house so that needs some tender loving care and don't get me started on the washing.'

'All work and no play makes Miss Walters crazy,' he says, giving me my surname. And yes, he is right. I might not have a ton of friends or a steady boyfriend, but I do like to let my hair down when I go out, which the four of us do pretty often. Or we did before Louise met Brandon. One day, Henry and Connor will meet some girl that they want to settle with, and I'll be Little Miss No Mates. It feels that way already. I need to start accepting the invitations I get from some of the staff that work here. I might give Luke a chance. He works in payroll with Mason and has asked me out a few times. Then again, I'm not sure if I can cope with his constant whining about not having a cafeteria in the building.

'Listen, I need to shoot.' He hugs me and then kisses my head. 'Love you.'

'Yeah, love you too,' I tell him. And I do. Both he and Henry I love like family. 'Ring me when you have time. And stay safe.'

'Yes, mother.' He rolls his eyes and presses for the lift. Once it arrives and I step in he gives me a wave and the door closes.

*

Friday evening comes around all too quickly, and I find myself at home alone. Work has been hectic as we put together the proposals for the new contracts we are chasing. I say we because it is a collective effort. We've all worked just as hard on them and I'm certain we have them in the bank.

Connor was unable to get tomorrow off and needed to be up early in the morning for another twelve-hour shift. Henry has a date tonight and another tomorrow, which he had forgotten about until he got a text message from Kate and Stacey, reminding him. So, our night out is out of the question. We met up on Wednesday though, which was nice. They came here when Connor had finished his shift, and we had a takeaway then last night we hit the local pub for a few drinks. It was lovely, nothing like when we are out at the weekend, but it was good to have a few hours out.

Deciding I'm not going to let this weekend go to waste sitting around eating junk food and watching shit on television, I finish the plate of chilli and rice I'd made for my tea then wash up the plate. It's seven in the evening so I hit play on my top twenty Spotify playlists, moving my hips in time to the music as I open up a bottle of pinot, then I make my way into the back room.

My grandparents used this room to store all sorts of stuff. Photo albums, lots of keepsakes of my mums, some antique ornaments, and paintings. There are plenty of other knick-knacks that they had accumulated over their fifty-one years of marriage and a drawer full of papers.

When Grandma died, my grandad didn't want anything thrown away and I respected that. I didn't want to get rid of anything either. It wasn't until Grandad passed away that I decided to get rid of some of their clothes, so I gave them to the local charity shop. It broke my heart but knowing someone else could benefit from them helped me in some ways.

When I glance at the old grandfather clock, which stands proudly in the corner of the room, an hour has passed, and I've drunk three-quarters of the bottle of wine and packed up three huge boxes. One is going to charity, one to the tip, and the other one I will be keeping.

Feeling a little buzzed with the wine, I top up my glass and stack the boxes under the window. It's dark out so I go to close the blinds. Just as I'm doing that the outside light turns on and I see a male figure loitering in the garden. My heart bangs against my ribcage, beating at twice the speed and when his face peers in the window, I step back, shocked. I land on my backside when I trip over the wine bottle I'd left on the floor. Cursing, I jump up quickly and that's when I realise, I know this man. I haven't seen him in twelve years. Not since I was fourteen.

The last time he was here, he and my grandad had argued. I remember hearing heated voices from my bedroom. I was used to seeing him a few times a week so when he stopped calling in, I asked my grandparents what had happened. My grandad said they had just had a silly falling out but not to worry because Uncle John was fine, and he had gone traveling abroad.

He didn't attend his own mother's funeral and when Grandad died, I had no known address to contact him.

'Are you going to let me in,' he shouts as he bangs on the window, shocking me again with the tone in his voice. The uncle I knew was always kind and had a gentle voice around me. A handsome man. This man obviously has aged somewhat since I last saw him. The years have not been kind but that's not what has me on edge. His eyes look hard and harsh, his tone aggressive.

'Just a moment,' I say to pacify him, while I get myself together. He used to look a lot like my mother even though there was a fifteen-year age gap and he seemed to have the same caring nature. There was a bit of an age gap between my grandparents too, with grandma being twenty-five when she gave birth to John and grandad being thirty-three. Fifteen years later they had my mum. Both of them were inconsolable when she died, and I don't think my grandma ever got over the loss of her daughter. They were all close, that's why I don't understand why my uncle stayed away when his mum died. I'm sure my grandad would've told him. Then again, as Grandad became increasingly frail, I asked him for my uncle's address. I knew it wouldn't be long and wanted to let Uncle John know. Grandad forbade it though so I let it be, not wanting to upset him.

Making my way to the back door, I turn the key in the lock and then open it.

'Uncle John,' I greet, trying to sound happy to see him after all these years.

'Meadow,' he grunts my name, pushing past me and making his way into the house,' Jesus, another arsehole in my life.

CHAPTER 3

MEADOW

'It's good to see you, Uncle John,' I say as I watch him flop down onto one of the dining room chairs. The wooden legs groan under the strain of his weight, so I brace myself, ready for the impact of it buckling under the heavy load. Luckily, the sturdy, old farmhouse chair, which has been around since my childhood, stays strong and upright. I let out a sigh of relief. He's put some beef on over the years, it would've taken more than me to lift him off the floor if he'd hurt himself.

He's changed so much in the last twelve years. I remember him being tall with a smart appearance. A handsome man. Clean shaven. Someone who took pride in himself. Well, that's certainly not the case anymore because that beard isn't doing anything for him, if anything it makes him look older than he is and his stained blue shirt which is stretched to max—buttons ready to pop—exaggerates his beer belly. Where his eyes were always warm and bright, they're now cold with dark circles. As well as his clothes being wrinkled and stained, there's a stale smell to him. Uncle John has clearly fallen on hard times.

He doesn't speak, just looks absently at me then his eyes shift taking in the room. The silence is uncomfortable, so I speak, trying to cover up the awkwardness.

'It's been a long time. I'm sorry you missed Grandma and Grandad's funeral. I had no way of contacting you. Grandad said you were working abroad and didn't have a contact address.' I ramble on trying to justify myself when realistically, I shouldn't need to. If he'd kept in touch with us, he would've known about his mother's death five years ago and then his father's. Eventually, he nods his head.

'Do you have anything to drink?'

'Yes, of course. Sorry, where are my manners? Would you like tea or coffee?'

'Neither. Something a little stronger.' His tone is disgruntled.

'Oh, I have wine.' I make my way to the fridge, ignoring the look of disdain on his face. If he doesn't like wine, then it's hard shit because that's all I have.

He doesn't say anything when I pour out a large glass of wine for him. Not even a thank you pass his lips. Rude. To be fair he's hardly said anything but to ask for a drink since he stormed through the door with a grunt and then headed straight into the dining room.

He puts the wine glass to his lips and chucks it down like he's drinking a pint of lager. He then picks up the bottle, which I had left on the table, and tops it up.

'So, you live here on your own now?' He asks, over the rim of the glass as he sits back in his seat, stretching his legs out.

'Yes.' He nods his head, his eyes becoming shifty. I don't like the vibe I'm getting from him, but he is my uncle, so I'll have to play nicely. 'When did you get back from—from wherever you've been travelling?' I ask, joining him in a glass of wine. Just a small one because I've already had my fill for the evening.

'Travelling?' The word rolls from his lips in a question. He lets out a humph and rolls his eyes. 'Two weeks ago. That's when I got back and found out about my parents.'

'If you found out two weeks ago, why haven't you been in touch?'

'Busy.' Jeez, he's a man of many words.

'Still, you could have called.' Not that it would've made any difference, Grandma and Grandad have been gone a while now and he looks as if he doesn't give a shit.

'About that.' He leans over and picks up the bottle of wine, filling his glass and emptying the bottle, shaking it to get the last drop out. 'I bumped into my dad's solicitor last week.'

'Solicitor?' What sodding solicitor? My grandfather never dealt with any solicitors.

'Yes. You know, a lawyer?' He sounds out the last words as if I am stupid.

'I know what a solicitor is. Grandad didn't have a lawyer or any other legal representation.'

'I think you'll find he did.' He folds his arms across his chest, lifts his chin and his lip rises at one side. He looks triumphantly as if he's just got one over on me. What is wrong with this guy? Cocky bastard.

As I wait for him to elaborate, he slips one hand into his pocket and takes out a packet of cigarettes before I have time to tell him there's no smoking in the house, he has one lit up and the smoke fills the air. I cough into my hand and stand, moving out of the way.

'Could you do that in the garden?' I wave my hand towards the door. He gets to his feet, pulling himself up with the help of the table, and then makes his way to the back door. I watch him step out into the garden, seriously considering locking him out. He must sense what I'm thinking because he quickly finishes his cig, throws it on the floor, and puts his foot on it. All the while he keeps a firm hold on the door.

'Are you going to enlighten me as to who this solicitor is and what he has to do with my grandad?' Why do I feel I'm not going to like what he has to say? This is not how I expected things would go if I ever met up with my uncle again.

When my grandma died, it hit me hard. She'd been like a mother to me for so many years. Losing her brought back memories of when we lost my mum. It was hard. Grandad was grieving for the loss of the only woman he had ever loved. They had been together for so many years. He had lost the love of his life and his best friend. Many times, I had wished for my uncle to return. Thinking he could help my grandad. We had my grandparents' friends but it's not the same as having a family. Or so I thought. Turns out I was wrong because their friends did a fantastic job of helping my grandad and me through the grieving process. And when my grandad died, they were there for me again. This man who I hardly know doesn't seem to care a rat's arse that his parents died while he's been away. Which means I shouldn't care a rat's arse about him. Or where he has been for the last twelve years. I should ask him to leave. Not give a damn about this so-called solicitor. It's Friday evening, getting late. I should tell him to go and come back tomorrow. Only I can't.

I was brought up to be a caring person. Love the people around me. Forgive people and give second chances to those amongst us who lack empathy. And he is the only family I have left.

'It turns out when my father died—your granddad.' He nods his head toward me. 'I came into an inheritance.' He reaches into the inside pocket of his jacket and pulls out a large envelope. I watch him take out its contents and lay it on the kitchen table, he then slowly slides it over to me.

'What is this?' I ask as I read the top line—last will and testament of Peter James Walters. I continue to study the piece of paper and I feel like my world is falling apart. The house. This house, 2, Westwood Court, is where I have lived all my life, built up so many happy memories and some sad ones too. A home that I thought was passed on to me when my grandad died, isn't mine at all. According to this legal document it belongs to my uncle.

My eyes cloud over, tears flood them, and my hands start to tremble. This isn't right. It can't be. But even through my blurred vision as I check over the contents of the Will again, everything seems above board. My granddad's signature is there. The signature of a witness and the solicitor of whom I have never heard of.

I shake my head. Not understanding. My grandad wasn't one for legalities. He'd never once mentioned having a solicitor. He didn't like people knowing his business. Even his bank account was kept to a bare minimum. Over the years, I'd told him he needed to put his savings into a bank account, not have it dotted around the house, hidden in various containers, and yes even under his mattress.

'I don't understand,' I say as I sit down on one of the dining room chairs, keeping hold of the piece of paper that has just ruined my life.

'What is there to not understand? This house was left to me and any money he had in the bank. But I daresay you will have spent that by now.'

I ignore him because I can't—I can't even look at him. My grandparents would turn over in their graves, knowing he was here, trying to take my home from me.

I'm not sure what to do so I just sit there, staring absently at the sheet of paper in front of me. This has got to be a mistake.

*

Five days later, I'm at my wit's end. I'm exhausted, I'm snappy and I just want my uncle gone. It's been a nightmare having him here and he's driving me insane.

I haven't a clue what he is up to, but I know he's searching for something. He creeps about the house during the night. Scurrying around like a sewer rat. I can hear him sneaking down the stairs and then the cupboard doors opening and closing and it's not just the kitchen cupboards. There are quite a few unused rooms up here and downstairs that I hear him in. I know he's been rifling through my grandparents' old room. He constantly bangs about and drinks alcohol.

Every evening when I arrive home from work, he slouched on the settee with a can in his hand. Then he demands I make him something to eat or order a take-out. I tell him I'm not his skivvy and to make his own, but this just riles him up and he becomes aggressive. He's disgusting.

He eats like a pig and my home has become his pigsty. I don't know how much more I can take from him or how much longer I can stay here. I don't want to leave my home but he's making it very hard to stay. It's clear he's after money. He's been selling things that belonged to Grandma and Grandad and now he wants me to pay him rent. Not on his life.

CHAPTER 4

KANE

What the hell is she doing? I do a double take and blow out a breath as I stare through the glass wall that separates my office from my secretary's. I watch her crawl along the floor on her hands and knees and those improper thoughts run rampantly through my mind. Such images of that firm behind would be the downfall of any hot-blooded male and even though she drives me to despair with her wacky ways and sassy mouth—even on a good day—I'm not immune to her womanly curves and the fruity fragrance that lingers in the air whenever she's around.

Meadow became my secretary almost two years ago. I didn't hire her. I wasn't even in the country when she was employed. I know for sure that if I had been here to interview Meadow Walters then she wouldn't have got the job and that's not because she's not capable of doing it because she is. No, I have my own personal reasons why.

My two youngest brothers had known her for some time—a friend from school. According to my brothers, she even stayed at our home. I don't remember her but then again with the fourteen-year age difference, I wouldn't have taken much notice. From the age of seventeen, I was hardly at home. I spent three years in the armed forces and then joined the police force when I came out. I had formulated a plan to open my own business along with Callum and Mason, my two middle brothers, with the idea that Henry and Connor would join us when they were old enough, so any leave or holidays I had, I was kept busy.

Being the eldest of five brothers when my father died before his time of a heart attack, I saw fit to take on his role and make sure my mother and four younger siblings were taken care of. My dad had always been the breadwinner, mum a stay-at-home mum. We didn't have much, but we were always fed, had decent clothes on our backs and we were loved. When he died it hit us all hard. My mum was inconsolable, and my younger brothers had no clue how to deal with his death or our mum's grief. We were all grieving. Struggling. Then if things weren't bad enough with the loss of our father, we had to sell our family home.

My parents had bought it when they married, and we had all been born there. He did have some life insurance which helped but it wasn't enough to pay off the mortgage. Mum knew she needed to come to terms with his death so she could get out there and look for a job. She found it hard to get employment because she hadn't worked since I was born apart from helping my father with the rota for his employees and a few other things.

He'd started his own security company back when being employed as a bouncer on nightclub doors and security at festivals or concerts was easier. An SIA license wasn't needed back then. It was only a small business that was owned by my father and uncle and had around twenty men on the books. I was fourteen and even though the loss hit me hard, I couldn't sit about moping. Dad was a good husband and father, who loved to spend time with his wife and sons. We had many happy memories, and I knew he would've wanted me to step up and be the man of the house. So, I went to school and worked hard on my grades. I helped my mum with my brothers and the housework and when I was seventeen, I joined the Army. I'd always wanted to join up for a few years. Serve my country, see the world, and get a trade but I had other reasons too. Two of them were one less mouth to feed at home and my mum wouldn't need to work as many hours as a waitress as I could send money home. Callum was fifteen and Michael thirteen by then, both of them old enough to help with the housework and take care of our four-year-old twin brothers. The other reason was payback.

My uncle had taken my mum for a fool when my dad died and fobbed her off with how the business was doing. According to him, it was going under as they were competing with other reputable companies and K&S Securities could not compete. Which was a pile of crap. My uncle had been talking out of his arse and pulling the wool over my mum's eyes. She believed him. Only I didn't.

Mum didn't realise I had heard the conversation that went down between her and Uncle Stuart, but I had. I also witnessed the despair and tears that she shed every night, not knowing how she was going to provide for her five sons. That is when I knew what I had to do.

A scream brings me out of my thoughts, and I watch Meadow the scatty mare place a glass on the floor and then rush across the room, nearly tripping over in the process. She snatches a piece of card from her desk then hurries back to the glass, where she proceeds to crouch on the floor and slides the piece of card under the glass then carefully lifts it making sure the card doesn't slip from the top of it. She looks around, biting her lip as she contemplates what to do next. She takes two steps towards the outer office door and then decides against it, turning towards mine. I step to one side as she barges in holding the glass out in front of her. 'Quick open the window,' she demands, pushing the glass further in my direction. That is when I see what she has in the bloody thing.

'Is that someone's pet?' I take a closer look and then step back from her not wanting the eight-legged creature anywhere near me. It's not that I'm scared of spiders, but this one could be a tarantula's offspring and with the way its thick, dark legs have taken on a defensive stance, it looks like it's ready to attack.

'Please take it from me,' Meadow pleads as she holds it out to me with shaky hands. If she's not careful she'll drop it on the floor. Her face pales and her shaking worsens. Quickly I snatch the glass from her with two hands careful not to lose the card which is stopping the arachnid from escaping.

'Why the hell didn't you just stand on it if you're scared of them?' I grumble, marching over to the window. I pop the glass on the windowsill and then turn to her as I open it. She stands there chewing on her fingernail, looking as nervous as a virgin bride on her wedding night—and that doesn't sit well with me.

If there is one thing, I know about my secretary is that she's not a shrinking violet. Meadow is confident, strong, and determined— she's also organised. Nothing phases her. She'll stand her ground against any of the staff here, including the management and that includes me.

'I don't like killing them,' she says her tone still having an edge about it. I want to ask her what is really bothering her because, over the last couple of days, she hasn't been her normal self. I know it's nothing to do with a stupid spider. I don't bother because even though she is close to all my brothers and gets along famously with all the staff, we don't get along. And who's fault is that? I ask myself.

Not wanting to dwell on the reasons, I close the window after tossing the thing out and shove the piece of card into the glass then move towards Meadow, holding it out for her to take from me. She grabs hold of the glass then without looking at her, I make my way to my desk and sit down. As I do, she thanks me and then closes the door behind her.

CHAPTER 5

KANE

'What are you looking at?' Callum moves to my side, curiosity getting the better of him.

'Meadow.' I nod my head in her direction as I tuck my hands in my pockets.

'Why? You don't give her the time of day usually, so what's different today? Well, the last few days actually because this isn't the first time this week, I've noticed you watching her. So, what gives?' He leans against the window, his arms folded across his chest, waiting for my answer.

'Something isn't right with her.'

'We know. Henry and Connor have noticed that she's not herself. She looks like shit, which we know isn't her. She's snappy. Which again isn't her. Well—apart from with you. We all know she'll give you shit to wind you up but—I don't know.' He runs his hand through his hair, his lips forming a fine line. 'Maybe it's the time of the month or something.' He shrugs his shoulders.

'How long has she worked here.' It's not a question. 'Almost two years. Which means it can't be that because we would've seen her like this before.' And I've never seen Meadow Walters so not put together.

'You're probably right.' We both watch her as she stares into space then after about five minutes of her being in deep concentration, she snaps out of it and lowers her head, focusing on something on her laptop. 'Maybe I should go have a word with her she looks so forlorn.'

'Leave her for now. Let's see how today pans out. If she doesn't show any signs of her returning to her normal self, then we might have to intervene.'

'Please behave yourself, the poor thing looks like she could just burst into tears,' Callum warns me as he returns to his seat and continues working on the figures for this year's tax returns. He doesn't normally work from my office but the one he shares with Mason and Henry is freezing. The heating has gone down so we're waiting on the engineer to come and take a look. He doesn't normally work with the accounts either, Mason and Henry are the number experts around here but they're in Birmingham. Well, they should be on their way back. We had a coach load of thirty men, travel there last Friday to cover a heavy rock concert. The same guys move around the country covering various concerts and festivals. They love the work and they've built up a remarkable reputation, so Summer Knights Security is always happy to supply them when needed. My two brothers wanted to tag along because they are into a couple of bands headlining the event. They should have been back Monday afternoon, but the coach broke down and the company we used couldn't get another one to them until this morning.

'I don't know why I agreed to do this, it gives me a bloody headache, calculating all these numbers.' I ignore his griping; he'll do what he can to save Mason and Henry from having to do it when they get back. They're all good like that. Will drop whatever they are doing to help each other out.

We both settle into our work in silence and when I look up again a few hours have passed. I'm surprised that Meadow hasn't come in to ask if we want a drink. We're quite capable of getting up to fetch our own but she likes to take care of us. She usually asks if we want a sandwich to be brought back when she's going out to lunch and that hasn't happened all week. I get up from my chair and open the door. Time to see if I can push her a little.

'Meadow, can you come in here, please?' I add please at the end because I'm unsure what type of crazy I'm dealing with today. Where she will usually just roll her eyes at me or shake her head when I don't use my manners, I'm sure with the mood she is in at the moment, I'm likely to be wearing that cup she has sat on her desk round the back of my head.

I watch her head snap up and those light blue eyes that are normally bright and full of life, today have heavy dark circles. She looks exhausted. Her hair always shines like gold, silky and tame, but today it's dull and tied up in a messy bun. And the suits she dons daily, either a skirt that sits just above her knees or trousers that fit her to perfection, showing off a firm behind matched with a short jacket and blouse or shirt have been nonexistent this week. Replaced with some tatty attire. Something pulls at my chest, and I have to look away. Something is wrong and she's reluctant to talk about it. Not that she'd talk to me, we don't have that type of relationship, although she would talk to my brothers, and even with them, she's tight-lipped.

I close the door and watch her from the window. There's a surprised look on her face probably due to me adding the word, please. I can see she's hesitant to get up. There's a debate going on. Shall I? Shan't I? Eventually she stands and makes her way to my door, so I quickly remove myself from the window and sit behind my desk, Callum eyes me curiously from his seat at the table where he shifts papers about, feigning interest.

'What do you need?' She asks, lacking any enthusiasm as she pushes the door open.

'I was just wondering if you had watered my plants this week. They're looking a bit wilted?'

'Oh, for god sake.' She scowls at me, stopping in front of my desk with her hands on her hips. My brother coughs into his hand, stifling his amusement. He knows I'm playing with fire. She's in no mood to be pressed today, hasn't been all week. However, I want to see what it takes to make her snap. Cruel, I know. But like I said she's not herself and if I push her far enough with my overbearing ways, she might just crack. And we might find out what has removed that beautiful smile from her face and replaced it with sadness.

'God forbid one of you had to do something for yourselves around here,' she mumbles as she gives the plants—which she bought for me, hoping they'd lighten my moods—a drink. She doesn't know I know this, but I have ears and I hear how she talks to my brothers about me being a grouch, and how she hopes the various plants that she has dotted around my office will lighten my moods. Maybe she should take a leaf out of her own book. 'Half the bloody time you complain about them being in here,' she grumbles, then storms out of the room, tutting.

'I can't believe you got her in here for that.'

'You want to know what is wrong with her then I'm your man. She hates me half of the time so if I prod her enough, she'll snap.'

His brow creases, not liking the way I go about things. I always get the job done, even if I do get a few backs up in the process.

'She doesn't hate you. If you ask me, you too have a love-hate relationship.'

'There's no love between us.'

'Oh, I wouldn't bet on that. We all see it.' He wiggles his eyebrows at me then he gets up from his seat and heads out of the door, leaving me contemplating his last words.

He's crazy. They all are because there's no love lost between Meadow and me. I'm sure she'd love to slap me across the face and tell me where to go. Whereas I'd love to pin her up against my office door and kiss that sass right out of her. But that's only because she loves to give me so much lip. And she has the most amazing kissable mouth. If that's all it is, then why does it bother you that she looks so unhappy? My inner voice asks, giving me reasons to question just what it is I feel for Meadow. Nothing. She's an employee just like the rest of my staff, I answer then I quickly stand, rubbing my face. It's time to get out of the office.

*

'Are we out tonight?' Mason asks as he spins around in his chair, tapping his pen on his teeth. He's talking to my brothers and me. We've just finished our meeting and finalized everything we need for our meeting with the council. I'm confident we have this in the bag. 'I thought we could try that new bar in town that's just opened,' he continues.

Wednesday is the night we get together and forget about work. Or try to but you can guarantee it never works out that way. A few beers and something to eat and maybe a game of pool just to break up the working week. Only work is all we chat about and who is getting laid.

'Count me in. I'm off until Saturday,' Connor one of my youngest brothers answers. He and Henry are twins and where Henry works full time for the company, Connor puts in hours where he can due to him being in the police force.

It shocked me when he told me he had applied to join but then again, I shouldn't have been surprised, he'd always looked up to me. He wanted a few years out on his own before he joined the company full-time and because I had been in the force for several years, the job appealed to him.

'I'm in,' Henry confirms.

'Me too,' Callum says, setting his eyes on me. 'What about you?'

'Yeah, I don't see why not.' I could do with something to take my mind off, Miss Walters. All day yesterday and this morning I've tried everything, hoping she'd break down—but like always she's proven to be a worthy opponent. Maybe she's more like me than I anticipated. Too damn stubborn for her own good.

Pushing back my chair, I stand and make my way over to the one-way window. Meadow sits at her desk, typing something into her laptop. She looks to be in deep concentration. As if she senses being watched, she lifts her head, glancing in my direction. I step to one side. Why? I don't know because she can't see me.

'Will you leave her alone,' Connor warns me, shaking his head. 'When she's ready to tell us what's bothering her, she will but until then don't wind her up any more than she is. Leave her be.' He has such a soft spot for her. It has me wondering whether it's because he looks at her as a friend or if there's something more. Another feeling cloaks me. Unease and hostility, creeping their way from somewhere deep within me. Clawing at me until my chest feels tight, and my hands begin to shake. What the hell is this? Jealousy. My inner voice suggests knowingly. I shake my head and take a few steady breaths because this is stupid. I could never be anything but caring toward any of my brothers.

'Now you've just made it worse,' Callum says, bringing me out of my hellish thoughts. 'This arsehole will torment her even more now.'

'I'm not tormenting her. Just like the rest of you, I want to know what is wrong with her. She won't tell any of you so I will have to intervene. And I'm afraid if that means being a little bit hard on her so that she flips then so be it. I don't mind being the bastard amongst us. You'll thank me in the end and so will she.'

'How so?' Connor asks, a confused look on his face.

'Meadow doesn't have many friends. The only girlfriend she has is sunning herself on some sandy beach. You two.' I point to the twins. 'Are her only two other friends and for whatever reason you are not pushing her enough, so she'll spill whatever it is that is bothering her. It might be nothing, but it could be something, and if we don't help her get it off her chest then...'

'He's right. She has no one,' Callum says and that tightening in my chest happens again only this time it's nothing to do with being jealous. For the last two years, I've shown her no respect as an employee or a friend of my brothers. I've pushed and pushed hoping she'd cave in and leave. Given her jobs to do that are not in her remit. Snapped at her. My rudeness would warrant human resources and the union to come down on me and rip me to shreds. And why have I been such an arse to such a sweet, beautiful woman? Because it's easier than giving in to the feelings that she evokes in me. I'm not a man to show my emotions, especially around women. Haven't for some time now but Meadow could be my undoing.

Just hearing she has no one doesn't sit well with me and although I know I still need to fight to keep my emotions at bay, I also know I need to break her so I can put her back together.

'Meadow, did you send my suits to be dry cleaned?' I speak through the office intercom system; Callum had it set up over a year ago and let's just say my secretary hates it.

'What the hell are you doing?' Henry questions, as he stands up quickly. I hold up my hand for him to give me a minute. I know what I'm doing. I think. This could go one or two ways.

'Yes,' she answers, her tone is calm-ish.

'And did you pick up my shirts?'

'Yes.' She answers briskly this time.

'Did you hang them in my wardrobe?'

This is one of the things she does for me that I am thankful for. Well, that and my suits. I hate to see them squashed up together when they've just been cleaned and ironed. They just get creased again and I have so many that it's hard to hang them without them being pressed together. Meadow does it just right. It's not in her job description—of course not—but when I first asked her, she seemed okay about it, and she's never said anything to me about her not being.

'Are you kidding me?' Her tone is now curt. Now we're getting somewhere.

'No, I'm not kidding Miss Walters. I've asked you a question I expect a civil answer.' My four brothers glare at me as if I've gone mad. Maybe I have. I almost chuckle at the wideness of their eyes. I don't because I can hear Meadow stomping across the room next to mine and towards my door. This is unusual because she normally walks with such elegance and grace, she looks like she's walking on air.

My door flies open, and one annoyed woman stands there. Her face is red, and her hands are placed by her sides, fists clenched. 'Are you seriously trying to piss me off? Is grating on my last nerve a game to you?'

'Excuse me?' I'm sitting down in my chair with Meadow standing extremely close by my side now. She glares at me and as she leans down, her mouth is but inches away.

'Oh, I excused you a long time ago because let's face it, you do not have one ounce of decency in that body.' Is she for real? I am a decent guy. I've always taken care of my family. I have great friends and I look after my staff. I'm quite taken aback by her outrage but for some reason, all I want to do is kiss that sassy mouth and if it wasn't for the fact that she is genuinely pissed at me, and my four brothers are here then I wouldn't be able to resist.

'Do this Meadow. Do that Meadow. Have you done this? Can you get me that?' She takes a deep breath and I watch her hands shake and her eyes fill with tears.

'Meadow…' She puts up her hand stopping me and leans in further; I can feel the warmth of her breath on my skin.

'Save it, arsehole. I've had it with you. I have done every menial task you have asked and still, you speak to me as if I am something you trod in.'

'You're contracted to work for me and the jobs I have asked you to do are in your contract.' I dig myself deeper into that huge hole I have opened up. Shit, this isn't going the way I wanted.

'Contract? Really?' Her eyes widen and her body stiffens. I can almost see the steam rising from her. I'm just about to try and calm her down, knowing I've gone too far when she turns swiftly on her heels and storms out of the room. She returns just as quickly with a hard copy of her contract. She slams it on my desk and glares at me again.

'Where in there—' she prods her finger hard on the contract as she stresses each word— 'does it say, drop off the boss's suits and shirts at the dry cleaners and pick them back up again then take them to his penthouse apartment and hang them up in his wardrobe? It doesn't.' The last bit she says through gritted teeth.

'Meadow.' Callum gets out of his seat, but she holds her hand up stopping him.

'Where does it say that it's my job to take endless calls from the brainless women who hang off your arm at the countless events you go on? Listening to their desperate pleas. How they can't live without you....' She glares at me with such animosity, I'm certain she would slit my throat if there was a knife to hand. 'The women I have turned away from that office door...' She stops and I think I'm given a reprieve—no such look. 'I can't do this anymore. I'm out.'

'What?' This wasn't supposed to happen. Well, what did you expect? Pushing her was never going to work. Deep down you knew this. My inner voice spits at me but I ignore it because now is not the time to decipher what it means. 'Meadow I'm....'

'No. You don't get to speak to me anymore. You can take that contract and shove it where the sun doesn't shine. I quit.' With that, she turns and storms out of my office, the door slamming shut behind her.

'Meadow!' Henry and Connor call as they jump out of their seats, vaulting over the table in front of them before they shoot out of the door.

'What the f**k?' I hold up my hands stopping Callum from giving me a lecture then bury my face in them.

'Well, that went well,' Mason says sarcastically. I lift my head from my hands, taking in the two pairs of concerned eyes. I don't need their concern. Meadow does. I need a punch in the face.

'I didn't—I mean—' I can't speak, and that's a first. 'I thought she would—hell, I don't know what I thought but I didn't expect her to quit.'

'We know,' Callum says. 'You thought she'd break down then you could ask her what was really bothering her, and she'd open up to you.'

'Well yeah. She takes my shit all day long and throws it back at me. God, I'm such a dick.'

'Yes, you are,' Henry says as he and Connor march back into the room.

'Is she okay?'

'As if you care.' Henry spits at me.

'Of course, I care.' I rub my face, racking my brain as to how I can put this right.

'Yeah, well she's gone home. She was so upset, Kane. Why would you wind her up like that?'

'I thought—It doesn't matter. I'll give her time to calm down.'

'Can't see that happening anytime soon,' Mason says as he closes his laptop lid and places some papers on top of it.

'I'll give her time to calm down then I'll call around to her house and apologise. Hopefully, she'll listen to what I have to say.'

'And if she doesn't?' Connor looks angry with me, and I don't blame him. I'm angry with myself.

'Connor, I'm sorry. I know you and Henry are close to Meadow.'

'She's not just a friend, she's like the sister we never had. You.' He points at me. 'Need to put this right. I've never seen her so upset and I've known her a long time.'

'I will. I promise.' I've always kept my promises to them when they were kids, I'm not going to fail them now. And I'm not letting Meadow go without a fight.

CHAPTER 6

KANE

I'm on my way to see Jake the night security guard. I was shocked when I got a call from him half an hour ago telling me he needed to speak with me urgently before he went home. It's unlike him to ring me at all so I'm concluding it's something serious.

I cross the foyer with a purpose in my step, taking in my surroundings. I still find it hard to believe that my brothers and I own this building. I stop for a moment to remember how shabby it was when we first took it over and how magnificent it looks now. The changes were extensive and costly but well worth it.

The ground floor of this building is sizable. As you walk through the glass doors, you're greeted with light walls and a marble floor. Dead centre is a glimmering waterfall feature, which attracts attention. To the left, we have the reception area. Visitors are greeted by our receptionist Grace who works nine till five and to the right of there is the visitor's waiting area. The seats are leather and mounted on the wall is a sizable screen that relays in sequence the six businesses that operate from here.

There are six sets of offices all run by family firms. I don't charge a mint for them, but I do get a healthy annual revenue. The bank of lifts will take you to whichever floor you want but the penthouses have their own. There's car parking on the lower ground and twenty-four-hour security seven days a week.

'Hey Jake, how are things?' I put my hand out in greeting, and he gives it a friendly shake. I met Jake during my time in the police force. We didn't work in the same department, but we did run into each other regularly during callouts, the cafeteria, and the police bar. Not long before I came out of the force his wife passed away. It hit him hard. So, understandably he needed time to grieve and reevaluate his life. He was in his late fifties then, which meant retirement wasn't too far away. A few years ago, we bumped into each other, and I could tell he was struggling to cope with his newfound freedom. Retirement or unemployment isn't for everyone, and I knew this was the problem he was having. Over a beer, he'd let it slip how with not having anything to occupy him through the day, he wasn't sleeping well at night. As luck had it, I had the perfect position for him in the company. We needed a CCTV operative who didn't mind working evenings. I explained to him that the company needed someone they could rely on to work from ten in the evening until six in the morning. He was overjoyed with the prospect of working again and accepted my offer straight away.

'All good apart from this.' He points to the CCTV screen, which shows the car park.

'What am I looking at?' I move closer to the screen; I don't see anything out of the ordinary.

'Watch.' He nods towards the screen as he clicks on the play button.

Nothing happens for a few seconds then the car park illuminates when a car pulls in. I don't need to ask whom the car belongs to, the red Renault Cleo belongs to my secretary, Meadow. I give Jake a questionable look then continue to watch as she gets out of the car, wearing a blue patterned onesie. She opens the boot and yanks out a bag. The picture isn't clear enough for me to see her face, but I do catch her wiping her eyes. My chest tightens and this time I know why.

She calls for the lift that takes you straight to the office and once it opens, she steps inside.

'I don't understand, does she leave again? Did you speak to her?'

'No. I must have been on my rounds or in the back making a cup of tea when she pulled into the car park, it wasn't until I was checking the live feed that I noticed her car, which hadn't been there earlier. I checked the time, and she came in at three fifteen.'

'Has she left?' I ask again. I think she probably called in while nobody was in the office so she could pick up some of her things. I did call round to her house last night, but she wasn't home. Her car wasn't outside, so I was hoping to call over this morning after my run. However, I didn't get to go for my six o'clock five-mile run because Jake called me to come at take a look at the CCTV.

'She's still here.' He says as he taps on a few buttons and the office appears on the screen. It's dark but as I look closely, I can see someone cuddled up on the sofa. 'Asleep.'

'I don't understand?' I lean closer to the screen so I can get a better look. 'Why would she turn up in the middle of the night in a onesie and then fall asleep on the sofa in the office?'

'I have no idea. When I noticed her car, it was about four o'clock. I went up just to check on her. To see if she was okay. She was already asleep, and I didn't have the heart to wake her, so I quietly left. I waited until I knew you'd be awake before I telephoned you. Do you think something has happened? A fallout with her boyfriend...?'

'She doesn't have one.' I'm quick to answer. 'Listen thanks for letting me know. And don't worry, I'll go up now and see what's wrong.' I'm sure I'm the last person she wants to see but she is in my office at five forty-five in the morning. She's normally here anyway around six thirtyish and I'm not far behind her.

'Do you want me to come with you?' Jake asks as he taps on the buttons again putting the monitors back to live feed.

'No, it's fine. Honestly, I'm sure she won't want us both there when she wakes up.'

'Of course, you're right. I'll leave you to it.' He slaps me on the back and turns to his screen.

As I step into the office, straight away there's a smell of smoke that assaults my senses, and not the nicotine type either. This smoke is from a fire, I've smelt it many times during my service years. I turn the lights on, making sure they are set to dim then turn the heating on because it's pretty chilly in here. I then make my way over to where Meadow is curled up on the sofa, covered over with one of my jackets.

Kneeling in front of her, I smooth my hand over her unruly hair. It's something I've wanted to do for so long now but fought against it, not wanting to admit to myself the feelings she evokes in me. I certainly never imagined doing it in these circumstances. She lets out a moan and curls into herself. 'Meadow,' I whisper not wanting to scare her. She looks too comfy to wake up, but I need to know what is going on with her.

'Mmmm,' she mumbles, pulling my coat up to her chin, her eyes still closed.

'Hey, sweetheart it's time to wake up,' I speak quietly, running my hand over her hair again.

'Don't want to.' It comes out croaky. I blow out a breath, rubbing my chin. She looks so peaceful and comfortable lying there covered with my jacket.

Contemplating whether to leave her a while longer, I slide her legs over and perch myself on the edge of the sofa, placing my hand on her foot. I rack my brain, trying to come up with reasons why Meadow has turned up here in the middle of the night, smelling like she's been around a bonfire and then fallen asleep in the office. I can't come up with anything.

I'm just about to get up to make her a cup of coffee—which is a first—when she stirs. Her leg moves first then the coat she had covering her moves from her shoulders and her head lifts.

Sleepy blue eyes stare at me, bewildered. When she rubs at them, recollection of where she is and who is sitting with her shows, and she scrambles to sit up.

'Meadow, are you okay?'

'Sorry, I never meant to fall asleep in here.' She makes to stand and then wobbles slightly so I take hold of her arm.

'Sit down.' I know how I sound so I add, 'Please.' She runs her hand through her hair and her eyes flicker.

'I'm okay.'

'No, you're not.' I gently squeeze her hand, which I didn't realise I had taken hold of. 'Sit down and I'll fetch you a drink.'

'Okay,' she says quietly. She looks defeated and my chest tightens. Not wanting to go there I dash over to the area where we keep the kettle and cups and in no time at all, I'm standing in front of her holding out a cup of coffee.

'Thank you.' She takes hold of it and puts it to her lips.

'You're welcome.' I sit down at the side of her and take a drink of mine then I place it on the floor and turn to her. 'Care to tell me what's going on with you?' She shakes her head and lowers it. 'Meadow,' I sigh. 'Meadow, I know I'm an arsehole but that doesn't mean I don't care.' She lets out a sarcastic laugh. I don't blame her; I've never once asked her how she is. Or taken any interest in what she does out of work. I have my reasons why but still; I could have been a bit nicer towards her. 'It might make you feel better if you get it off your chest.' I'm the last person who should be giving advice. I've never listened to anyone but myself.

'I doubt it.' My chest tightens again at how forlorn she sounds. The Meadow I know is a happy soul and full of life.

She lets out a tired yawn and then places her cup by her feet. I watch her as she tries to lift herself from the sofa. She doesn't succeed because her legs give out and she collapses backwards. I'm quick to catch her.

Cradling her in my arms, I feel her shoulders shake so I hold her tightly, letting her sob against my shoulder while she grips my shirt with one hand. I gently soothe her as I stroke her back. We sit there for a few minutes while she lets it all out. I'm still no wiser as to what the hell is going on with her and why she ended up here, I'm hoping to rectify that soon.

'How are you feeling?' I ask as she moves from my arms, sitting back on the sofa.

'I'm okay,' she sniffles. 'I haven't been feeling well all week and I've been off my food.' She's definitely been feeling something, and it wasn't tummy troubles. She's lying. 'I'm just feeling a little lightheaded.' She lowers her head, focusing on the floor.

'Okay. I believe you might be a little lightheaded but this feeling unwell doesn't wash with me Meadow so do you want to tell me the truth? What is it that's been bothering you?'

'Nothing is bothering me and I'm not a liar.' When she lifts her head and her eyes meet mine, I can see a whole world of worry there. I widen my eyes at her, daring her to test me. She knows I can see straight through this charade. Not only a minute ago she was crying in my arms. Even if she had been poorly, it wouldn't warrant her bawling in front of me and accepting my comfort. I'm surprised she didn't slap me and shrug me off when I wrapped my arms around her.

'Mr Summer, I'm fine, and seeing as I no longer work for you then I'll just go. Thank you for being here for me, I'll be okay now.' Who is she trying to kid? Even her voice sounds weak.

'I didn't accept your resignation, Meadow, as well you know,' I say, as she makes to stand, still unsteady on her feet. 'Meadow, sit back down.' I'm shocked when she does what I say without hesitation or giving me any grief.

As she sits down, she rubs her hands up and down her face and blows out a long breath. She looks pale and her eyelids look heavy. Besides this, there's still the fact that she smells like a bloody bonfire. 'Listen, Meadow, what I'm about to say I don't want you taking it the wrong way. I'm concerned about you' —she gives me a don't give me that look— 'we all are. This isn't you. You look exhausted. It's obvious you aren't sleeping right. You're irritable. I agree you do look unwell but it's not the poorly kind. I think whatever it is that is troubling you has brought this on, and you stink of smoke.' She stares at me, her brow furrowed. 'And I need to ask, why you'd turn up here in the middle of the night and fall asleep on the sofa? Care to share?'

She shakes her head and plays with her fingers, that's when I notice her usually-polished, manicured nails are broken and chipped. 'You wouldn't understand.' She worries her bottom lip as she turns away from me.

"Try me."

She stays quiet for a while then turns so she's looking at me and when she speaks, tears fill her eyes. 'My home. The house that my grandparents left me—where I grew up. Every memory of my mum is in that house.' Her lip trembles, stopping her and I have to fight the urge to wrap my arms around her. I can't understand this need to comfort her. This isn't me. That's because you don't want to fight this anymore. You've fought it long enough…Shit, now I'm having difficulties shutting down my inner thoughts. I bite the inside of my cheek and focus on what she is saying.

'When my grandparents died, they were the last of my family except for an uncle that I hadn't seen for years, he'd been working abroad since I was fourteen, Uncle John.' She spits out his name as if it's poison on her tongue and I don't need a clairvoyant to tell me, he's the cause of her troubles.

Not knowing where this is going or how long it's going to take for Meadow to unburden what it is that has been worrying her, I stand and hold out my hand. 'Come on.'

'What?' she looks confused and those tears in her eyes are killing me.

'Let's take this upstairs.' She knows I mean my penthouse. It might be early and usually there is only Meadow and me that turn up at the office before seven but who knows there's always a first time. I don't want anyone to see her like this, not even my brothers. Not yet anyway. Once she's told me everything and had a few more hours of sleep as well as a shower and a change of clothes then I'll bring them in on this.

Without any arguing from my secretary, she stands with my help. No sooner does she slip her hand into mine than my whole body tingles and heats up. Another thing that I don't understand. It's not like I didn't take her hand in mine only a few moments ago. I push down these confusing thoughts, pick up Meadow's bag, and lead us out of the office towards the lift.

In no time at all the lift door opens and we make our way to the entrance of my apartment.

'Why have you brought me here Mr Summer?'

'Will you knock it off with the Mr Summer shit, you make me sound like an old man.' Granted I have a few years on Meadow, almost fourteen to be precise, but I'm the only one in the company that she calls Mr, and I'd love to hear her say my name. 'Please call me Kane.' She nods her head as she slips off her trainers, revealing her bare feet. It's not like I haven't seen how she pairs up whatever nail polish she is wearing on her fingers with her toes and how delicately petit they looked before; she wears sandals all the time in the warmer weather. However, seeing how she wiggles them into the pile of my carpet, is something I could get used to. Shit, now I have a thing for toes. Is there such a thing?

'Well?'

'Well, what?'

'Why am I here?' Oh yeah, I forgot she'd asked me that. Too engrossed in her bare feet.

'I just wanted to make you more comfortable. I thought—I mean there's a spare room with an en-suite if you want to freshen up a little, get changed, or if you want to shut your eyes for a while. You look shattered, that is all, and I thought it might make you feel a little better.' I make my way through into the open-planned living area, and Meadow follows me.

'Thank you. I'd love a shower and to be able to change my clothes.' She looks down at herself, pulling on the material of her onesie. A small smile graces her lips, but her eyes are still watery.

'Okay then, let's get you sorted.'

I show Meadow through to the spare room. I know she's been here many times to put away my shirts and suits. God, I'm such an arsehole. Why the hell did I push her into doing that for me? You know why. Comes out of nowhere reminding me of the feelings she arouses in me and how I have denied them and tried to push her away.

'There's shower gel there. A spare toothbrush and toothpaste in there.' I open the cupboard above the sink to show her. 'And the towels are in the cupboard under the sink.' I point it out. 'I'll leave you to it, call me if there's anything you need.'

'Thank you Mr,' she hesitates for a split second then follows up with 'Kane.'

CHAPTER 7

KANE

Meadow using my first name does something to me, something I'm not used to feeling. Yes, I hear my name said daily, not just by my brothers, friends, or colleagues, the women I share some of my time with love to say it however, it doesn't have the same appeal as hearing it roll off Meadow's tongue. The sound of it is more attractive to my ears and sends those weird tingling feelings through me again. My whole body feels lifted. And instead of feeling like a coiled spring due to Meadow's predicament, I'm feeling a lot lighter knowing we are getting somewhere. And as I walk into the kitchen, switch the kettle on, and retrieve two cups from the cupboard I have a smile that only one woman can put on my face. I laugh out loud because as crazy as it sounds it's the same woman whom I have scowled at for almost two years.

Fifteen minutes later, Meadow appears freshly showered. Her hair is tied up, she's wearing a black pair of leggings and if I'm not mistaken the T-shirt, she is wearing is one of mine. I tend to leave a few spares in there for when my brothers come to stay over. They don't stay often but when they do they raid my wardrobe so I started to leave some of my old clothes in the guest room in the hopes they'd leave the bloody good stuff alone.

'I hope you don't mind,' she says, pulling at the black T-shirt. 'I was in a rush and forgot to pack any tops.' She looks embarrassed. She needn't be. My clothes look hot on her. Where the hell did that come from? Interesting. I rub my chin, knowing that was never the issue. Meadow is an attractive woman, definitely hot but I chose to ignore my attraction to her.

'Not at all. Come and sit down.' I point to the chair on the other side of the breakfast bar. 'Feeling any better?' I ask as I pass her a cup of coffee and a plate of hot buttered toast. 'I thought you might be hungry.' I take a piece, so she doesn't feel awkward. I understand being here with me might be a bit strange especially under the circumstances and with what went down in the office yesterday.

'A little.' She picks up a piece of toast and thanks me. Once she's eaten it, she gets up from her seat and grabs a piece of kitchen roll to wipe the butter from her fingers then she returns and sits down.

'Would you like to continue with what you were telling me?' I take a sip from my cup, watching her run a finger over the rim of hers. She nods her head.

'I hadn't seen my uncle since I was fourteen. My last memories of him were of my grandad and him arguing while I was in my bedroom. I had no idea what it was about because when I went downstairs, he was gone. I didn't say anything to my grandparents, I could see they were upset but later my grandad told me we wouldn't be seeing John for a while. He was going to work abroad, and he didn't say where and I never asked. I was fourteen and too involved with what was going on in my own life. You know, friends, school, that sort of thing. Years later when my grandma became ill and we knew she didn't have long to go, I asked Grandad to call him. He refused, telling me he wasn't welcome. So, when Grandad died, I had no way of contacting him.'

'That must have been hard on you, having to go through the death of your granddad alone.'

'I had my friends and family friends rallied around also.' Friends, meaning my two twin brothers. I remember how upset she was when he passed. She was given time off and I did send her flowers, I don't think she realised they were from me.

'Anyway, I'd not seen my uncle for many years until a few weeks ago when he turned up at the house. He wasn't as put together as he used to be. He always kept his appearance smart—took care of himself and was always kind to me. The twelve years hadn't been kind to him. He'd piled on weight; his clothes were filthy, and he was vile towards me.' I place my hands at the side of me, hiding my clenched fists. I know I'm not perfect and I have been hard on her at times but hearing someone has treated her in such a way that she has made herself ill, makes me want to hurt someone. She picks up her coffee cup and takes a sip while I wait for her to elaborate on what she means.

'What did he do?' I ask before she gets the chance to tell me.

'He walked in as if he owned the place, ordering me to get him a drink. His whole attitude gave me bad vibes. Then he told me he had bumped into my grandad's solicitor—' she rubs at her nose— 'only he didn't have a solicitor. I knew my granddad and he didn't believe in doing anything official—he didn't even believe in banks. The fewer people that knew anything about his business then all the better, in his book. He wasn't dodgy, he was just brought up that way.'

'Where did he keep his money if he didn't have a bank account?' I have to ask because I know he left Meadow a tidy little sum.

'Oh, he had a bank account and he had money in it, but the bulk of his money was kept under his bed in suitcases and under his mattress. He always told me what he had was mine when anything happened to him, and I always laughed and told him he wasn't going anywhere any time soon.' She lets out a small laugh. 'Well, you can only imagine my surprise when old Uncle John produced a will from this supposed solicitor that had been signed by my grandad. And get this, my grandad had left everything to that poor excuse of a man.'

'What do you mean? Was it legit?'

'He handed it to me within an hour of him coming to my home.' She prods at her chest on the last two words. 'It seemed to be. I mean all the T's were crossed and I's dotted. My grandad's signature was on it.'

'Can I see it?' She shakes her head.

'In a fit of fury, I ripped it in half and threw it on the floor of my bedroom. When I had to leave, I was in a hurry and left it behind.' She bites her bottom lip, holding back the tears. So, I let her have a few minutes.

'What do you mean when you had to leave?'

'I had no other choice. He was making my life a living hell. He wanted me to pay rent—me pay rent to him.' She spits the words out. 'I couldn't sleep due to the god-awful music he'd play night and day. He ate like a pig and drank alcohol as if it was going out of fashion. If that wasn't bad enough, he was ticking things off to sell that belonged to my grandparents. My grandma's antique vases and pictures. My grandad's baby grand piano.' She covers her mouth with her hand and closes her eyes for a brief moment then continues. 'My desk. He ranted and raved wanting to know where it was. I know it's worth something to an antique dealer, so I told him Grandad had sold it years ago and he flipped.'

'Did he hurt you, Meadow?' If he's hurt one hair on her head, I'll strangle the bastard.

'He didn't hit me, but he pushed me and was aggressive towards me a lot. Getting in my face all the time. Threatening he'd throw me out. Taunting and tormenting me. I'd had enough. He'd only been there five days and I couldn't take anymore…'

'Why didn't you tell anyone? You could have come to me.' I realise what I just said when she raises an eyebrow at me. Why would she come to me? 'You could have said something to Henry and Connor.'

'I was embarrassed.'

'Why?'

'He's the only family I have left. My mum's brother. My grandparent's son. I was hoping he'd calm down or at least once he had some money he might just piss off. He'd sold a few things, and I knew they were worth a bit. He didn't calm down though; he became even more desperate than he was when he first arrived.'

'I understand about family loyalty Meadow, but you owe him nothing. For whatever reason, your grandad didn't want him in your lives so something must have happened.'

'I know but I don't know what it was. I wish I did. I tried to reason with him, but it was futile. I think he might have gotten himself into a bit of trouble and owed money to someone, so I was fighting a losing battle. When he drank, he got worse, and he was usually well-inebriated when I got home from work. Last Friday, I was dreading going home so I went for a drive around and stopped off at a small café for a bite to eat. I needed to get some milk, so I went to the shop once I had eaten. I thought hopefully he'd be in a drunken stupor by the time I arrived home, and I wouldn't have to put up with him. I didn't go to my usual shop because of the roadworks—I ended up at that row of shops by the Black Bull pub.'

'Jesus Meadow, that area is no good for a woman on her own.' Drugs, prostitution, attacks, and even murders have happened in the Greenwood estate.

'I know that now, but I didn't realise it was that bad.'

'What happened?'

'The shop had a notice up for a flat to let. I was desperate. So, I enquired about it and the shop owner showed me around. It was a one-bedroom flat above the shop. No bond was needed and no contract to sign, just a month's rent upfront. I told him I'd take it.' I rub my face, shocked. I can't believe this. Meadow is an intelligent woman; she comes from a good home. She must have been desperate to want to move out of her family home into such a dive. I haven't seen inside the flats above the row of shops, but I know the area very well.

'I paid the month's rent upfront, and he gave me the keys. I thought if things got worse, I could just take a few things and move into the flat while I sorted out the predicament, I was in.'

'Have you spoken to a solicitor?'

'I was going to. I made an appointment with Brown & Co. But it's not until next Tuesday. I thought I could get some advice. I need to know where I stand with the house. John can't get any of the money my grandad left me because the majority of it was left in cash and what was in the bank was transferred to me as his only living relative.' Sounding defeated, she shrugs her shoulders and I want to take her in my arms and tell her everything will turn out okay.

'Your uncle sounds dodgy,' I say instead of comforting her. 'The will could be a fraud.'

'There is that. It seemed legit but then again what do I know about wills? At the moment I don't know what to do for the best.'

'You said you ripped it up and threw it on the floor. Was that into tiny pieces?'

'No, just in half.'

'Well, that's one good thing. As long as your uncle hasn't gotten his hands on it again, it could be taped together, and we could have it checked out. It's a shame you can't remember the name of the brief who wrote it up.'

'I'm not going back to the house where he is,' she stresses, her body tensing up.

'Hey.' I place my hand on hers. 'You don't have to do anything you don't want to. Leave it to me.' I squeeze her hand gently, causing her to look down at how my hand encompasses hers. I lift it off not wanting to make her feel uncomfortable.

'Thank you,' she utters.

'So, you moved into the flat then.' I'm not asking because from what she has already said she's made it clear. She nods her head.

'And how's that going?'

'I'm not sure which is worse. Staying with my uncle or living in that flea-bitten, damp cesspit.' She scowls then rubs her forehead and closes her eyes. The stress of everything has probably given her a migraine.

'Would you like some painkillers?'

'Yes, please.' She rubs at her eyes and then her temples.

Retrieving the tablets from the kitchen cabinet and a bottle of water from the fridge, I'm back in no time, handing them to her.

'Thanks.' She swallows the tablets with a swig from the bottle and then places it on the breakfast bar.

'I can only imagine how bad it is.'

'Well, whatever you're imagining times that by ten,' she says, as she fiddles with the bottle of water. 'No hot water. That's the first shower I have taken since last Friday. I was in such a hurry to find somewhere I didn't even realise it didn't have a washer. I'd only managed to grab a few things when I had to leave…'

'What do you mean had to leave?'

'When I eventually arrived home on Friday night John was zonked out on the settee. I was quiet because I didn't want to wake him. I went up to my room and locked the door behind me. I'd already packed a small case so knowing he was still asleep, I crept downstairs and out to my car and placed it in the boot.'

'Was you that scared of him?'

'Not when he was sober but when he was drunk, he was volatile, a ticking time bomb, he could go off over the slightest thing. Sober, I could handle him but most of the time he'd had a few too many.'

'So, what pushed you to leave? What happened?'

'Once I put the case in the car, I went back to my bedroom, I didn't see him at all Friday evening. Saturday morning when I went downstairs, he wasn't there, he'd gone out. Later in the afternoon, he came back, and he was in the foulest of moods. Ranting about someone letting him down. He'd had some buyer lined up for my grandad's piano and he hadn't shown up. He asked me for money, and I told him I didn't have any. That didn't go down well either and he started smashing things in the kitchen. I wasn't sticking around to see how it played out, so I picked up my keys and my handbag, ran out of the house, and drove to the flat.'

'You did the right thing, getting out of the house, Meadow.' I was in the police force long enough and saw enough psychological abuse, coercion, and physical abuse, it makes me sick to the pit of my stomach, knowing how much domestic violence there is. Meadow might not have had a partner, but a member of the family could deliver the same abuse, this being her uncle. 'I just wish you had said something when he first turned up then you wouldn't have been alone.' My heart squeezes in my chest. It's unsettling that she felt as if she couldn't come to one of us.

'What happened last night?' I ask, hoping she doesn't notice how her being upset is tormenting me.

'There was a fire.'

'In your flat?'

'Not in mine. One of the others but it was bad enough that the smoke was spreading into mine and the one on the other side of it, so the firemen and police told us it was unsafe to stay there. They didn't give me and the other residents much time to get out. I just grabbed what I could and came here.'

'Jesus, Meadow.' I blow out a breath. 'What a bloody nightmare.'

'I know. I had nowhere else to go.' She looks so sad and defeated. When her shoulders start to shake and tears flood her eyes, I'm up and out of my seat, taking her in my arms. I hold her tight, shushing her as she grips hold of me, buries her face into my neck, and sobs like a child. Holding her in my arms is one thing I have longed to do but due to my insecurities, I pushed her away. Not wanting to experience those feelings again, the ones that led me to be taken for an idiot, I buried them deep inside and become her arsehole boss. I wanted her to hate me and hopefully leave my company. I hate myself for being so callous towards her—for my own selfish reason, I made her hate me. Even at the moment while she clings onto me for comfort, I know her true feelings towards me and to be fair I deserve her loathing. However, if she'll let me, I'll make it my utmost priority to find out what her uncle is up to, make sure she is rid of him and can claim her home back and I will keep her safe from harm while I'm doing it even though I know she will fight me on it.

I'm unsure how long she stays clung to me but when I feel her tensed body relax into me, I place my lips on her head, letting them linger for a while before I pull her away and place my hands on her shoulders.

'Listen to me, Meadow. I know you have every reason to hate

me.' She lifts one hand and wipes the tears from her eyes. 'Believe me, I had my reasons, which are stupid and immature, and I will explain myself to you one day with the hopes you can forgive me.' Her light blue eyes gaze at me, confused. I move my hands from her shoulders and cup her cheeks, running my thumbs under her eyes, removing the wetness that still lingers there. 'If I could take back everything I've ever said or done to upset you, I'd do it. I hope one day you can forgive me, but right now we have more important things to sort out.'

She closes her eye for a split second and bites her lip then she nods her head. Taking her hand, I assist her in sitting down then pass her a tissue.

'Meadow, I think you should go get some sleep while I make a few phone calls,' I tell her, passing her the bottle of water she had placed on the breakfast bar. She takes it from me and puts it to her lips. 'I need to call in a few favours as well as call my brothers.' She looks up at me and places the bottle back down. 'They will want to know, and they will want to help in any way they can. What do you say?'

'Okay.' She agrees.

Tracey Gerrard

CHAPTER 8

MEADOW

I throw the cotton sheets back, feeling more refreshed than I have for a long while then I sit up and take in my surroundings. I'm reminded where I am—my boss's penthouse. The huge space with its queen-sized bed, delicate cream walls, and high gloss fitted wardrobes, I could get used to. This room alone is bigger than the flea-bitten pit I just fled from.

I bury my face in my hands unable to believe I came here last night. Mind you, desperate times call for desperate measures and I was desperate.

Being woken up in the middle of the night—not that I'd been asleep long because I hadn't. The argument I'd had with my boss had played heavily on my mind. The cheek of him. How dare he question me on whether I've sorted out his blasted suits? Who the hell does he think he is? It's not even my job but for whatever reason, I've taken care of them without batting an eyelid. And has he ever been grateful? Has he hell. It's a moot point now though because telling him a few home truths about himself as well as telling him to stick his job where the sun doesn't shine, sealed my fate—I'm now unemployed as well as homeless. However, that might not be the case.

Pouring my heart out to him, disclosing what had been troubling me for nearly two weeks, surprised the hell out of me. What shocked me even more was his reaction. Attentive. He was kind to me and that is a first. He offered me comfort when I cried then brought me into his home, so we had privacy then he listened some more. Hung onto my every word, showing concern for my welfare. I haven't had that for such a long time. As I told him everything that had gone on with my uncle and then the fire at the flat, his eyes were sympathetic

Protecting Her

to my misery. And then he did the unthinkable. Something I'd never have thought of—not even in my wildest dreams would I have expected him to kiss me while he held me tightly as I soaked his shirt with my tears. It might have only been a kiss on my head, but his lips lingered there long enough for me to feel the heat radiating from them. His words caught me off guard. Telling me he had his reasons for being an arsehole, and that we'd discuss that some other time, threw me into confusion. I was too tired, too distressed to decipher what they meant. Now I'm awake, I'm still confused about what he said and the meaning behind it because I doubt what I'm thinking is not what he meant. I'm sure my boss, Mr Kane Summer, although showed another side to his usual demanding ways, hasn't gone soft. He was probably shocked to find me in the office asleep and then unloading my troubles to him.

Needing the toilet, I get up from the bed, leaving my thoughts there. A hot shower and a few hours of peaceful, undisturbed sleep have given me the energy to push on with my day. I have a lot to sort out and sitting around here won't get it done.

I use the loo then wash and brush my teeth. Feeling a bit chilly, I rummage through the drawers in search of a jumper or something I can pull over the T-shirt I had the cheek to pick out when Mr Summer or Kane, which he has told me to call him from now on, offered me the use of his shower. I like that name. It sounds strong and although spelled differently to the biblical bad boy Cain, it really does suit him.

I find a hoody and pull it on then I open the bedroom door, peeking out before I step out into the unknown. I say unknown because I'm unsure what today will bring.

Loud voices grab my attention and I'm pulled toward the rowdy sound of the five brothers I have come to know and love—well four of them anyway. The jury's still out on Mr Summer. Let's see how well he can behave himself.

'Here she is.' Callum is the first to spot me as I step into the room. I'm taken aback by the amount of concern that is filling the room. Apart from Kane and his four brothers, there are also two other men that I know are part of the security staff and both of them look worried too. Callum shakes his head at me, he has that look of an older brother who is disappointed in his younger sister. I give him a tight smile and then walk into his open arms. I've looked at the twins as family for a while now and since working for Summer Knights Security I have grown attached to Callum and Mason. He hugs me tightly. 'Why the hell didn't you tell us what was happening?' I don't get to explain myself because I am pulled into another pair of strong arms. This is Henry.

'I'm not happy with you young lady. You should have come to us.' Geez, he sounds like my dad. If I'd had one that is.

'What he said,' Connor says, taking me from his twin brother and pulling me into his chest.

'All right you lot give her some air,' Mason tells them all. I step out of Connor's embrace, turning to see Mason's brow furrowed. God, he looks so much like Kane when he's being all serious.

'Seriously, Meadow, you couldn't come to us?' He's stopped from saying anymore when big brother speaks.

'Stop hounding her you lot. Come and sit down Meadow.' I look up to see Kane pulling out a chair for me. He gives me a reassuring smile, which does reassure me. I know Callum, Mason, Henry, and Connor are on my side. Yes, they're upset with me at the moment, and I don't blame them but knowing Mr Summer, I mean Kane—I'm still not used to calling him that—is still in my corner, means so much, I don't think anyone would understand why. I don't understand why.

'Coffee with milk and sugar,' he offers as I sit down, he places a cup in front of me.

'Thank you,' I tell him, and I'm rewarded with a cheeky wink. Wow, did he just flirt with me? I blush a little but cover it up by picking up the cup and taking a drink from it.

'You must be hungry.' Yes, I am.

'Mason brought the sandwiches, help yourself while I update you on what we think of your predicament.' Whether I like it or not, now I've told Mr Summer, I know he will have shared everything with his brothers, and they will want to help me in any way they can. This is why they are all here.

'Lovely, I'm starving.' I help myself to one and bite into it. Chicken, salad, and mayo. Nice, I haven't had breakfast apart from a piece of toast when I was first brought here. I don't even know what time it is until I glance at the laptop screen that is open on the table. Blooming heck, it's eleven fifteen. 'Wow, I've slept well.'

'You needed it. It looks like you needed that too,' Kane mentions as he nods his head to the piece of sandwich I have left in my hand. 'Help yourself to another.' He pushes the plate towards me.

'Thank you, don't mind if I do.' His lip rises at one side as I pop the rest of the first sandwich into my mouth and then help myself to another. I'm not one to shy away from food but I haven't been myself lately, which has played havoc on my usual healthy appetite.

'Okay Meadow, I'm sure you're aware why everybody is here.' I nod my head. 'Well after discussing what you told me happened last night and this is your decision, Connor thinks you should go to the police.' I glance at him, and he shrugs his shoulders.

'If your uncle has threatened you Meadow then it needs reporting. We can't do much about the house at the moment because if the will is legitimate then you don't have a leg to stand on. The house belongs to your uncle.'

'I am aware of that.'

'That's not all Meadow. Even if it isn't, if your grandad didn't make a will then John has got as much right to live in that house as you.' He's not telling me anything I didn't already know.

'Is the house in your name?' Callum asks as he stands with his back against the wall. That's when I notice the whiteboard, a lone picture of my uncle sitting in the middle of it.

'No. My grandad died before he had the chance to sign it over to me. He always said he would but—' I shrug my shoulders and get up to take a look at the picture. The picture is a close-up and shows John leaving the house. It's a recent one too. 'What's this?' I place my hand on the board and stare at the photo. The shrubs that surround the front garden bring a tear to my eye. Planting them was the last thing the three of us got to do together. Grandad, Grandma, and me, a year before my grandma died. 'When was this taken?' I turn to look at Kane.

'This morning,' he answers as he comes to stand by my side. It makes a change to have him in such close proximity and not get the feeling that he doesn't want me anywhere near him. The vibe I'm getting at the moment from him is warm and welcoming. I like it. 'It's certainly clear from what you told me that this man is not the same man you remember. I mean he's your uncle John, but something has changed.'

'I agree.'

'Before we go any further.' Kane's eyes meet mine. There's a softness to them that I haven't seen before. 'I need to know do you want the police involved?' I look at Connor and he gives me a sympathetic smile, meaning it's up to me.

'It's your call, Meadow.' Connor is as straight as an arrow. If he thought the police were my best option, then he'd be badgering me to call them.

'Meadow, your uncle's been aggressive towards you. He's pressured you to do what he wants. Coercion is a criminal offence, as is his abusive behaviour, so if you want to report him then we'll stand by you. However, I think there's more to this. He's shifty, that's for sure. He's changed since you were a teenager and your grandad—who was a good judge of character, so I've been told—didn't want him anywhere near the house. There's a reason for that. I can promise you, Meadow, if you leave it to us, we'll leave no stone unturned.' He stares at me for a moment, his blue eyes holding mine hostage. Pleading for me to trust him. I have no reason not to. He wouldn't be helping me if he didn't want to. I know he'll keep his word. But how? Kane runs a security company, not a bloody private investigating company. I don't want them getting into bother over this, over me. When I snatch my eyes back and look around the room, everybody else is waiting for me to say something.

'Mr Summer—Kane—I don't want anybody getting into trouble. I know you were in the police but none of you are private investigators. Only Connor has the authority to find out things about my uncle. You've already said he's shifty, I don't want any of you getting hurt.' The room erupts in raucous laughter, and I'm thrown a few looks that say, Come on Meadow don't be so bloody stupid.

'Don't you worry.' Callum comes to stand beside me, throwing his arm around my shoulder. 'We have it all in order.'

'You do?'

'Yes, we do,' Kane answers, turning to the picture on the board. I turn too and Callum drops his arm from my shoulders. 'As from nine o'clock this morning, I have a team of four men tailing your uncle and keeping eyes on the house. They'll each take turns on who will be shadowing him and who will keep surveillance on your home.' Wow, a stakeout. 'You know Damon and Chris.' Kane points to the two men who are sitting at the other side of the table. They both smile and give me a little wave. I smile and wave back at them. Yes, I know them, they have both worked with Kane for many years. I think they came on board when he first set up his company. 'They're part of the surveillance team along with Antony and Sam'—I know them also— 'who are keeping tabs as we speak. They took the picture of your uncle an hour ago as he was leaving the house and forwarded it to me. Sam is now tailing him while Antony keeps tabs on any comings and goings from the house. We don't know what he's been up to since you left so we need to cover all bases. We're also waiting for some info to come through on your uncle, we should have it shortly.'

'What info and where from?'

'Between us, we are owed a lot of favours and let's just say we cashed a few of them in. I don't think your uncle has been working abroad all this time, Meadow. There's more to this than just an angry member of the family who's pissed off because his niece has been living in the family home and got the inheritance that he thought he was entitled to.'

I have to agree with him. It's hard to believe my uncle has changed so much. None of my family, small as it was, had an aggressive bone in their body. From what I remember, my mum was always happy. Caring and kind to others. I can't remember a time before she died when she didn't smile. My grandma was the same. She was always happy to give to others, helped at the local charity shop, and gave her time at the church fair. Grandad, I never heard him curse or argue with anyone until the argument he had with John. That is why I was so shocked when I heard their heated voices. Then years later my grandad seemed to get irritated when I mentioned him. I don't understand what's gone on over the years, but it saddens me to think the only family member I have left is such a horrible person.

'I agree. He's not the man I remember and even after the fallout with my grandad, he could have still contacted my grandma before she died. He had plenty of time, but he never did.' I chomp on my lip trying hard to stop my chin from quivering. I've cried enough over the last week or so, It's time I toughened up.

'Hey, come here shorty.' I chuckle as Henry wraps his arms around me. He named me that when we were fourteen. Not that I was incredibly small because I wasn't. It was he and Connor who were overly tall, standing well over a foot taller than me. 'Everything will work out.' He kisses the top of my head and lets me go.

'I know. I'm fine. Just exhausted with it all.'

'You're bound to be. Maybe you should grab another nap and we'll wake you as soon as we have any information.' I look up at Henry knowing he is right but there are things I need to do first.

'I can't. I need to go over to the flat to see what's happening. I hardly had any time to gather anything together. I don't have a change of clothes or any toiletries.' Everyone turns to Connor, a strange look passing between them all. He blows out a long breath as he places his hands on the table and stands up. When he moves to the side of me and sits down, he takes hold of my hand.

'About that. You can't go back to the flat Meadow—well not today anyway.'

'Why? I'm sure they had the fire under control before I left. It was just smoke damaged.'

'Yes, that's correct. But the police are not letting anybody in until the Specialist Fire Safety Officer presents the report on his findings and the SOCO team too. They think it's an insurance job.'

'Oh, my, God. Someone could have been killed. This just gets worse.' I can't believe this. Things are just going from bad to worse.

'Don't worry it won't take them long but at the moment you can't go back there. If you need anything getting—personal stuff—I can see if they'll let me in to get them, but I can't promise anything.'

'I suppose that would be okay. Thank you.'

'You're welcome.'

'Meadow, you're welcome to stay here as long as you need to. Connor will go and collect your things. If they allow him in, that is.'

'I'll go with him,' Mason offers.

'Good.' Kane turns to Damon and Chris. 'You two might want to go home and get your heads down because you are both on the night shift.' Then he turns back to me. 'Callum is going to man the office and I'll be working from home just so you have someone here.'

'You don't need to do that. Honestly, you've done so much already, I'll be fine. In fact, I have my bank card with me, I could book in at the hotel across from here.' I watch his brow crease.

'Don't be silly. Why would you do that when I have enough room? Plus, we're all set up in here.' He waves his hand to the board which holds a solitary picture of my uncle. My mouth rises at one side.

'Yeah, granted it doesn't look much at the moment, but we intend to make progress on 'Operation Bring Down Uncle John.' He gives me that dynamic smile, the one he uses when he and his brothers know they are in the running to win a big contract. When he knows they have it in their grasp. His determination to win should be bottled and put on sale. My stomach flutters, knowing he's willing to do this for me. Bring on board people he trusts to find out what my uncle is up to. He knows I never wanted to bring the police into this. I told him so early this morning. Stupid as it is, until I know what is really going on, I'd rather do it this way. Kane has shown me another side to him today that I didn't know existed. Nevertheless, I need to remember what an arsehole he can be—has been—and that smile he's just shown me, he's held back from me so many times in the past but for now he's playing Mr Nice, so I'll stay here for now but if he reverts back to Mr Arsehole then I'm out of here.

'Thank you, I'd love to stay.' It's not a lie, part of me really likes the idea of living with Mr Summer.

'Good.' This time when he smiles at me his dimple comes out to play. It's beautiful. Kane is beautiful. As well as being shocked, I feel the heat covering my cheeks as I blush. 'Then we should all get on with what needs to be done,' he instructs as I turn my face from him.

*

A soft knock at the door stirs me and I turn over, pulling the sheet back over my head. 'Meadow, are you awake?' I recognise the voice, but it doesn't match the caring tone. Am I dreaming? Could this be the same man? Maybe aliens have taken over his body and made him into a better person.

'I'm awake,' I croak, lifting the sheet and sitting up against the comfy pillows. The door is already open, and Kane stands there at the foot of the bed, his hands in his pockets.

'How are you feeling?' He moves around the bed, sitting down at the side of me on the edge. His manly scent and the close proximity have my stomach fluttering again and I rub at my face, trying hard not to show his presence is affecting me. 'I'm good. What time is it?' I say once I shake off the feeling he is arousing. What the hell is wrong with me? Gazing around the room for any signs of a clock, I give myself a little pep talk. Remember who he is? Do not start crushing on your ex-boss. It won't end well.

'Five thirty,' he answers, the low tone of his voice does not help with my predicament.

'Wow, I've slept the day away.'

'You needed it.' He shifts nearer to me and places his hand on my cheek. He stares at me, his warm eyes, searching my face. For what I don't know but like the idiot I am, I lean into his touch. It's warm and gentle and that is what I need at the moment. 'Mmmm.' He breaks the silence then removes his hand and stands quickly. 'There's Chinese waiting. You must be hungry.'

'Yes, I am.' My belly rumbles on cue.

'We have new information too.' He walks to the door, and I call him back.

'Thank you.' I am grateful for his help. For all their help.

'You're welcome, Meadow.'

'Oh, Kane,' I call him back again.

'Yes?'

'Was Connor able to get into the flat?'

'No, I'm afraid not.'

'Crap.' What the hell am I going to do? I have nothing here but a pair of leggings, a onesie, and a pair of knickers.

'Don't worry, he went shopping with Mason, they've bought you a few things to get by. When you're feeling up to it one of us will go shopping with you to get whatever else you need.'

'I can go on my own.' I throw back the covers and stand up.

'I don't want you going anywhere on your own, one of us will go with you.' I don't get to tell him that I'm a grown woman and I don't need babysitting because he strides off, closing the door behind him. I should fight him on it, but I won't. Not today anyway.

It's not long before I've changed into a pair of jeans and a vest. The boys did well. Some decent underwear, a few pairs of jeans, and a couple of tops. No joggers or hoodies though. During the working week, I'm used to wearing suits and blouses but relaxing at home, I like my comfy clothes. I can get by with jeans, but I need something to keep me warm. So not having anything, I pick up Kane's hoodie that I had on earlier and make my way out of the bedroom.

I find Kane and his brothers minus Connor, all tucking into the Chinese food as if they haven't eaten all day.

'Come on, sit down,' Callum says, around a mouthful of salt and pepper king prawn. He uses his foot to pull out a chair between him and Kane and I slide in between them.

'This looks delicious,' I comment picking up a plate and a fork. 'I could eat a horse, I'm that hungry.' My eyes light up as I tuck into the first carton that is passed to me. Chicken fried rice.

'Here try these,' Mason offers, smiling as he passes me the tray of barbecue ribs. My favourite. In no time my plate is full of small amounts of everything. I love my food and I'm not ashamed to show it.

We all sit there inhaling our food like starved animals, no words are spoken, just the sound of us enjoying a meal together. I've eaten with Kane's brothers many times but never with him. It should feel awkward due to the hostility we've shared for so long however staying in his home, talking with him, and eating at his table seems nice. I find he's not irritating me like he normally does, and he seems at ease with me. It could all change in a flash.

'So, what did you find out?' I ask as I help clear the empty plates and cartons away. I'm fit to bursting and probably don't need to eat anything else until next week. The guys are too. Kane had ordered far too much but it won't go to waste. Anything that was left has been claimed. Everyone has something to take home, Kane has even put some aside for Connor, who is working until six in the morning. He'll eat it for dinner tomorrow.

'Come on let's go into the office,' Kane suggests. Following him from the dining area down the corridor to his home office, it surprises me how I haven't noticed before the number of rooms this place has. I can be quite nosey but then this is Kane's place, and in the past, I wouldn't have dreamt about nosing in his space. Now I'm here I might just have a little snoop around. I'll leave it until he goes out, of course. I know he's supposed to have a jacuzzi in his bathroom. I wouldn't mind having a soak in that.

Kane holds the door to his office open for me to enter first, everyone else follows behind me. Nothing has changed, the whiteboard is still standing with just one lonely picture in the middle of it.

'Sit down Meadow and we'll run through what we have learned today about your uncle John.' He points to the chair at the head of the table, so I take a seat. I realise I'm sitting in his chair and that makes me feel special. And maybe a little nervous.

He gets to it straight away. 'Our sources have informed us that John hadn't been travelling or working abroad as you thought. He'd been residing at His Majesty's Pleasure.'

'Excuse me?' I almost choke on my words. Did I hear I'm correct?

'He's been in jail Meadow,' Callum says, simplifying it for me, and the words sink in. Just my bloody luck. The only family I have left is not just an aggressive arsehole but a bloody criminal as well.

'What for? How long? When did he get out?' I'm rambling. My questions are quick and abrupt which gives Kane a concerned look.

'Calm down Meadow,' he says as he comes to stand by my side, placing his hand on my shoulder. 'We'll get to that in a minute. Just give yourself a moment to let it sink in first.' I don't know why he's being so kind about this, I have a criminal in the family. I've been working for him for the past two years and I know just what a stickler he is for making sure every one of his staff is as clean as a whistle and they do not associate themselves with known criminals. I hadn't seen my uncle for years, I didn't know.

'I didn't know,' I mumble against my hand.

'What?'

'I didn't know he was a criminal.' I look up, meeting Kane's soft eyes. He doesn't seem annoyed; all I see is warmth in them and a little confusion on his face.

'Meadow, we know you weren't aware of this.' He crouches down and takes hold of my hand, the half-smile that crosses his face tells me I'm being silly for thinking such thoughts. I nod my head, giving him a tight smile as a silent thank you.

'What did he do?' I ask. Kane lets go of my hand as he stands up and crosses the room back to the whiteboard where he picks up a marker.

'He was given a seven-year sentence for three cases of fraud; he spent four of them in prison and was released on parole.'

'However.' Callum rises from his seat and joins his older brother. 'He was rearrested on some more charges of the same kind and was remanded in custody due to him being out on parole. He was found guilty and had to serve the rest of his sentence plus what he'd been handed out for the new charges that he'd been found guilty of.'

'I don't know what to say. Do you think my grandparents knew?'

'We're not sure, Meadow,' Henry says as a sad smile crosses his face. 'Once we'd found out he'd been in prison, we were able to source most of the information from archives of the local newspaper. So given that it was local knowledge then it's a possibility.'

'Maybe that's what the argument was about,' Mason offers. 'You know, if he was out on bail at the beginning of the trial then he may have told them, and your grandad lost it and kicked him out of the house.'

'With the type of fraud he'd committed, it's understandable,' Henry adds.

'What was it? You said trial, that's serious, right?' Mason gives me a slow nod of his head.

Kane reveals how my uncle and two known associates had swindled three elderly couples out of their pensions with another two being looked into. They had all received the same amount of time for the first charges of fraud, my uncle getting out early on parole for good behaviour. And then was arrested straight away due to the police having enough evidence on him to secure a guilty charge on two more accounts of fraud and one of identity theft.

God, I feel sick. How could he? No wonder my granddad didn't want him near the house.

By the time Kane had finished telling me what prisons he was sent to and the dates, my head was swimming with everything I had learned this evening. Kane had written some of the information on the whiteboard as well as two drawings, I think they're the two prisons because he'd also written the names of them underneath and the dates my uncle resided there.

'Here drink this.' Henry offers me a glass of wine. He must have nipped out to the kitchen to fetch the wine and glasses while Kane was telling me everything.

'Thank you. You'd better leave me the bottle.' I let out a nervous laugh as I take a long drink from the glass. 'It's a lot to take in. Has Antony and Sam reported anything back yet?'

'Yes. John left the house around eleven this morning and got the bus to town. He spent two hours in the betting office and then walked down to The Crown. He's back now and just had a pizza delivered.'

'So, he's a gambler then?'

'Looks that way,' Henry answers, topping up my glass.

'Why would he do that, rob old people of their hard-earned

money, I mean? I don't understand.'

'Meadow, you're going to have lots of questions. At the moment we don't have all the answers, but we are doing our best to find out what he is up to. If I were to hazard a guess to your question, I'd say greed or desperation. It's clear he's desperate for money again from what you've told us. We're watching him now so if he steps out of line then we'll have him on that and we'll try our damn best to get your home back.'

I don't know why but saying thank you doesn't seem enough and before I know what I'm doing, I'm in front of Kane, standing on my tiptoes and kissing his cheek. 'Thank you,' I tell him when I pull away. Then I return to the table, taking the glass of wine Mason is holding out for me.

CHAPTER 9

MEADOW

My head throbs as I sit down at Kane's dining room table. I bury my face in my hands, regretting drinking the best part of a bottle and a half of wine, last night.

After I kissed Kane on the cheek and said thank you, things seemed a little weird between us. No one said anything but I did feel his body tense when I placed my hands on his biceps and brushed my lips ever so quickly across his stubbled cheek. His response was zilch. Nothing but a nod of his head then he turned back to that bloody board. I'm sure I blushed as I padded back to my seat, feeling slightly embarrassed. Mason handed me another glass of wine and because he and Callum had an early start this morning they went home, leaving me with Henry and their older brother. Kane informed us he had work to do so we left him alone in his office and went into the living room with the wine.

We sat for hours putting the world right and reminiscing about our school days as we opened another bottle of wine. I'm not even sure what it was, but Henry did say it was good stuff. It was late when he fell asleep on the settee, so I covered him with a throw-over and went to my room. On the way there, I stopped outside Kane's office and knocked lightly on the door, there was no answer. I'd wanted to say goodnight to him but then thought he'd probably gone to bed. I also wondered why he hadn't come to say goodnight to us before he went.

'Here take these,' Henry offers me a couple of painkillers and a glass of water. I take them and thank him, gratefully. 'I needed some when I woke up.' He rubs at his bare chest, yawning. 'I don't even drink wine. Now I know why,' he moans as he rubs his forehead.

'You want to put some clothes on,' Kane orders as he strides into the room, wearing only a pair of joggers. I do a double take as he strides past me holding the board he was writing on last night then plants it on the other side of the room. My lady parts snigger and my eyes seem to be glued to the strong muscles that define his back. I prize them away, but the bloody things have taken on a life of their own and are now happy with being stuck to his fine firm arse.

'I bet you wish you had a body like this.' Henry flexes his muscles standing there in just his boxers shorts, smirking at his brother. I try to take control of the senses that are only used to seeing Kane in a suit and tie and then bite my lip to hide my amusement. Jesus, when did I become one of those women? It's not the first time I've seen Henry strutting around in his underwear and I'm sure it won't be the last. I've been friends with Henry and Connor for a long time, we've even shared the same bed after a night out. Nothing sexual, that would be just gross. But seeing Kane shirtless does do something to me that I can't seem to control because when he states he is going for a shower, my baby blues follow his every movement.

'Are you eyeing my brother up?'

'I might be,' I answer in a daze as I lean to one side, my head tilted so I can get a better view of the fine specimen of a man. Henry leans with me—both of us practically hanging off our seats as we watch his brother move with confidence out of the dining room and down the corridor that leads to the bedrooms and bathroom.

'Does he know you gawp at him when he's not watching?' As if I've just been slapped in the face with a wet fish, I sit up startled at what just happened. Then I turn to Henry who is ginning at me like a bloody idiot.

'I was not gawping.' I slap his arm and try to sound convincing, but I fail miserably because I was gawping.

'You were giving him the once over,' he jokes with a knowing look on his face.

'I was not. I was just shocked to see him parading around shirtless. I'm used to seeing him all suited and booted.' I try to defend my wondering eyes.

'Yeah, I'm sure that was it,' he smirks at me picking up his coffee cup and taking a drink. 'Your secret is safe with me.' He mimics zipping up his mouth and throwing the key away. Geez that's all I need Henry thinking I fancy his older brother and giving me shit about it.

I'm given a reprieve when his phone vibrates on the kitchen island, and he gets up to answer it. I try to put what just happened to the back of my head and focus on the mess my life is in at the moment. I don't know how long I've sat there feeling sorry for myself but when I look up, Kane is back fully dressed, and Henry has finished his phone call.

'Right, I'm going to get some clothes on.' He gives me a cheeky wink then he smacks a kiss on Kane's forehead and takes off out of the room, leaving me alone with Mr Grumpy or is it Mr Sexy?

Kane rolls his eyes and then fiddles with the whiteboard that is propped against the wall. He has his back to me as he stares at what is written on there. The silence is awkward so after a few minutes, I get up and ask him if he'd like a cup of coffee. God knows I could do with one.

'Yes,' he says, and just when I think he's reverted back to the man with the huge attitude problem and no manners, he turns to me. 'Thank you, that would be nice,' he says politely, and just like that the ice is broken again and I have a huge smile on my face as I venture into his kitchen.

*

It's just after twelve when Connor, Mason, and Callum turn up. Henry decided he needed to head off home once he had dressed, telling me he'd be back around lunchtime to catch up with whatever we had learned about my uncle then Kane went downstairs to the main office, taking his coffee with him and only returned when his brothers arrived. So, my smile was short-lived due to being left alone, bored to tears, and wondering whether this was all worth it. I want to know what John is up to and I want my home back but involving Kane and his brothers might just drive me to despair.

'So, what have we learned so far?' Callum asks as he worries his tongue between his teeth.

'Not much at this point other than he has just met with this woman at a bar in town.' Kane passes his mobile around the table, showing my uncle shaking hands with a woman who's probably in her mid-thirties. She has shoulder-length, wavy black hair, wearing a smart dark blue two-piece suit and is carrying a briefcase.

'Any idea who she is?'

'I've never seen her before in my life,' I answer, passing the phone back to Kane. 'She looks professional. She could be a solicitor.'

'It's a possibility,' Callum offers. 'However, there's no point in us sitting here surmising, is there?' He's quick to rise from his seat, picking up his jacket from the back of it.

'What are you doing?' Kane asks, a look of confusion on his face.

'That bar is a ten-minute walk from here. Sam might be tailing him, but I could do with a pint and a bite to eat. You never know I might just bump into a nice lady.' He wiggles his eyebrows and smirks at me.

'Do you think that's wise? I mean, I don't want you putting yourself in any danger.' He laughs and places his hands on my shoulders.

'What danger am I going to get into? We're talking about your uncle who likes conning old people and enjoys bullying his niece.' I cringe at the thought of him—my uncle— taking money from helpless people. 'I'm sorry, Meadow, I shouldn't have said that.' He gives me a sad smile, picking up on my reaction.

'No, you're right. He is a conman, and he did push me around but what I meant is I don't want you getting in any trouble. I don't want any of you ending up in bother because of me.'

'Hey, you're like family to us. As far as I'm concerned you are family.' Connor gets up from his chair and places his arms around me. 'And we look after one another. Okay?' I nod my head and let out a soft sigh.

'What's your plan?' Kane asks as Connor sits back down, and Callum shrugs his coat on.

'Well, I just thought I'd get in on the action. Women like to go to the ladies, so I just might bump into her on her way out. Apologise, flirt a little'—Kane rolls his eyes—'Hey you're not the only one who can pull the ladies.' He's right, they were all at the front of the queue when God was giving out looks and charm. 'You never know I might get her number and I'll take it from there.'

'Okay but stay away from Walters. I have Sam on him. Just find out who she is and what she's doing with that lowlife.'

'Leave it with me, boss.' He salutes Kane mockingly then hurries out of the door.

'Are they still in The Hopping Frog?' That's the new bar and restaurant that opened a couple of months back. I've been in once. It's a popular place.

'Yes. I'm just going to print this off.' Kane holds up his phone. I presume he means the picture of the woman who has met up with my uncle.

'So, what do we do now?'

'Well, I have some work to catch up on,' Mason comments as he pushes up from where he is sitting. He probably has. They all will have and I'm keeping them from it.

'Is there anything I can help you with?' I ask, taking a look behind me just to make sure Kane isn't on his way back. We haven't spoken about my employment with the company since the other night, so I don't know where I stand.

'No, it's fine don't you worry about it. Honestly Meadow you need the rest. I know you're not used to sitting around doing nothing but with what you've been through I'd say it's well and truly needed. Plus, you and Kane need to discuss the argument you had the other night before you come back to work. What he did and said wasn't out of malice—he was truly concerned about you and thought if he wound you up enough, then you'd flip and probably break down and tell us what was going on. I don't think he thought it through properly.' He gives me a tight smile. 'Don't be so hard on him, he means well.' I'm shocked Kane would do that. He's never shown any emotions around me—well not until the other night. Maybe I've misunderstood him.

'I'd better go. Henry's on his way, he's just messaged me; his car had a flat, so he's had to sort it out. He's meeting me at the office. He said sorry for not making it back on time, he'll catch up later. There's no point in him coming up here until we know more. In fact, I don't know why we are up here when we could just as easily work downstairs.'

'That's because Meadow needs the rest,' Kane states as he strides across the room towards the notice board, he pins up the picture of the pretty, smartly dressed woman.

'I'm feeling a lot better now, thanks to all of you. If you want to work from the main office, then I'm good with that.' I might have a little hangover, but I've slept well for the last couple of days, and

I've eaten well too. I don't feel lightheaded anymore.

'You still look pale and tired. We'll work from here for now.' He turns back to the board, pondering over the two photographs the conversation is now over. Still the arsehole.

Once Mason left Kane followed, stating he'd be back later. Connor stayed for another hour, then he left too. I knew they had work to do and would be back once they'd finished. But all of a sudden, I felt all alone, and the tears started to flow again.

I'm not sure how long I curled up on the settee, feeling sorry for myself as I contemplated my sad life. No family, and not many friends. Yeah, I have Louise, Henry, and Connor but when they're away or busy with whomever they are dating then I have no one. At the moment, Callum, Mason, and even Kane are showing they care but once this is all over, what will I be left with? Who knows if I will even have a home to go to? Will I be able to get the rest of my grandparent's things that I have saved, or will my uncle have sold them all?

I must have fallen asleep at some point because I'm suddenly awakened by a slam of a door. I sit up quickly, smoothing my hair down with my hands then rub them up and down my face. I make a quick sprint to the bathroom before whoever it is, makes it through into the living room. I presume it's Kane and I don't want him to see my tear-stained face and red eyes.

'Meadow.' His deep voice calls, my presumption correct.

'I'm here,' I call out as I come out of the main bathroom, shutting the door behind me. I know I look a mess but what can I do about my swollen eyes in such a short space of time? 'I'm just going to my room,' I holler, hoping he doesn't come to find me. If I stay out of his way long enough my eyes will go down and I won't get asked any awkward questions. Then again, he might not be bothered by what my eyes and face look like.

'What's wrong?' Looks like I was wrong. Kane stands in front of me, his hands on my shoulders, his face full of concern. 'Are you okay, Meadow?' His normal hard exterior has been replaced with a softness that was present the other night when he brought me here.

'I'm okay, just feeling sorry for myself.' My answer has him moving his hands to my face. They cup my cheeks and as he gazes into my eyes, he runs his thumb under them. I don't know what is going on here, but something passes over his face. Is that desire I see in those electric blue eyes? Does he want me? I'd like that. I'm shocked at this notion because yes, he's attractive. A god some women would say but he's also an arsehole who winds me up no end even if he is trying to help me out. However, when his mouth moves towards mine, I throw the usual loathing of this man out of the window and with thoughts of this morning I accept his lips.

The softness of them as they brush across mine sends a tingle through me and a shiver down my spine. He tests the water again and when I comply his tongue strokes the seam of my lips. I open up for him not having the power to say no. Do I want to say no? Should I say stop? Something in me is saying yes but when our tongues meet the sensation that runs through me is something I've never felt before, and my core tightens. Kane is a confident man, who likes to be in control, and at this very moment, he's controlling this kiss. Controlling me. He deepens the kiss angling my head and moves one of his hands to my hips. His lips brush across my jawline and then down onto my neck. The heat between us grows and my body presses into him as his lips meet mine again. This kiss is powerful, filled with fire, and something that belongs in the bedroom. And that is when I know I need to stop this.

I'm not Kane's type. There's no way he can be attracted to me. The women he beds are one-night stands. Women with silicone implants who are tall and leggy. That's not me. Most of the time he doesn't speak to me. He doesn't even smile at me, scowls yes, many times. He's only just started being civil to me and wanting to help due to my predicament. Does he feel sorry for me? Is that it?

I pull back and push on his solid chest for him to stop but he's too into it to realise and continues to trail soft kisses along the column of my neck. When I push harder, he steps back, and our connection is broken.

'What was that?' I ask, still trying to catch my breath.
'What?'
'You kissed me?'
'I did.'
'Why?'
'Because it's something I've wanted to do for a long time.' His hand reaches for mine and I step back out of his way.
'But... You don't even like me.' I place my hands on my hip. 'For almost two years, you have barely given me the time of day and

when you have it's with an attitude. Most of the time you're brusque, bad-tempered, and damn right mean…'

'I know.' He lowers his head, taking a deep breath. When he looks up, he looks ashamed of himself. Is he for real? Does he think I'm stupid? All he wants is a woman to warm his bed.

'You know?' My tone is bitter. 'You want me? You've wanted me for a long time? Well, it isn't happening buster. I will not be one of your floosies…. Is that why you brought me here, so you could get me into your bed?'

'What? No.' He runs his hand through his hair. He looks frustrated with himself. 'I brought you here because you were in trouble. I needed to know you were safe, Meadow.' He reaches for me again, and I smack his hand away.

'This isn't happening Kane.' I point between us. 'I will not be made to feel small and used. I refuse to be like those women that I'—I point at my chest— 'that I have turned away from the office door or made excuses for you when they have telephoned the office. I will not be made to look like a fool.'

'Meadow that's not—' Before he has a chance to finish what he is saying or see the tears that are building in my eyes, I turn and rush off to my room, storming through the door. It slams behind me, and I lean against it then slide down until my behind hits the floor.

I bury my face in my hands annoyed at myself for crying again. Even more annoyed about what just happened. I'm so ashamed of myself. I don't know how I'm going to face him later. I feel as if I should collect the few things, I have with me and just leave to save any awkwardness but where would I go? My home is out of the question and so is the flat. I could stay with the twins, Connor and Henry, they'd be happy to put me up. Then again, questions would be asked and I'm certainly not getting into how I let their older brother kiss me. They'd know I was hiding something. And I could never hide the fact that even though I know I shouldn't have liked him kissing me, I did. I more than liked it.

CHAPTER 10

KANE

I sit at the far side of the table, listening to Callum explain our findings today. Earlier today we were able to gather some intriguing information on Meadows's uncle, so things are becoming extremely interesting indeed.

I'd normally be the one adding information to the board as we try to figure out what his game is but for the first time in my life, I'm taking the coward's way out.

When I returned home after being at a meeting, I didn't expect to witness Meadow in such a state. She'd tried to cover up the fact that she'd been upset and crying but her beautiful eyes were puffy and red and knowing she was still hurting pulled on my heartstrings. I'd only meant to comfort her. I'd decided last night that anything with Meadow other than friendship would be out of the question. She's too close to my brothers for one thing and that could cause a rift between the twins and me if anything went wrong. I can't allow that. I'm also her boss and not a very nice one as she reminded me earlier and although she did quit the other day before all this and even though I haven't accepted her notice, I can't see her wanting to work for me now. You got what you wanted. My inner voice interrupts me, but I ignore it, not wanting to get into the whys and wherefores. I'm supposed to be helping her not taking advantage of her while she's feeling vulnerable. However, those lips called to me. Like a siren calling the sailors to their deaths, I succumbed to her beauty. My downfall because now she can't even look at me. I don't blame her. If I'd had been her, I'd have punched me in the face.

I know it was wrong of me, and she told me so, but I wouldn't be lying if I said part of her enjoyed it as much as I did. Her soft lips fused with mine—our bodies pressed together as if we were meant to be. I could feel her heart drumming against her rib cage, hard and fast, and I felt the heat between us. But she pulled away and berated me for being the arsehole I am. When she stormed away, I knew it'd be a mistake to go after her, so I left my apartment and buried myself in work for a few hours. When Callum called to tell me, he was on his way back and that he had informed the others to meet at my place, I knew I needed to man up. Go and apologise. Then I decided against it because to be truthful I'm not sorry about kissing her. It's the timing that was all wrong. I was going to act as if nothing had happened but no sooner did, I walk in here and see her face, I knew I needed to give her a wide birth. She didn't want to look at me while I reeled off the information that we'd been able to find out about her uncle, so I feigned a headache and asked Callum to step in for me then I sat at the far end of the table out of her view.

'So, this is Marie Simpson, whom John met up with. Their meeting didn't last long due to her not being happy with him.' Callum gets my attention as he points to a photo of her, which was taken by Sam when she first arrived at The Hopping Frog and shook hands with Meadow's uncle.

'What gave you that impression?' Connor asks.

'Her body language and the fact that she called him a waste of space and stormed off.'

'How did you find out her name?' Connor lifts his eyes to Callum as he stands to reach for the jug of water and a glass from the table. He pours a drink and then sits back down waiting for an answer.

'That was easy. When I arrived, I was just in time to witness her giving him a mouthful. She picked up a file and bag from the table. I surmised she was ready to leave, so I backtracked out into the car park and then accidentally bumped into her. Using my God-given charm, I was able to put a smile on her face and once she saw that John was leaving the pub too, she took me up on my offer of a quick drink.'

'I can't believe you were able to get her number and find out where she works in such a short space of time,' Henry comments.

'It's a gift,' he says with a smug smirk on his face. 'Anyway, over a drink, I found out her name and that she works at a small privately owned gallery on the other side of town. She'd been approached by John last week about some prints he said he had. He was supposed to bring them with him today only he fobbed her off with some lame excuse that the person he was getting them from had let him down.'

'Do you know what they were?' Meadow asks. She sits up, seemingly interested in knowing what the photos were of.

'Well, that's the thing, Meadow. I know you're grandma had lots of paintings, but it can't be any of them because this woman.' He points at the picture on the board. 'Deals in nude photos.'

'Oh.' She seems shocked.

'Exactly, and John knew this, which has me asking the question, does he have the photos or not? And if he can get his hands on them, where is he getting them from?'

'Are they intimate photos?' It's me who asks this time because I am interested in what he is up to, and I've met a few people who love to have pictures of sexual poses around their homes.

'Yes, but not just sexual poses. As long as the photos don't depict anything that would be frowned upon or against the law, Marie will display them in her gallery. She does private showings to wealthier collectors and opens to the public most days. I'm calling in tomorrow just to see what she's got.'

'So, who's the other woman?' Henry asks as he leans back and puts his hands behind his head.

'This is Judy Williams. Sam called me after I had left Marie at her car. I was just getting into mine. He'd followed John who had called into the betting office then when he came out, he made his way to a small café where he met this woman.'

'And did you pull your charm on her?' Meadow asks, smiling at him.

'Of course. I was in my element. I love doing this. I might become a private investigator.' We all laugh at his enthusiasm. He'd probably make a good PI. To be fair, whatever my brothers turn their hands to they do it with passion. 'I was able to find out that she works as a journalist for the local rag.' I sit forward in my seat because this is getting interesting. Why would he be meeting with a journalist?

'And what was she doing meeting with my uncle?'

'Haven't the foggiest. I never got the chance to ask. I don't think their meeting went to plan. I only just got there in time to witness a heated discussion but couldn't hear what was being said then John got up and walked out. Before Miss Williams had the chance to leave, I went and sat at her table and struck up a conversation. At first, she seemed a bit taken back.'

'You know you could get arrested for stalking.'

'Connor stop being so dramatic. I only asked her to join me for a cup of coffee. She was happy too. She told me her meeting hadn't gone the way she wanted and when I enquired as to what it was, she was very tight-lipped about it. The only thing I managed to obtain from her was what she did for a living and where she worked. If I'd had longer then maybe I could have gotten more but her phone rang, and she told me she had to leave.'

'I think you've done really well, Callum.' Meadow smiles at him, giving him the thumbs up.

'Thank you, my lady.' Callum mocks dipping his cap.

'I'd love to know what his game is and why he's associating with a journalist.' She worries her lip as she looks up at Callum.

'I think we all would.' He gives her a tight smile as he makes his way to sit down.

'I have something to add.' Connor pushes his seat back and stands then he makes his way to the front of the table. 'I'm waiting on the name and some information on John's cellmate.'

'Why?' Henry enquires.

'Because it's a well-known fact that when prisoners are locked up for a considerable length of time together, they tend to get to know each other extremely well.'

'Who are you waiting on?' Henry questions as he sits up straight and takes a drink from his glass.

'Can't tell you."

'Why?' He narrows his eyes on his twin brother.

'Because it's classified, and I'd have to kill you.' Here we go. My twin brothers will often take the piss out of each other. Wind each other up then get into a fight. It's not malicious just them goofing around. No one gets hurt. I wouldn't allow it.

'Even with my eyes closed and standing on one leg you couldn't take me.' Henry tosses a piece of chewed-up gum at him which Connor catches in one hand, causing Meadow to laugh. The sound is music to my ears. Knowing she's not stewing on what happened between us makes me feel better, but should I really be happy that she could dismiss such passion so easily? I'm not sure what to think anymore.

'Idiot.' Connor throws it back, hitting Henry on the side of the head.

'Will you two pack it in,' Mason intervenes, grabbing the gum out of Henry's hand and lobbing it in the bin. 'You're like two bloody kids sometimes.' They both wear the same smirk as they settle down, which is somewhat disturbing. They've always had that weird telepathic bond going on. As if they can read each other's mind and usually they're concocting some devious plan to get back at someone. Callum, Mason, and I have all been on the receiving end of it many times. When they were teenagers, they were always pulling pranks. I remember one day Callum was asked to take them to school by our mum because they were running late. He said he would but rather than dropping them at the school gates he dropped them half a mile down the road by the shops. They were both fifteen minutes late and got a warning in their planner. That evening while Callum was sitting in the chair watching the TV, they both crept up to him, tipped the chair over, and through the gaps of the chair arm covered him in foam by using the small fire extinguisher that we had in the garage. The poor man nearly shit himself. Mason and I saw the funny side of it, and we pissed ourselves laughing. Mum on the other hand didn't. Both the spare extinguisher and the one that was kept mounted on the wall for emergencies were almost empty and the chair was soaked through. They were both, along with Callum made to buy two new ones as well as clean the chair. Mum was always careful, knowing we had flammable liquids amongst other combustible things in the garage, she liked to be prepared for any eventuality.

'When will you have this information?' Meadow's soft questioning voice brings me out of my musing.

'Hopefully, tonight or first thing in the morning.'

'At least we're moving forward.' I rise from my seat and join Connor. Meadow seems to be fine, so I don't feel as much of a dick as I did and if there is one thing about me, I hate sitting around twiddling my thumbs. I like to be in charge, working the room. Meadow knows this, my brothers, too. 'We might not know why John is meeting with a journalist or where these so-called photos are from—but he's going to reach out to these women again. If he's meeting with a journalist, then he might have information for sale. Or it could have something to do with the illusive photographs. These things will all present themselves in good time. As for his cellmate, Connor is right to obtain as much information as possible, it might throw some light on a few things. What we need to be doing is focusing on the will. We can't take it as gospel that it's real.' I turn to Meadow. 'Your uncle is as dodgy as they come so it wouldn't surprise me if it's fake. And if it is then John must have known your grandparents were leaving the house to you otherwise, he could have just waltzed right in without one, knowing he had as much right to that house as you, if not more.' She stares at me thinking for a moment while she plays with her top lip.

'Shit, your right. He wouldn't need a will. Why didn't I think of that? Come to think of it, why didn't any of you?' She rolls her eyes. 'You two are police trained.' She's right, we should have realised it before now but to be fair, all this has only recently come to light, and we were all a bit shocked by what Meadow had gone through on her own. I still don't think she's told us everything.

'You're right Meadow, we are, and we should have realised this before now.'

'We did,' Mason interrupts. 'Yesterday we all but said it was fake.'

'Yes, but we didn't join the dots, did we? We assumed it was fake but didn't make the connection that he didn't actually need one, so why has he presented one now?'

'Because he knows the house was left to Meadow,' Connor finishes.

'Exactly.'

'So, what do we do now?' Meadow asks.

'We wait until Connor's info comes through and see if we can get anything from it. We could do with getting our hands on that will—and if there's anything else you can tell us, Meadow, anything at all that you haven't already, that would be a great help.' She chews on her thumbnail, thinking, as she stares at me.

'I'm not sure.' She takes a long moment, now chomping on her bottom lip. Yes, I'm affected by it. It was only a few hours ago I was biting the same bottom lip. Our eyes connect and for a fleeting moment, I think she's remembering the same. She looks away and blows out her cheeks. 'When he first turned up at the house, I'd been going through a lot of my grandparents' things and boxing them up. They were things I would never get rid of—keepsakes such as antique vases and ornaments. Other trinkets and personal possessions. Things that reminded me of my childhood and the happy times we'd spent together. I'd boxed up some old tat that I was going to take to the tip and another box for the charity shop. John went through the lot that weekend. He seemed to be searching for something. I heard him through the night opening cupboards and banging about and when I questioned him on what he was doing, he told me to shut up and keep out of it.' I breathe in deeply through my nose, trying to combat the anger that is brewing within me. Callum gives me a sideways glance but says nothing.

'He'd even pulled back the carpet and ripped up floorboards in their old room and when he couldn't find what he was looking for he'd get angry and start cursing and throwing things around.'

'Could he have been looking for money? You did say your grandad hid his money under the bed.' She shrugs her shoulders.

'Probably. He never said what he was looking for, but I knew he wanted money. He sold some of Grandma's vases and he tried to get his hands on her rings. She was buried with her wedding ring, but she always said her engagement ring and eternity were mine. When she died my grandad gave them to me. I never wear them. I put them in an old trinket box that belonged to her. He must have found it because I saw he had the rings in his hand. I grabbed them off him and he pushed me to give them back, but I wasn't letting him sell them. So, I gave him money for them,' she says awkwardly.

'Shit, Meadow what else haven't you told us?' Callum asks, as he places his arm around her shoulders and kisses the top of her head. I don't react because I now realise how much my brothers care for her.

'Do you think he owes people money?' She plays with her fingers, looking exhausted with it all.

'I do,' I answer her, and my brothers all agree. 'I think we wait to see if anything comes back from this cellmate and if Callum can get any more out of Miss Simpson when he calls into this gallery of hers tomorrow. Mason if you can look into Judy Williams—find out what she's like. It might throw some light onto why he was meeting her. Henry, can you keep in contact with Sam and Antony tomorrow morning up to lunchtime? I'm in a meeting first thing then I have a Zoom call with Michelle the council events manager, and some jumped-up suits from the council, so I'm not going to be available until after that.'

'What's that all about? I thought they'd got everything they needed from our side.' Callum tilts his head, looking at me.

'They have. I think they just want to tie up a few loose ends before they make their final decision.'

'I'd let her tie me up, she's hot as hell,' Henry says, a gleam in his eye. I wouldn't say she was hot. Pretty yes but then Henry's taste in women is different from mine.

'You're such a pig.' Meadow jabs him in the side with her elbow, giving him a look of disgust.

'Have you seen her, Meadow?' He widens his eyes and has a stupid look on his face. 'She has legs up to her neck, even women give her a second glance.' He exaggerates.

'I've seen her,' she says sarcastically rolling her eyes at him. Yes, my little secretary has met with the extremely tall and confident Michelle who has a stick up her arse.

'Let's call it a night and hopefully, we'll have more to go on tomorrow. I have some work to do.' It's not a lie but the main reason is, I don't trust myself around Meadow. So, I'm going to confine myself to the office, hoping she'll go to bed before I get finished.

'Have you heard anything about the flat, Connor?' Meadow asks.

'I'm afraid it's still out of bounds for the time being.'

'Then I'll need to go buy some new clothes tomorrow. I've got nothing with me except the few bits you got me. I could do with some hoodies and other things.'

'I don't want you going alone, Meadow,' I state with urgency in my voice. It's welcomed with a frown from her and a questionable look from my brothers. 'Your uncle has been seen around town— I don't want him seeing you and following you here. Not that he'd get within a foot of this place. We need to be careful is all I'm saying if we're to keep our surveillance on him a secret and you safe.'

'I agree with Kane. We can't let him know where you are.' She listens to Mason and then turns to me.

'What if someone comes with me?'

'I still don't think that's wise.'

'I can take you now. The shopping centre on the other side of town is open late and from what the security team has said, John is in the pub just up the road from where your house is.' Meadow looks to me for my opinion. Her blue eyes now sparkling, pleading for me to agree. It's good to see them smiling again.

'That's fine.' I take my wallet out of my pocket and toss the company card at Mason. 'Use this.' He catches it but Meadow is quick and snatches it from him. She places it on the table.

'I have my own money.'

'Company perks.' He beams at her, picking it back up. 'Come on cupcake, we'll even buy whatever you need to bake some goodies because I for one am having withdrawal symptoms from your baking. Seriously it's been nearly two weeks woman.' She laughs and my brothers all agree with him. I do too. Meadow loves to bake and would normally bring different types of cakes of various flavours into the office on a Monday morning, my brothers devour them in no time at all. I pretend I'm not into them but to be truthful I do like to indulge in a small slice of the chocolate and raspberry cake she makes.

'I have as well. I couldn't make them with him around. I'm sorry.'

'Hey don't be, we understand. But if you want to whip a batch of those lemon cupcakes or even a lemon drizzle cake while you're here, then feel free. I'll even help you.' Mason offers.

'Will you make that chocolate sponge cake with the raspberry filling?' Henry gives her a wide smile. I have to agree with him, it is my favourite.

'I'd love to. To be truthful, I've missed baking.'

'Come on then let's get going.'

They both leave quickly, Meadow I'm sure is eager to get some fresh air. She's been stuck here for the last few days. She's desperate for some of her own clothes, she's probably desperate to get some space from me too.

*

With my meeting and Zoom call finished, I'm confident Summer Knights Security has done its utmost best to secure the council deal as well as the new close personal protection contract. The council contract will start in three months, with my team and a few subcontractors that I use often, covering all events run by the council. The personal protection team starts next month and runs for six months. The businessman who has hired us had a few threats, which he thinks is an ex-employer, but he can't be sure. He informed the police but when they investigated the matter there was no evidence to support his suspicions. They did, however, advise him to hire a security team if he was still adamant that they were a threat and to contact them if he had any more information to go on. He's really only hired us because his daughter who lives in the US is coming home for six months, and he wants a team around her just to be on the safe side.

Raised voices have the chocolaty treat that I was just about to indulge in suspended in midair. I place it back on the plate and then push my chair back ready to seek out who it is. I don't have time to rise from my desk when the door half opens. I can't see who is behind it but the woman's voice I know only too well.

Meadow pushes through the door still cursing and when our eyes meet, I see one angry-looking woman.

'You!' She exclaims, pointing a finger at me. 'I can't believe you'd do that.' She moves towards my desk, slamming her hand down hard on it just to prove she's not very happy with me. I'm not sure what I have done to warrant such anger from Meadow, she seemed fine last night when she came back from shopping with Mason, loaded down with five bags full of new clothes and the ingredients she needed for her cakes. She was eager to get on with making one straight away and when I woke this morning my kitchen smelt sugary and sweet. She'd cleaned up and set out five plates with all our names on them. I brought mine down here and hid it away from my brothers. It's not unheard of for one of them to eat what is not theirs.

Needing to know what I've done and make sure she hasn't hurt herself; I push back my chair and rise from my seat.

'What have I done now?' I ask as I move around to where she is standing and try to take her hand. She slaps mine away and takes a step back from me.

'What have you done?' She winces as she places her hands on her hips. 'You told me you hadn't accepted my notice. You made me feel as if you cared about my welfare—about me.'

'What are you talking about?' I move slowly towards her, not wanting to freak her out and have her move out of my way again.

'My job is what I'm talking about. You made it clear that it was still mine. I don't believe this—I trusted you.'

'You can trust me.' I step into her space, and she shakes her head, glaring at me. I can't help but focus on that mouth of hers. Her lips calling to me. I hear her cursing at me. Calling me for something I'm not sure I've even done. She drives me crazy when she goes off on one, but I'm still focused on those beautiful kissable lips to give a shit. I know I shouldn't be. The last time didn't end well.

'Trust you! No sooner is my back turned than you employ somebody else. That desk is mine. Not yours or hers. Mine!' She grits her teeth at me, but I'm too far gone to care and the next thing I hear is her moaning against me as my mouth covers hers.

Moving us so she's backed up against the wall, and my body is pressed up against hers, I angle her head and deepen our kiss. She might think she hates me, but her body tells me differently.

I don't let up, desire cursing through me, electrifying every nerve in my body. Her smell is intoxicating, and I can't believe I have resisted the urge to make her mine for so long. Pushed her away and made her hate me just so I didn't reveal my true feelings. The feel of her body, her smooth skin under my rough hands as they explore under her shirt without reservation, drives me wild with need. Her quiet moans surge me on and I'm a man at her mercy. I'd do anything to make her happy, make her mine, even if in the past I have shown her no such devotion.

Reluctantly, my mouth leaves hers when I feel her push on my chest. I take a step back from her, my chest heaving. Her pupils are dilated, proving she's just as affected as I am.

'What do you think you are doing?' She pushes off the wall, taking a step to the side out of my reach. But I'm not letting her go that easily. I know she feels it. That passion. That spark. That is now ignited and cannot be diminished.

'I know you feel it Meadow so don't try to deny it.' I take her hips pulling her into me and my lips skim across hers. She doesn't move so I trail them across her chin and down her neck. She shivers in my arms, as she holds on to my biceps. When she lets out a little whimper, I know I have her. I kiss along her collar bone then make my way back to those lips I crave so much. 'Please tell me you feel it,' I say against her mouth but before she has time to answer, I lead us into a kiss so passionate, I fear we might burst into flames.

'Oh, sorry, I'll give you a minute.' It's Callum's voice, his tone playful as he closes the door behind him. I didn't even hear it open. Too engrossed with the woman in my arms. Well, that was until she just pushed me away.

'Shit,' she curses, running her hands through her hair and straightening her top. She turns to me, opens her mouth then closes it again. I smile inside knowing I've actually made her speechless.

'Why do you keep doing that?'

'Doing what?' I brush past her toward my desk, trying hard to calm the ache in my boxers.

'Kissing me. Why do you keep kissing me.'

'Because it's the only thing that will shut you up.' Her shocked expression almost makes me laugh but I hold it back knowing she'd probably go for my throat if I made a joke of this situation. I sit on the edge of my desk. 'Come here, Meadow.' I put my hand out and I'm surprised when she doesn't ignore me. I take the hand she slapped on the desk and turn it over. It looks red and sore. 'Does it hurt?' she shakes her head.

'Liar.' I gently kiss the palm of her hand. 'Truthfully, Meadow, I can't fight this anymore. You're beautiful inside and out and I've always been attracted to you. Only it's not just a physical attraction. It's more.'

'Oh.' Again, she's lost for words. 'I don't know what to say.'

'Don't say anything. Not now anyway. We'll talk later.' She nods her head agreeing with me.

'Who's the woman sitting at my desk?' This time she asks calmly. I must have kissed that attitude out of her. I'm sure her sass will resume shortly.

'She's from the agency. Callum called them. We needed someone while you're recuperating at mine and while we're getting all this shit sorted with your uncle.'

'Oh. I'm sorry for jumping to conclusions. And for shouting at you.'

'Hey, don't ever be sorry for putting me in my place.' I take her hips, pulling her between my legs. She doesn't stop me so I lean forward our lips so close a breath couldn't pass through. 'I like that you don't take my shit.' I brush my lips across hers then stand, reluctantly taking my hands from her hips as I make my way around the desk and sit down. 'Why did you come down anyway?'

'Oh, I forgot. Well with all—with everything I forgot.' She blushes.

'Sit down Meadow.' I want to invite her to sit on my knee, but I don't think she'll take me up on the offer. Plus, Callum will be back any minute. He won't stay away for long. He'll be chomping at the bit wanting to know what is going on with Meadow and me. He won't get anything from me because I don't even know what is going on with us.

Meadow sits down opposite me, making herself comfortable. 'I came down because I think I remember something about my grandad. Well, I'm not sure if it's a memory or something I've dreamt up.'

'What is it?' I ask then turn towards the door when there's a light rap.

'You both decent?' Meadow's face heats up as Callum walks through the door a knowing smirk on his face. He rounds the desk, pulls up a chair, and sits down at the side of her. 'You ok cupcake?' He winks at her and then takes out his phone, turning his attention to me, his eyes dancing with humour. I give him a stern look, hoping he'll take the hint and knock it off. I don't want Meadow to feel embarrassed because he saw the kiss we shared. 'I have news,' he says, taking the hint.

'Can it wait a minute? So does Meadow.'

'Oh. Of course, go ahead.'

'I'm not sure if it's anything worth getting our hopes up but it might have some connection to the art dealer and the journalist. That is if it's not just my imagination.'

'What is it?' Callum asks the same question I did just before he waltzed through the door.

'I was looking over the information and the pictures that are on the board upstairs and a memory of some sort suddenly came to me. When you mentioned that Judy worked for the local paper and Marie was into photography, it sort of pricked at something, but I wasn't sure what it was. Then this morning while I was looking over everything again it came to me. I remember my grandma telling me something, years ago when I was in primary school.'

'What did you remember?'

'She told me that when she first met my grandad, he loved photography and that he worked as a freelance photographer. I'm almost sure she mentioned he'd worked for a few newspapers.'

'How sure are you?'

'I'm not sure that's just it. I couldn't have made it up, could I?'

'Do you remember, why she told you?'

'Yeah, I think so. I think I was doing a project at school, and I wanted to take some photos of our local area. It had something to do with the environment we live in. Something like that anyway. I remember asking if I could take some pictures with my grandma's phone and that's when she told me about how my grandad used to enjoy photography.'

'Was there anything else? Any indication who he'd worked for?' She shakes her head at Callum.

'Not that I can remember, and I never saw any signs around the house that my grandad still did photography, I only ever remember him working as a paramedic.'

'It might hold some significance to something your uncle is up to and to why he is meeting with these two women. What that is, who knows?' Callum reassures her.

'I think there's something. We'll find out what eventually, don't worry. You were right to bring it to our attention. I'll see what I can find out about your grandad, with your permission that is.' I wait for her to give me the go-ahead. If she gives me her grandad's full name and date of birth, it's quite easy to find out things about a person.

'Yes, you have my permission.'

'Good. Write down your grandad's full name, date of birth, and where he was born, and I'll see what I can find out. What did you have for us.' I look at my brother.

'Connor sent me the name of John's cellmate. Jeremy Horn. He's served four years for fraud. Before that he was—and this is where it gets interesting. He worked for Adle & Co Solicitors. He was struck off and then he went and lied under oath, so the judge also held him in contempt of court.'

'What does this mean?' Meadow asks, glancing between us.

'It means the will your uncle provided could have been drawn up by a bent lawyer.' She props her elbow on my desk, sighing.

'Just as you thought. How could I have been so stupid to fall for it? I'm used to seeing legal documents, I should have known.'

'Don't beat yourself up about it, Meadow, it's not that easy to see the difference. Sometimes fraudulent documents look real enough. Anyway, it was you who said you thought he was lying.' I try to reassure her. She's had enough on her plate without feeling stupid for falling for his lies.

'Is he still in jail?' She turns to Callum.

'No. He was released a few months ago,' he informs us as he glances at his phone screen. 'Connor has his address and wants to know do you want him to pay him a visit?'

'Let's see what else we can gather over the next forty-eight hours then we'll pay him a visit, if needed. If he's still in contact with John, then we don't want him tipping him off.'

'You're right,' Meadow says. 'We could do with getting our hands on that will. I can't believe I left it behind.'

'Don't worry about it. We could always lean on Mr Horn and get the information we need when the time is right.' Both Callum and Meadow agree with me. 'Did you get anything from the gallery?'

'Not much. She has a nice place. Decent size with lots of black and white prints on the wall. I don't know much about art, but I can see the appeal to collectors.'

'Were they nude?'

'Yes, but tasteful. I did notice she had a small area cornered off. There were no pictures hung on the wall but there was a plaque there. Some sort of title. It said, 'Beyond Beauty'. According to what she told me the guy she had met yesterday had let her down big time. Promising her seven black-and-white prints of various poses of a woman during pregnancy. Different trimesters and a couple of mother and baby after the birth.'

"I don't understand," Meadow turns to me.

'Neither do I Meadow but there's definitely a connection between, John, the Will, and this Jeremy Horn, that's for sure. The memory you have—the details of your grandad working as a photographer and for the newspaper, I'm not sure yet what this has to do with John, Marie and this other woman Judy—but we'll get to the bottom of it that is for sure.'

'I hope so because I'm not letting my home go to him or anybody else.'

'That's the spirit, Meadow,' Callum beams at her. 'You're strong and a fighter. What he did to you—scaring you into running—we all understand that you didn't have a choice. But you have us now and no reason to feel scared anymore.'

'Thank you, Callum. I know that.' He gives her a warm friendly smile and pats her hand.

'I think I'll go back upstairs; I didn't sleep very well last night, and Henry and Connor are coming over later.' Her eyes move to mine. I'd forgotten that they'd arranged to have a few drinks and watch a movie. I think they're planning on Face Timing Louise, whom they have known since high school, she's gone travelling with her boyfriend and I know Meadow misses having her friend around.

'There's paracetamols in my bathroom cabinet. Help yourself and rest. We'll talk later.'

Her smile is genuine as she walks out of the door, her eyes full of affection. My heart swells in the hopes such affection is for me.

CHAPTER 11

MEADOW

'So, you and Kane seem to be getting along well. Have you called a truce?' Connor takes a swig from his beer, watching me over the neck of his bottle. There's a gleam in his eye and I wonder what he knows.

The kiss Kane and I shared today was on fire. It held so much passion. A hunger that I've only read about in books or seen in films, and it sucked the anger I had built up for him right out of me, leaving me weak at the knees as well as wanting more. After he'd kissed me the other day, I warned him to stay away from me, assuming he just wanted one thing. Now I think it's more.

I was furious at him when I entered the office thinking he had gone back on his word and employed someone to replace me. My anger brought something out in him, an animal side, and he soon made it clear that I was wrong but not before he pinned me against the wall and kissed the hell out of me. At first, I was surprised, and I wanted to push him away and even though he made my heart beat out of my chest, bringing me to life, I did push him away. But I soon welcomed him, the warmth of his body and the softness of his lips. The way he made me feel—the way my body melted into his felt right. He confuses me. I am confused. He'd shown many times that he didn't care for me. He just tolerated me due to being employed as his secretary by his brother but now I see how he watches me with affection. He has displayed a tender side that I haven't seen before, and I fear he wants what I said he wouldn't get from me. Although now, my fear has come back to bite me on the arse because I now want him just as badly. He wants to talk. Air out our dirty washing so to speak. I can't see that happening until all this is over.

'Yes, he is proving that he does have a heart after all and not a swinging lead weight in the middle of his chest.' I play it cool.

'Oh, you don't mean that.' Henry laughs, wiggling his eyebrows at me. I hope he doesn't mention what he witnessed the other day, I'd never live it down if Connor knew I was ogling his brother. 'He's not that bad, he's always looked out for us.' He points between Connor and himself. 'All of us.'

'I know, I'm only messing. As my boss, he was abrupt, unpredictable and unbearable a lot of the time. I only stayed because he runs the ship like a military operation, all the staff are lovely and it's been a blast working with you two, well mainly you, Henry. Callum and Mason are the best, we get on well and we've become really good friends. Oh, and the pay is good.'

'There is that. It's always good to get a fat wage at the end of the month,' Connor agrees.

'I must admit since Kane found out about my uncle and the fire at the flat, I can't fault him.' I don't mention our little but extremely hot encounter in his office today or in his apartment the other day.

'Louise looked well,' Connor states, changing the subject. We've just finished a video call with her on Messenger. She looked good and was happy to hear from the three of us.

'She did. I'd love to be with her.' I take a sip of my wine thinking when this is all over, I should take a little holiday. Somewhere in the sun.

'Well, you're more than welcome to come away with us when we go again,' Connor offers, grinning at me.

'Like hell, I will. I'm not sitting around while you two party with your mates and countless women. I've heard all about the nude parties and they aren't my thing.'

'Hey, we don't share women and I certainly don't let any man see my junk. They'd be envious.' Henry tosses another bottle at Connor rolling his eyes at him. I know they're not that bad really, but they do like to party as often as they can and I'm just not a party girl. I'm more of a sip a couple of cocktails kind of a girl or a few glasses of wine. I like to dance in the clubs but then it's home to my bed. Not on to an all-night party.

'Louise seemed shocked when you told her about your uncle, had she met him before?' Henry takes a sip from his bottle.

'Yes, many times when we were at school. She saw a different man to what he is now so I can understand her being shocked.'

'She seemed even more surprised that you are staying here with Kane,' Connor comments.

'Well, she's also aware that there's never been any love lost between us.' I shrug my shoulders.

'I'm more shocked that you chose to stay here when you could be staying with one of us." Henry points between him and his twin.

'I know, it shocked me too,' I laugh. 'Kane's pulled out all the stops for me. I feel safe here. I know I'd be safe with you as well but honestly, I'm just happy that I don't have to put up with my uncle or that annoyingly loud music that I was subjected to at the flat.'

'Was it that bad?'

'Yes.' I nod my head and then take a sip from my glass. I place it back on the table and cross my legs, making myself comfortable on the couch. 'It wasn't just the music. There was lots of arguing that went on until the early hours of the morning. Drug selling and taking. The steps up to the flat were disgusting. Smelt of piss. It was revolting.'

'I can't believe you didn't tell us straight away. When have we ever not told each other when something is bothering us?' Henry gives me a sad smile. I know he's right and I do feel bad about it.

'In all honesty, I didn't think things would get as bad as they did. Then as I said I felt embarrassed. John is my only living family member.'

'Well just so you know you should have come to us straight away and as long as you're happy here then we're happy,' Connor speaks for Henry and himself.

'Thank you, I am. But if things don't work out, I could always use the birthday present you got me and have a few days away.' It was my birthday a few months ago and I still haven't had the time to book in for the spa weekend that they paid for me.

'What was that?'

'The spa weekend.' I watch as a what the hell is she on about look passes between them.

'We didn't get you a spa weekend,' Connor states.

'You didn't? I just assumed it was you two.' If it wasn't them then it must have been Callum or Mason. Since I started working for Summer Knights, I've had two birthdays and two Christmases with them. Each time I've been handed a birthday gift bag or Christmas bag containing perfume, chocolates, gift vouchers for manicures and pedicures, bottles of wine, prosecco, that sort of thing. And a signed card from all four brothers, it never bothered me that Kane's name wasn't on there, much. On my last birthday, I was surprised to get a spa weekend break and just like every other time Connor, Henry, Mason and Callum were present to hand it to me. All the gifts were placed in one bag and the bag was signed by all four brothers so I could never be really sure who got me what. I just presumed it was from my two best friends. 'It must have been Mason or Callum then.'

'Nope.' Henry lifts his chin, an amused look.

'Mason got you the chocolate from a shop in York, Callum bought you that overpriced bottle of fizz and we chipped in together for the perfume and gift set.' Oh, I forgot about the gift set.

'Then who was the spa weekend from?' They both raise their eyebrows at me as if I should know. Then the penny drops. 'No, it couldn't have been.' I refuse to believe that Kane would buy me such a gift. He might extend such kindness now but then no. 'Kane?'

'Mmmm,' Connor, smiles with a glint in his eye and Henry nods his head.

'I don't believe it.'

'Well believe it because it was him and he went out to buy it himself.'

'How do you know that?' I'm shocked.

'Well, he couldn't ask his secretary now, could he? And it wasn't any of us.'

'Why does it surprise you, Meadow? You do work for him so of course he's going to buy you a gift on your birthday and for Christmas.'

'He doesn't or didn't come across as someone who'd go out of his way to get me such a nice present. You know, half the time he didn't...'

'We know he's been a dick.' I chuckle when Connor interrupts me. He was definitely a dick, but he seems to be making up for it now. 'When it comes to special occasions, he's always been one of the first to muck in.'

'I didn't know. I'll need to thank him.' And I will as soon as I see him. I feel stupid, but how was I supposed to know when the gift bag and card didn't have his name on it? 'Is there anything else I should know?'

'What do you mean?' Henry asks.

'Besides what he's doing now, which I have thanked him for, and the spa weekend, which I will thank him for, is there anything else I should be thanking him for? You know, who bought me the gift card for the manicure and pedicure last Christmas?'

'It was probably Kane. That's not our thing. Chocs, perfume and bottles of bubbly then yes. He knows you work hard for our company so why shouldn't he treat you?'

'I wished I'd known. I feel awful.'

'Don't feel bad. If he'd wanted you to know it was from him, he'd have put his name on it. Plus, you're getting along fine now, so you can explain you didn't know it was from him until tonight, and then thank him.'

'Yes, I will.' I ignore the way Connor is looking at me, I know he's after gossip, but I refuse to tell them anything about Kane and me. I know he won't have mentioned anything, it's not his way or mine. So, I sit quietly reaching for my glass then finish off the rest of the wine.

'Right, I need to shoot.'

'You do?'

'Yeah, I'm up at six in the morning. You coming?' Connor asks his twin.

'I think I'll stay a bit longer and have a few more.' He waves his bottle in the air. It's only nine o'clock so he's more than welcome.

'Do you want to watch a movie, Meadow?' Henry calls as I close the door behind Connor. I make my way into the room, noticing he has drunk his fair share of beer.

'What do you have in mind?' I ask as I pick up a few of the empties and carry them into the kitchen. Kane would have a fit if he saw them scattered about his living room.

'Well, we haven't watched Superman for a long time so I'm up for that if you want.' He knows I love Superman. Henry Cavill is to die for in Man of Steel, but my favourite is the original Superman. I adore Christopher Reeves. I've had a crush on him ever since we were fourteen and were having a film day. I'd watched Superman before with my grandparents, but when I watched it with the twins and Louise, I became besotted with Clark Kent. Those black-rimmed glasses make him hot.

'Original Superman and you're on.'

'Sweet. I'll sort the film out while you see what snacks Kane has got hidden away.'

'I'm on it,' I tell him, feeling a little more like myself. It feels normal to be watching a film and having a few drinks with my besties. It's a shame the four of us aren't together.

'Have you ever noticed how much Kane looks like Clark Kent?' Henry questions as he switches back and forth between Superman and Man of Steel.

'He does not,' I say with humour in my voice.

'He does, we've always said it, I'm surprised you haven't noticed. Look.' He switches the films so we're now watching Superman and fasts forward to a scene with Clark Kent. 'He's the double of him especially when he's wearing his reading glasses.'

'Who Kane? I didn't know he wore reading glasses. I've never seen him wear them.'

'He wears contacts most of the time but now and again if his eyes are sore, he'll wear his glasses. Look, imagine Kane with glasses on then look at Clark Kent—spitting image.'

'Mmmm, there's some resemblance,' I say, trying to hide the fact that he is right. I can't believe I've never noticed before because even without glasses on it's clear to see that they do look alike. Maybe that's why I've always harbored a little crush on my boss even if half the time I've wanted to wring his bloody neck. And now he's showing that he isn't an arsehole and that he has some sort of feelings for me, my little crush is becoming more. I agree with Henry then we both settle down to watch the movie.

The film finishes and I rub my heavy eyes. Two glasses of wine, a film, and a bowl of popcorn and I'm ready for my bed. I turn to Henry, and I'm not surprised he's fast asleep. His head is lying on the chair arm as he snuggles up to the cushion. I turn off the TV and cover him with a throw over then make my way into the kitchen to get a glass of water. My mind wonders about Kane and where he is. I'm surprised he isn't home now. I rid the thoughts of him being out with a woman and also rid the thoughts of what we shared meant nothing to him. 'He wouldn't do that to me,' I whisper to myself as I place the glass in the sink and then wander into the dining area where the whiteboard stands.

The picture of my uncle standing outside my front door angers me. How he treated me and my home, I can never forgive him. The two women, Marie from the gallery and Judy from the newspaper, why did he seek them out? Is there any connection between what is going on and my grandad's past? I need to find out what he is up to, and I need to get that will, not that it matters now with what we have learned so far. Saying that, if we did have it, we'd know for sure whether it was legit or whether it had been put together by Uncle John's cellmate.

I make my way into the bedroom that Kane is letting me stay in and as soon as I switch on the light, I spot my bag on the floor. I know what I'm about to do would have the Summer brothers and half the security team that works for them, seriously pissed but I want to do my bit instead of sitting around the penthouse twiddling my thumbs. And if I don't do it now then I might not get another chance.

*

Instead of turning onto my street, I make a quick left onto the road before mine and park by the trees. Turning off the engine, I step out of my car, close the door quietly and make my way toward the narrow unlit passage that joins the two streets. It's a short walk, one of which I have walked many times with my grandparents coming home from the park, and although I don't remember I probably did the same with my mum. Choosing to enter through the back gate rather than the front will hopefully not alert John if he's not in one of his drunken stupors, that's if he is in at all—he could be up the road still in the pub. And I won't be seen by whoever is on surveillance tonight.

Like a ghost, I pass through the gate silently, stepping into the garden. There are no lights on at the back of the house and I can't see any indication that there are any at the front. But still, I tread carefully not to make a sound. Reaching the garden shed, I wonder if I should turn back. This is stupid of me to come here alone not knowing what state or mood he is in. I push myself forward until I'm crouching down by the ceramic plant pots. I've never been one to back down or cower away without good reason and I want that will, so this is a no-brainer.

Just as I'm about to stand, something brushes past my leg. I fall backwards onto my behind, my back hitting the wall. It doesn't hurt but my heart is beating faster than an Olympic sprinter.

'Suzy, you nearly gave me a heart attack,' I whisper to the next-door's black cat as she meows and curls around my legs. 'Go.' I gently push her away but she's reluctant to move. She's used to me petting her and giving her treats. Giving her half of what she wants, I let my fingers run down her back, through her silky fur then gently push her again to go away. This time she listens to my command, and she takes off through the hedges. Calming myself, I take a few deep breaths and contemplate my next move. Do I hang around until I'm certain he's gone to bed, or do I take my chances now? This is my house I should not be scared of entering—but yet I am. Sighing, I sit on the edge of the large plant pot wishing I had the courage Callum and Kane say I have. I'm no stronger than a cream cracker—easily broken.

'You will be the death of me, woman.' My legs turn to jelly—my heart thudding like a jackhammer against my ribcage. The scream I release comes out muffled as a hand is placed over my mouth. 'What the hell did you think you were doing, coming here alone?' That deep voice and the woody scent blended with vanilla and the essence of apple has me shrugging off the man who has me wrapped in his arms, my back to his chest as he whispers in my ear. He releases me, his large hand moving from my mouth.

'You idiot, I almost peed myself.' I push at his chest annoyed at him for sneaking up on me then because he has me feeling like a fool due to the fact it could have quite easily been my uncle instead of Kane, I kick him in the shin.

'Ouch. What was that for?'

'For scaring me half to death.'

'And how do you think I felt when Henry sent out a message, asking if anybody knew where you were?' Oh, hell no wonder he looks pissed. I can only imagine Henry would have been going out of his mind, waking to find I wasn't there. They all will have been. I'd seen the way Kane looked yesterday when I wanted to go shopping. The concern on his face was there for all to see. And even though it's dark out it's apparent now in how he stares at me and in his voice.

'I'm sorry, I didn't think.'

'No, you didn't. But never mind now, you're safe. I suppose you came back here'—he looks up at the house— 'for the will.'

'I did.'

'Well seen as we're here then we might as well get it.' He wraps his hand around the drainpipe, testing how secure it is to the wall. 'There's a small window open, I should be able to put my hand through and open the bigger one. How good are you at climbing?' I ignore his question.

'We don't know if my uncle is in. He could be watching the TV although I'd bet my life, he's in a drunken heap.'

'Oh, he's drunk all right but not in there.' He nods towards the door. 'He's still in the pub up the road—Sam has eyes on him. Tell me Meadow, how did you get past Antony?' Oh, yeah, if Sam is watching my uncle up at the pub, then Antony will be parked up somewhere at the front in the street. He'll be furious with me.

'I came through the back gate. It's usually locked but the day before I left, I'd unlocked it just in case I needed to flee quickly.'

'You know?' He places his hand on my cheek, stroking his thumb over my cheekbone. 'If you'd have come to me when all this started, I would've made my presence known to him, he wouldn't have dared hurt you or treat you the way he did.' His tone is caring and full of sincerity. If I didn't believe him before, I do now.

'I know.' I don't say anything else because now is not the time to get into a heated discussion. He moves his hand and tests the drainpipe again.

'How well can you climb?'

'It's been a while since I climbed a tree but I'm certain my monkey skills are still good. Why?'

'Because I don't want to leave you alone down here so if you can shimmy up this and onto that ledge, you'll be able to put your arm through the window and open the other one so we can climb through. I'll be right behind you.'

'I have a key,' I whisper, giving him a childish grin. Bless him, he has it all planned out. Ready to help me.

'What did you say?' I rummage in my pocket and pull out the key, holding it up in front of him. 'I don't believe you sometimes, Meadow.' Hearing him say my name does something to me. It's not like he hasn't said it thousands of times since I became his secretary—do this Meadow, do that Meadow—but now when he says it, there's something in his tone that has me wanting to hear him say it over and over again. I shake off the feelings that are running rampant at the moment when he takes the key from me and places it in the lock.

Kane pushes the door open and walks inside, I follow behind and turn on the light. I've no sooner taken my hand away than he reaches out and turns it off again. 'What are you doing,' I whisper.

'We don't want to alert anyone. Your uncle might be out, but we don't know who might be watching.'

'Oh, yeah, I never thought of that.'

'Come on.' He takes my hand in one of his and in the other he holds a small torch. As he turns it on, I hear him speak. 'Do we still have eyes on the target?' I look at him stupidly then realise he's speaking through his hands-free. 'Good, keep me updated, I need to know as soon as he makes a move to leave.'

'He's still in the pub I take it.'

'Yes.' He glances at his watch. 'We've probably got twenty minutes if that before he's thrown out, the last orders have already gone.'

'We better get a move on then; it only takes a few minutes to walk down here from the pub even if he is pissed.'

'Lead the way.' Kane holds his arm out for me to go ahead all the while he keeps the light from the torch low, so it illuminates in front of us. Manoeuvring through the kitchen, I step over a set of drawers that have been pulled out of the kitchen unit and just thrown on the floor. As my eyes adjust to the darkness, I'm unable to believe the state of my usually tidy home. Besides the things that are scattered on the floor, cups, plates, and pans are piled in the sink, waiting to be washed—it takes everything in me not to set about cleaning, and putting it back to the way it was. The smell of stale cigarette smoke and the pungent stench of the rubbish that he's too lazy to throw out makes my eyes water—and it's not just the odour that is causing it.

'We don't have time to hang about Meadow,' Kane states as he steps over the mess and makes his way to the other side of the kitchen.

'It's annoying and upsetting to see it in such a mess.' I follow him and point down the hallway toward the bedroom stairs. 'I wish he'd put things back when he's finished looking for whatever it is he is trying to find and clean his bloody mess up.'

'He's definitely looking for something.' Kane stands by the front room door, inclining his head for me to take a look inside.

'Just look at the state of it in here.' Every cupboard door is wide open with all the contents cluttering the floor or thrown onto the settee. I wipe at the tear that rolls down my cheek. My grandparent's possessions—things they had collected over the years that I had wanted to keep safe are just tossed to one side. Discarded like an old rag.

'Come on, once we've got everything sorted out and rid of your uncle, I'll help you clean the place up.'

'I'll hold you to that,' I smile, trying to make light of a dark situation.

We bypass the other rooms and head for the stairs to the bedrooms. Entering my room, it's easy to see even in the dark that there's been no leniency spared. My mattress has been tipped over and the bedding thrown in a heap. Just like downstairs, drawers, and wardrobe doors have been pulled open with the contents strewn about. I wish I knew what he was searching for. Maybe Kane is right and he's just looking for money.

'Where did you leave the will?' Kane asks, striding over the mattress so he is standing beside the window.

'I ripped it in half and threw it on the floor so it should be under this lot somewhere.' I kick at my underwear that has been pulled from the chest of drawers. I should be embarrassed that my uncle has seen and handled them, but I can't bring myself to care. Neither do I care that Kane is picking them up as he searches for what we came for.

'Are you sure it was the floor you threw it on?'

'Yes, but John could have picked it up.'

'It doesn't look like John knows how to pick anything up.' He moves the mattress out of the way the light from his torch proving it's not hiding there either. I crouch down and feel under the bed but find nothing at that side so I continue to crawl on my hands and knees, my hands feeling for anything that will resemble the sheet of paper that my uncle tried passing off as my grandad's last will and testament. Finding nothing at the bottom, I stand and make my way to the far side, squeezing between the bed and the wall. Just as I put my foot down, something pierces through my trainer and I scream out as it enters into my foot, the pain stabbing under the arch.

'Meadow.' Kane rushes to my aid and I hear him cursing into his phone. He rips out the earpiece, puts his phone on the loudspeaker then places it on the bed. Tears spill from my eyes as I try to breathe through the pain. I reach down to feel around then without thinking pull at the wood that has attached itself to my trainer. I scream again when a nail—I think it is anyway— is released from my flesh and the trickle of blood fills my sock.

'Sam, can you hear me, what is going on?' Kane lifts me from the side of the bed, his strong arms holding me until he places me on top of it, taking my foot in his hand. 'What have you done?'

'I think I stood on a piece of floorboard that's been ripped up and one of the nails went through my foot. Ouch,' I moan as Kane removes my trainer.

'Sorry.' He removes my sock, running his thumb over what I think is the puncture wound. 'We'll need to get it looked at once we get out of here. Can you stand?'

'I'll try but it hurts like hell.' I make to stand with Kane's help, and no sooner do I put any weight on my right foot than the pain becomes unbearable and tears flood my eyes again.

'Let's get your sock and trainer back on it might help.' Kane gently slips my foot into the trainer and fastens the laces. He picks up his phone and calls for Sam again. When he gets no answer, he curses under his breath.

'What's wrong?'

'I can't get hold of Sam,' he says with concern. 'We need to find that will and get out of here.' He turns from me and starts to rummage along the floor, moving around clothes he'd already looked under. 'It must be here somewhere,' his tone now impatient." He moves the bedding again, giving them a shake and something floats to the floor.

'Found it, I think.' He reaches down and picks up the two pieces of paper, shining his torch on what is in his hand. 'Got it.' He shoves it in the pocket of his black combats. 'Now let's get out of here.' He puts one arm under my knees and one behind my back.

'What are you doing?'

'Carrying you. Don't object, it will be quicker this way. Put your arm around my neck.' I do as he says. I wasn't about to argue with him, my foot is throbbing like hell. Plus, I've come to like being in his arms.

Kane's phone beeps and he answers it. 'Antony, where the hell is

Sam, I haven't been able to get hold of him?'

'Listen, Kane, we have a problem. Uncle John is on your doorstep.' I hear him say through the loudspeaker.

'What? How has this happened? Where is Sam?' Kane sounds angry.

'There was a brawl up at the pub and Sam got dragged into it. He was able to call me, and I flew up there to help him out. While I was helping Sam, John must have slipped out of the fray. By the time we realised and made our way down to the house, it was too late. He's coming through the door as we speak.

'Okay, stay where you are, and we'll hide out until he falls asleep. How's Sam?'

'Just is pride hurt, thank god.'

'Good...' Kane stops speaking when we hear my uncle downstairs. The rattle of plates and the beeping sound of the microwave give us the benefit of knowing he's in the kitchen.

'Kane my foot is killing me,' I whisper so I don't alert John. Gently he places me on the bed, taking hold of my foot, and then speaks to Antony.

'Radio silence until I say otherwise.'

'Roger that.' Then all goes silent. I forget half of the time that these men have spent time either in the armed forces or the police and in some cases both.

'I don't suppose you have a first aid kit or painkillers in here, do you?' He keeps his voice low as he runs his hand over my shin. I shake my head.

'Out of ten, how bad is it, one being not too bad and ten being unbearable?'

'I'd probably say eight but I don't deal with pain well so it might not be too bad if it had been you who had stood on the nail.'

'I'm sure it hurts like hell but if you can hold out without screaming or moaning for a while longer that would be great. We'll be out of here as soon as John goes to bed but that does mean we'll need to move from here. If he comes up the stairs and looks in here, the door is open, he'll spot us straight away. I propose we get comfortable on the floor on the other side of the wardrobe then once he's asleep we can leave and get your foot looked at.'

'Okay.' He lifts me off the bed, collects a pillow off the floor, and moves stealthily across the room with me in his arms. Although I'm in pain and quite nervous about what could happen if my uncle were to find us here, I'm still affected by Kane's masculinity. His smell is intoxicating, and his muscular arms do something to me. Those tingles and flutters in my stomach are back again and I'm tempted to bury my face into his neck and breathe him in. I don't because now is not the time. We need to focus on getting out of here as soon as possible without being caught. Uncle John might be much older than Kane and nowhere near his build but drunk he thinks he has the capabilities of ten men. He wouldn't think twice about having a go at me, angering Kane and pushing him in the hopes he'd hit him. I'm unsure of how much Kane would hold back if that were to happen. And now I know what my uncle's intentions are, I'm sure he'd do it on purpose so he could claim some compensation for it. He's turned out to be a little weasel and I'm ashamed to call him family.

Placing the pillow down first, Kane then sits me on it, placing another one under my foot. 'Comfy?'

'Yes, thank you.'

He smiles at me and then glances at the door. 'Was that open when we came up here?' I ask, not able to remember. He nods his head and places his finger on his lips. He tilts his head to the side, listening carefully. I can't hear anything, so I think we're safe from being found out for now.

'It was open. If he looks in, he can't see us.'

'What if he comes inside the room?'

'Hopefully that won't happen. However, if it does then I'll have no other choice than to put him to sleep myself.' Kane's smile is wicked as if he'd relish hurting the man who has hurt me. It might be something my uncle deserves but it's something I don't want.

'Well, let's hope that doesn't happen.' I give him a tight smile and he nods his head understanding what I mean.

Kane settles next to me, crouching like a tiger ready to defend or attack, whichever might be needed if my uncle comes in. While we sit there with my foot raised the pain lessens to a dull throb. I lay the back of my head on the wall and close my eyes, the tiredness I felt before I came up with this stupid plan has now returned.

I feel Kane's warm hand gently squeeze my leg and when I open my eyes, he has his finger on his lip. Sitting up, I listen carefully but my nerves have the better of me and all I can hear is the beating of my heart, thudding against my chest. I breathe in deeply then let the air out slowly as I count to ten in my head. In the darkness I seek out Kane's hand, needing him close. He senses my search and helps me out, taking my hand in his. It helps and the rhythm of my heart seems to return to a regular beat.

The creaking of one of the floorboards that should have been replaced years ago gives away John's movement. He's definitely on the landing. Holding my breath, I listen to his footsteps. He makes his way into the bathroom, the noise of him peeing then the flush of the toilet as well as a very undignified burp and another bodily noise that I'd rather not have heard, gives away his whereabouts. He pads along the landing after relieving himself of about two pints of beer, his footsteps stopping right outside my door. I stiffen, fearful of him coming in. Kane tightens his hold on my hand, placing his finger on his lip again, reminding me not to make a sound. There's no fear of that happening, if anything I might pass out. The darkness, the throbbing in my foot, and the situation we are in have my nerves on edge.

I'm soon given a reprieve when the sound of John's footsteps lets me know he's heading towards the old room that he claimed when he came back. The door opens and I can just make out the sound of clothes rustling then him flopping down onto his bed. If he sticks to his usual ritual, he'll be out in seconds, snoring like Grizzly Adams.

Ten minutes pass by slowly, it feels more like ten hours but once Kane knows it's safe to get out of here, he's on the move with me in his arms.

He manoeuvres the landing in seconds, cautious not to step on the loose floorboard then covertly attempts the stairs. Almost at the bottom, I want to sneeze. I bury my face into the crook of my arm to limit the sound just as I do, my foot catches on the banister. The sound of me sneezing mixed with the muffled whimper is enough to alert my uncle that there is not just him in the house. However, due to the amount of ale he has drunk and the pig-like grunts that are emitting from him, we go unnoticed.

Kane stands stock still until he feels it is safe to move. Once we're in the kitchen he switches on his torch, so he doesn't trip over anything. Without a sound, he opens the back door and we're greeted with a relieved look from Antony.

'What has she done? Here let me take her.'

'I'm okay just stood on a nail,' I whisper at the same time as Kane says, she's fine where she is. He takes the key from his pocket and locks the back door all the while keeping me held against his chest.

'Where's Sam?'

'He's round the front, keeping a lookout.'

'I need to get Meadow to the hospital.'

'We can't all go out of the front. If we're seen someone might call the police.' Kane nods his head in agreement with me.

'Is there a road at the back?' He inclines his head toward the back gate.

'No, it's an alley that leads to the next street.'

'Take my keys and bring my car around, it's parked at the bottom of the street,' he says to Antony.

Antony and Sam are already there when we come out of the dark passage.

'My car is over there; I can't leave it.'

'Give me your keys,' Sam suggests, supporting a nice shiner on his right eye. 'If Antony follows me, I'll drop yours off at Kane's and he can bring me back.'

'Don't come back tonight, he's not going anywhere. Go home and get a good night's sleep. The lads will be here at eight in the morning. I'll call them and ask if they can get here a bit earlier,' Kane suggests.

'Are you sure?' Sam asks as he takes my keys from me.

'Yes. He's dead to the world.' Kane opens his car door and places me in the passenger seat. 'Make sure to get that eye looked at if it gets any worse.'

'It's fine,' Sam tells him, waving his hand as he squeezes his six-foot-four frame into the front of my Renault Cleo. Antony gets in his and both of them stay put until Kane sets off. Once we're on the move, they follow behind us until we are on the main road.

CHAPTER 12

KANE

Just as I finish buttering a round of toast, and plating up scrambled eggs, placing them on the tray alongside a cup of coffee, Meadow limps into the kitchen. She looks well-rested after her eight hours of sleep and that soft smile on her face suggests that she's not mad at me anymore.

It was four in the morning before we got home from the hospital, which I suppose wasn't bad going on how busy the A&E was when we got there. The doctor and nurses were absolutely fantastic with her. I hadn't realised just how delicate Meadow is. Her pain threshold is zero and she is frightened to death of needles. This became a bit of a problem when she had to have a tetanus shot in her bottom. The medical staff had checked out her foot—Meadow's little moans and whimpers were quite cute. She wasn't happy with me when I let out a chuckle and told her to stop being a baby, the scowl she threw at me soon had me biting my lip to stop any amusement.

The medical staff were happy that the nail hadn't caused any internal damage to the foot but did prescribe her a course of antibiotics as a precaution just in case it became infected. When she was asked if she'd had a tetanus shot lately, she couldn't remember that last time, which meant she needed one.

I was asked to leave the room as she didn't want to bare her bottom in front of me. I was soon called back in to hold her hand when she saw the needle. According to her, it looked like something they'd use on an elephant which was an over-exaggeration because I'd seen my mum sew up holes in our school uniforms with bigger ones.

Anyway, I stood at the other side of the bed with my head turned away and when they gave her the jab, I laughed at her again when she let out a scream and squeezed my hand tightly. This didn't go down well, and I was met with another scowl from her. Then as soon as she was told she could go home, she wouldn't accept my help back to the car and hobbled all the way, grumbling about me being an arsehole. I didn't want to remind her that this arsehole had given her a place to stay when she needed it, was pulling out all the stops to find out what her uncle was up to and saved her from an altercation with him when she thought she'd be okay turning up at the house alone. Neither did I remind her that I had carried her from the house to the car and then out of the car and into the hospital.

'How are you feeling?' I ask, testing the water.

'Not bad.' She stands opposite me, biting her lip.

'You should have stayed in bed. I was just about to bring this through to you.'

'It's after twelve, I think I've slept long enough.' She picks up the coffee cup and takes a sip then returns it to the tray. 'I—I owe you an apology for my behaviour last night. I'm a bit of a wuss and when I'm tired, I can be a bitch.'

'You're fine. I don't have the best bedside manner.'

'Well, you did pretty well with me last night even if you did find my fear of needles to be funny.'

'And your zero tolerance to pain,' I add, chuckling.

'Arsehole,' she laughs too, picking up a piece of scrunched-up kitchen roll, I'd used earlier and throwing it at me.

'Come on, you need to take the weight off that foot if you want the swelling to go down.' I help her into the living room, making sure she has her leg elevated on the settee then I return to the kitchen to fetch her very late breakfast.

'Are you not eating?' she asks as I place the tray on her knee, and she tucks into the scrambled egg.

'I've already eaten, just a coffee is good.' I hold up my cup.

'Did you check the name on the will? I know I should have asked last night but I wasn't in the right frame of mind to talk plus those painkillers had started to kick in. I went out like a light as soon as my head hit the pillow.'

'Yes, I did. And don't worry about it. Yes, it is Horn's name on the will and Connor is checking him out because this could land him back in prison.'

'I never thought about that. If he's been struck off as a solicitor but used his name as if he's still in the job then that's against the law, right?'

'Yes, that's correct. Connor has asked that we let the police deal with Mr Horn.'

'Definitely. Now we know the truth about the will, we can focus on the art dealer, the journalist, and just what my uncle is up to.'

'Yes, and hopefully we'll know a bit more about that soon.' I finish my coffee and stand to take it in the kitchen. 'I have some work to catch up on, so I leave you to watch mindless daytime TV.' She shakes her head as she takes a sip from her coffee cup.

'I need to go down to the office,' she says putting her cup down.

'What for?'

'I was pretty abrupt with your new secretary yesterday, I should apologise.'

'Let's get one thing straight, Meadow.' Sitting down at the side of her, I place my hand on the leg that she has resting on the settee. 'She's not my new secretary because I still have one, who will be back at work once she is up to it.' She nods her head when I raise an eyebrow at her. 'She's just filling in, Meadow.'

'I know and thank you for not taking my outburst seriously. Any other boss would have.'

'Maybe I'm not the arsehole you portray me to be.'

'Oh, you're still an arsehole but I forgive you because you've proven to be one of the good guys too.'

'Well, thank you so much, Miss Walters, that is ever so kind of you.' She rolls her eyes at me when I put on my telephone voice. 'What did you actually say to her because she never mentioned anything when you left?'

'I think I told her not to get too comfortable because that desk and chair are mine.' Her face heats up and she bites her lip to stifle her laugh. 'I might have mumbled a few unladylike words when she told me I couldn't just walk into your office without an appointment.'

'Yes, maybe you should go and apologise. To be fair, she hasn't said anything, so I don't think you've upset her.'

'What's her name?'

'Kaylee.'

'Can you hang on ten minutes, and I'll come down with you?'

'Of course. Have you finished with this?' I point at the empty plate, not a crumb left.

'Yeah, thank you. I was starving.' I take the tray from her and help her up. She accepts my help and fifteen minutes later, we are strolling into the office, Meadow linking my arm.

Kaylee looks up from her computer when I place a chair on the opposite side of the desk telling Meadow to sit down.

'Good afternoon Mr Summer,' she smiles then gives Meadow the same genuine smile. I nod my head at her and make my way into my office, leaving Meadow to it. I do keep my door open just in case I'm needed to stop a catfight. I laugh to myself because seriously I can't see that happening, Meadow doesn't usually have a bad bone in her body, and up to press is normally very professional. And I have no complaints about Kaylee.

Turning on my laptop, I keep an ear on what is going on in the room next door.

'Hi, I'm Meadow, Kane's—Mr Summer's secretary.' I casually glance through the window and see her offer her hand to Kaylee.

'Oh, I know who you are, Mason and Callum speak very highly of you.' She shakes Meadow's hand.

'That's good of them, they are lovely men. Anyway, I just wanted to come and say sorry for my outburst yesterday. I shouldn't have spoken to you like that and I'm truly sorry.'

'Oh, nonsense. If this desk belonged to me, I wouldn't want anybody using it. It's gorgeous. Have you found all the secret compartments yet?' Kaylee gushes over the ugly monstrosity and Meadow's eyes light up in surprise.

'I don't think so. It belonged to my great-grandad who passed it on to my grandad and he gave it to me. I've found ten but I do think there's more to be found.'

'I've always had a fascination with antique desks, especially this kind.' She opens one of the drawers and then closes it quickly. 'Oh, I'm sorry. I've only looked in the ones that I needed to.'

'It's fine there's nothing in them of any importance or any personal possessions. It's just work stuff. But feel free while you are here to search for more of the secret drawers because the bloody thing has beaten me.' They both laugh and just like that due to having that one thing in common, they become friends.

*

Protecting Her

I climb into bed, put on my reading glasses, and pick up *As The Crow Flies*, opening it on the last page I read. It's a crime fiction novel that Callum bought me which I started reading before all the trouble with Meadow. I find reading relaxes me and I need to relax and clear my mind, even just for an hour or two. Too much going on all at once: late nights, early mornings, meetings after meetings. I have a business to run but all I can focus on is Meadow. What she has gone through, what she is going through and that bastard of an uncle of hers who has caused it. I blow out a breath and try to forget about the woman who is lying asleep in the next room but it's futile. Just knowing, she's there and I can't touch her has me wound tightly. All I want to do is hold her, feel her body pressed against mine while I breathe in her fruity fragrance and kiss those full lips of hers. That's not all I want to do but I'd be truly satisfied with that, for now.

Flicking the page over I let out a sigh when I'm unable to concentrate, so I close the book and place it on the bedside table. I'm just about to get up to pour myself a drink when the heavy rain starts to batter at the windows, and the lightning illuminates the room. Pulling back the sheets, I climb out and make my way over to the balcony doors and view the city as it lights up like Bonfire night.

My mind ponders over the day as I watch the blades of lightning streak across the night sky and set it alight.

It's been quiet on the John Walters front. Damon and Chris watched the house from eight o'clock this morning. Then Sam—who is feeling much better after the brawl in the pub last night which left him with a black eye—and Antony took over. Apart from John venturing into the garden for ten minutes, he hadn't left the house all day. We still have no news on why he met with the journalist and Connor is struggling to gain any more information on Mr Horn. At the moment he's keeping his nose clean. He hasn't been seen to be fraternizing with any shady characters, but we are keeping an eye on him just in case he meets up with Meadow's uncle.

I haven't seen much of Meadow since she left the office. She sat and had a coffee with Kaylee, and they chatted for about an hour and because they were getting along so well, I was able to get on with some work. She came and told me when she was leaving, and I walked with her back here. Her foot was throbbing, so she took some painkillers and went for a lie-down.

I did message her throughout the afternoon just to check she was okay, and I also ordered takeout so neither of us would need to cook.

When I eventually finished answering emails and looking over contracts, it was almost nine o'clock, so I decided it was time to come home.

The lights were out in the apartment, Meadow had eaten, and she had left a note saying she had gone to bed. I'd have liked to have seen her this evening, but I understood it was late and the painkillers the hospital gave her made her drowsy.

As a crack of lightning forks through the sky the clap of thunder that follows is enough to wake the dead. At the same time, my bedroom door bursts open and Meadow flies in. She stops, awkwardly staring at me, and mumbles something about Henry being right, I do look like Clark Kent with my glasses on then she darts towards the bed, lifts the sheets, and buries herself under them.

I stay where I am for a few minutes and when she shows no sign of coming out from under where she is hiding, I join her sitting on the side of the bed.

Lifting the bedding, I climb in and then use the torch on my phone so I can see her face. 'So, you don't just have a fear of needles you are scared of thunder as well.' She chews on her thumbnail and glares at me.

'I don't have a fear of needles, I just don't like them being stuck in me.'

'And thunderstorms?'

'I might have a little fear of them. But I do have a genuine reason for that.'

'Do you want to talk about it?' I ask because I genuinely care about Meadow and if I can help her overcome her fears then I will.

She sits with crossed legs still chewing on her nails as our heads hold up the sheets like a tent. She opens her mouth to speak then closes it again as her eyes search my face. Letting out a soft sigh she removes the sheet and crawls up the bed, sitting back against the headboard.

I stay where I am, in the middle of the bed appreciating how Meadow looks at home in my bed, wearing one of my old T-shirts with black shorts. It's something I never thought I wanted but now she's all I want.

'When my mum died, my grandparents told me she had gone to heaven to live with the angels. I was only six, so of course I believed them. Every night I'd look out at the dark sky from my bedroom window, hoping and wishing that I'd see her dancing amongst the stars. I missed her, really missed her. I missed how she'd read to me at bedtime and sing to me. I missed her stroking my hair, her cuddles, and how she'd always call me her gift. I just wanted to be close to her.'

The shimmer in her eyes calls to me and without hesitation or any fight from her, I make my way to the top of the bed, lift her into my arms and place her on my knee. She snuggles into me as I stroke her hair, placing a gentle kiss on her head.

'One night when I was looking out of the window, I noticed flashes of light in the distance. For whatever childish reason I thought it was my mum calling out to me so without thinking I tiptoed downstairs, not wanting my grandparents to hear me then I made my way into the kitchen. I unlocked the back door and ventured out into the garden. To cut a long story short, the storm that had been brewing a few miles away soon descended overhead and I was caught in it out in the garden with claps of angry thunder and even angrier flashes of lightning.'

'Why didn't you run inside the house?'

'I'd gone down to the bottom of the garden and when the rain and thunder came, I set off running but my foot went down a hole and I twisted my ankle. I was in too much pain to move so I just sat there crying and alone as the thunderstorm did its worst. Lightning struck one of next door's trees and the branches lit up. I was scared to death. I must have screamed at that point because the next thing my grandad was lifting me into his arms and rushing me into the house. I was soaked to the skin and my ankle hurt like hell.'

'I can only imagine how frightened you must have been.'

'It was frightening. And since then, I've hated being alone when there's a storm.'

'Well, you're not alone now. I have you.' I hold her tightly reassuring her and she smiles at me. Her smile is beautiful, and her lips look soft and inviting. However, as much as I want to kiss her, I know at the moment she just needs me to hold her.

'Thank you.' She turns in my arms, her eyes gazing into mine. 'You know, you're not the arsehole that you're portrayed to be,' she grins, her eyes gleaming with mischief.

'I know'—my eyes widen and I feign a shocked expression—

'some woman with a huge attitude started the rumour around the office.'

'Maybe she just needed to get to know you.' Her eyes stay locked with mine as her tone takes on a more serious approach.

'No, she was right in her assumption. But if she'll let me,' I lean over and rub her nose with mine. 'I'll make it my life's work to make it up to her.'

'She'll let you.' We stare at each other for a long moment and I'm finding it extremely difficult not to make a move and make her mine. I know I need to tame it down and be the man she needs at the moment. Taking advantage of her when she's in such a vulnerable state just isn't my thing.

'Thank you.' I gently lift her from my lap and place her on the bed. 'I'll go put something on.' She looks at me in just my boxers and her cheeks flush. I give her a flirty wink then turn and make my way over to the walk-in wardrobe. Picking up a pair of PJs, I then make my way back to her as I put them on.

'Come with me.' I put my hand out for her to take and she gives me a questioning look. 'The sky is beautiful, come and see it. We can watch the storm from the balcony, you will be safe with me. You no longer need to be afraid Meadow.' She takes my hand and walks with me to the glass doors. The curtains are open from when I was looking out before she blew in like the wind.

'You will be fine,' I tell her when I step forward to open the door and she stops in her tracks. 'Trust me.'

'Okay.' She moves slowly to my side, and I place my arm around her shoulders. I feel her shiver, so I pull her into me letting her back rest against my chest.

'We'll stay just inside the doorway, if it gets too much for you, we can close the door,' I whisper against her cheek. She sighs lightly and holds tightly onto my arms. 'You know, I've always loved watching storms from up here. You can see for miles as the heavens light up, it's a beautiful sight.' Not as beautiful as the woman who is in my arms, I want to add but I don't.

Meadow stays silent in my arms as we watch the storm. Now and again, she jumps when there's a clap of thunder, but the trembling has stopped.

'This is the first time I've watched a storm since that night.'

'It's understandable that you're afraid of it. How do you feel now?'

'Well, I don't think I'll ever go out in it again or stand and watch it alone but being here with you is a step forward from where I was half an hour ago, so you never know.'

'I'm glad I was here to help,' I tell her as I close the balcony door. 'Come on, pick which side you want to sleep on.' I smile at her as we walk over to my king-size bed.

'Oh. I'm sorry you must think I'm crazy.' Her cheeks heat up. 'I'll be fine now it's calming down.'

'And if it starts up again?' I cock an eyebrow. I'm not going to pass up the chance of having her in my bed. I'm happy to hold her all night if it will make her feel safe. 'Meadow sleep in my bed. I'm not going to make a pass at you. Not that I don't want to.' She blushes again. 'I don't want you on your own if it starts up again.'

'I'll come back if it does.'

'You might as well stay then at least you won't be scared.'

'Okay.' That didn't take much persuading. It's obvious she's still afraid, her fear isn't going to disappear overnight.

We climb into bed, Meadow taking my usual side which I'm happy to give up for her. After saying goodnight, she turns on her side, facing away from me. Settling on my back, I know I'm in for a long night. I'm not used to having a beautiful woman sharing my bed all night long but now I've resolved to the fact that I want Meadow, I'm sure I could get used to having her in my bed every night. In fact, I know I could.

CHAPTER 13

MEADOW

'How are you feeling?' Kane asks as I walk into the office. 'Does your foot feel any better?' I nod my head and then hold out one of the cups of coffee I'd brought down.

I came down to thank him for his kindness last night. I didn't get the chance this morning because he'd left when I eventually woke. I'm glad in a way. Barging in on him in his bedroom last night made me feel foolish. I know I shouldn't because he understood when I explained why I was afraid of thunder and lightning, and he was happy for me to stay with him. Having him hold me while we watched the storm made me feel safe, it also had me feeling other things. Things that could be dangerous if I was to act on them. Kane has now kissed me twice and told me that he wants me. And boy does he know how to kiss. Even though I've pulled him up on both occasions, I'm struggling because I love the way he makes me feel and I'm certain with the way things are going between us I won't be able to deny him, and I'll end up in his bed. And it won't be because I need him to hold me due to the thunderstorm. I can't believe I let it slip how much he does look like Clark Kent with his glasses on. I'm sure he heard me even though he didn't say anything. And I can't believe I have never noticed it before.

So yes, when I woke this morning, I was glad he'd already left for work however I knew I needed to thank him for being there for me.

'Are you okay?' he asks, taking the cup from me, placing it on his desk then leaning back in his chair. 'You don't seem to be limping today.'

'Yes, I'm fine thanks and my foot does feel much better. It's still tender but the swelling has gone down a lot.'

'Good. At least you'll be able to wear your shoes soon.' He looks down at the grey rabbit slippers on my feet that Callum bought for me. They have floppy ears and a little pink nose and are so comfy.

'Oh, I don't know, I've got used to these.' I sit down on the chair opposite him and pop my feet up on his desk. I really am pushing it because if one of his brothers was to do it, he'd blow a gasket. He raises an eyebrow at me, so I wiggle my toes, which allows the rabbit's ears to move and the little pink nose to twitch. I let out a childish giggle and he shakes his head at me. But I don't miss his lip rising at one side as he lifts the cup to his mouth or the way his eyes are smiling at me over the rim.

'Aw come on; you've got to admit they're cute.'

'Okay, I'll admit they are cute.'

'See that didn't hurt, did it?'

'I guess not.' Wow, I'm on a roll with him this morning. I haven't been told to take my feet down off his desk and he agrees with me. In our office environment, this never happens but I guess things have changed considerably for us. 'Did you just come down to bring me coffee or did you need something?'

'Yes… Yes, I came to bring you coffee and to say thank you for last night.'

'It was nothing, Meadow, there's no need to thank me.'

'Yes, there is. You were there for me the other night when I stupidly went to the house and again last night. So, I'd say a thank you is definitely necessary.'

'Well, I'd say anytime you need me then I'll be there for you.' Our eyes meet and things suddenly take on a more serious note and I'm at a loss as to what to say next. It's hard to see at the moment that the man who is sitting behind his desk now is the same man who throughout the last two years, has shunned me when we have both been in the office together. Just gave me a nod of his head in greeting then turned it the other way. Only spoke to me when needed and annoyed the hell out of me when he did. The menial tasks he put on me—taking his suits to the dry cleaners and picking them up as well as putting them away in his wardrobe. The number of women I've had to turn away for him be that over the phone or at the door and never once complained. And I do have to ask why. Why did I continue working for him? To be truthful, I love the company. His twin brothers are like my brothers. Callum and Mason have become good friends. The rest of the staff who work within the company, as well as the employees from the other business that rents office space in the building, are all caring and brilliant people to work amongst. In all fairness, I've enjoyed working here even if Kane has made it difficult. However, putting all that aside he has changed over the last few days and things have changed between us…

'Meadow have dinner we me this evening?' Kane's question comes out of nowhere and brings me out of my thoughts.

'Pardon me,' I say needing him to repeat what he said just to make sure that I heard him right. I put down my cup and sit up straight in my chair watching him run his hand through his hair.

'Listen, Meadow, I know that I've been a bastard to work with these last couple of years and you have every right to hate me, but like I said the other night I will try and explain myself to you with the hopes you can forgive me. The reasons behind my behaviour are juvenile but I'd love to be able to explain myself, if you'll let me.'

'And you want to take me out so you can explain all this?' I'd love to know what has caused him to behave so badly towards me.

'Yes. Apart from that, I want us to spend some time together, just you and me, so we can get to know each other better. You've had a lot going on lately. Upsetting things and I wanted to take your mind off it all. There's nothing we can do at the moment about your uncle or your home, that is unless you want me to go around and pay him a visit. I'd have him out on his arse in seconds and he wouldn't have the balls to come back.'

'You'd do that?' I'm shocked.

'Absolutely. Just give me the word and it's done.' Kane's confident and calm tone leaves me with no doubt but to believe him. That and the way he looks at me as if to say, 'You must know this.'

'Thank you but let's wait to see what happens. Hopefully, we'll find out what he is up to.' I smile softly at him.

'Okay, whatever you want. What about spending some time alone without my brothers?'

'I can't go out anywhere.' I lift my foot and give my toes a wiggle, causing the rabbit's ears to flop about. 'Can't get my shoes on.'

'Oh, yes of course. I didn't think.' His eyes lower and he looks a little awkward and if I'm not mistaken a little sad.

'How about we stay in, and I rustle us something up.'

'Are you sure? If your foot is still sore, I don't want you standing on it too long.'

'Hey, I'm not going to be cooking anything up Michelin style.' His mouth curves upwards and the corners of his eyes crinkle as he gives me that beautiful smile.

'Well as long as you're sure then that would be wonderful. I'll even try and get finished early so I can give you a hand.'

'Don't worry about it, I'll be just fine on my own.'

'Thank you, Meadow, for doing this. I would've understood if you found it awkward.'

'Are you crazy? I'm looking forward to what you have to say,' I chuckle and he rolls his eyes.

'I bet you are.'

*

'Well, that was delicious,' Kane delights as he pushes his plate away placing his knife and fork on top of it. 'It's very rare I get a home-cooked meal. The last time I had a lamb hotpot was probably when my mum made it a few years back.'

'I'm glad you liked it. I haven't made it since my grandad died. It was one of those dishes that I loved to watch Grandma making and when she died, I thought I'd make it for him.'

'You're grandma taught you well because it was tastier than my mum's but don't tell her I said that.' He throws me a cheeky wink as he stands to clear the plates away.

'Thank you,' I tell him, watching him lift my plate from the table. 'I promise not to mention it the next time I see her.' Not that I've seen her recently. I think the last time I saw Mrs Summer, I must have been seventeen and just started college. It was probably just before Louise, and I lost contact with Connor and Henry. 'How are your mum and Ray?' Ray is Kane's stepdad well sort of stepdad, I don't think they ever married.

'They're well. I haven't seen them for a while. Since they both took early retirement, they're always jetting off to some warmer climate or sailing off on a cruise.'

'I don't blame them. If I'd brought up a family and worked all my life, I wouldn't want to sit around doing nothing.'

'I guess not,' he says ending the conversation about his mum and Ray as he swills the plates then opens the dishwasher and puts them in. I don't think he has anything against the man who took his father's place but from what the twins have told me, Kane, Callum, and Mason idolized their dad, and it took them a while to get used to having the man their mum had met some six years after their dad died. Connor and Henry don't remember their dad because they weren't even a year old when they lost him so to them Ray is all they have known.

'Here let me help you.' I pick up the cutlery to pass to him.

'I'll do it. Go sit down and take the weight off that foot,' he orders taking hold of my shoulders and turning me so I'm facing the way out of the kitchen. 'You did all the cooking, so I'll clean up.' I open my mouth to speak and then close it again when he gently taps my bottom. 'Go.' He widens his eyes at me, daring me to challenge him then he shows me that cheeky smile. I'm a little shocked by his playfulness and contemplate reminding him of his forwardness. Deciding not to bother because I do like his playful manner—I haven't seen it often—so I do as he suggests. I make my way into the living room, making myself comfortable on the settee—I have been cooking all afternoon.

When I told him I'd cook, he mentioned he'd try to finish work early so he could help. With such a workload to get through, he didn't arrive home until six. He'd called me to let me know he couldn't get away early. To be honest, I wasn't bothered, it gave me time to whip up a lemon tart, another one of my grandad's favourites.

Ten minutes later, Kane walks in holding up a bottle of wine and two glasses. 'Care to join me?'

'Why not,' I answer, sitting up and removing the foot I had resting on the couch. We'd both only had water with our meal, so a glass of wine would be lovely.

While we were eating at the table there was some distance between us but now, he's sat down beside me, I can feel his presence. Not that I couldn't feel it before but with his body this close, sharing the same space it's hard to ignore his manliness. I'd have to be devoid of all my senses not to react to him. The sound of his deep voice is enough to put my body on high alert. The feel of his hands on me, caressing my skin ignites something within me that I know I should extinguish but to be truthful I don't want to. Seeing his face light up, and getting to watch that beautiful smile, I feel privileged to witness such beauty. The taste of him when he kissed me is addictive and I crave more of his lips on mine.

'So, we should talk about us.' I cough, choking on my wine as I'm suddenly snapped out of my wayward thoughts by Kane's voice. 'Are you okay?'

'Yes,' I croak, leaning forward to place my drink on the table, he takes it from me and then gently pats my back.

'All right now?'

'Thank you. Yes, I am, it went down the wrong hole.' I wipe my mouth with my hand feeling like the biggest fool ever. I shouldn't be having these thoughts about him. Whatever he wants and however I feel, it wouldn't work between us. And now he's witnessed me using the back of my hand to wipe my mouth, he's probably having second thoughts about it anyway.

'I am genuinely sorry about being such a terrible boss,' he says as he leans his elbows on his knees. So, I guess we're going there first.

'You mean arsehole.'

'I was definitely an arsehole.' He turns his head, his blue eyes meeting mine and he does genuinely look sorry. But I'm not letting him off that easily. It doesn't matter how my body reacts to him; I want to know the reasons for his behaviour towards me.

'At least we're on the same page so spill it.'

'Truth?'

'Always.'

'Okay then. Truthfully, I was attracted to you the first day I walked into my office and saw you sitting there, looking all at home in my surroundings. I'm a confident man Meadow you know this, but I almost swallowed my own tongue when I looked at you. I actually think I tried to speak to you, but you took my breath away and I became tongue-tied, so I walked away and hid in my office for the rest of the day.' He turns from his position on the settee, so he is facing me. He doesn't look embarrassed about telling me this. Whereas I am shocked and I'm sure the expression on my face gives it away. 'I think it was the way your eyes smiled at me that first caught my attention. You must have been laughing about something and they were all watery—and glistening they reminded me of a starry sky. Then there was your smile. Who wouldn't want to be smiled at like that every day?' His thumb strokes over my bottom lip and I just sit there unable to move. 'Artists would pay big money to capture such a work of art—such beauty. I came to hate it because of how it made me feel. That perfume you wear is subtle but luring. The combination of your scent mixed with what you wear is seductive. When Callum introduced you to me you. Your first words were, 'Hello Mr Summer, it's nice to meet you.' That was all it took to lure me in, and I didn't like it.'

'Why?' I finally say something.

'Why?' He tilts his head; his eyes lock with mine.

'Yes.'

'Falling for someone makes you weak, clouds your judgment and in my experience leaves you open to be taken for a fool.' His words and the way he says them have me believing he has experienced this firsthand. 'Plus, I'm your boss and you're good friends with my youngest brothers—it'd never work. That's what I told myself anyway and through my frustration of not being able to have you I become this awful person. An arsehole, hoping you'd leave.'

'I don't know what to say. All this time I thought you hated me.'

'I never hated you, Meadow.' He takes hold of my hand. 'If anything, I hated myself for treating you the way I did. If I could turn back the last couple of years and change my behaviour, then I would. I'm sorry, I hope you can forgive me.'

'What changed?'

'Seeing you upset. It pulled at my heartstrings.' My chuckle has him raising an eyebrow.

'What's so funny?'

'Until this week, I didn't think you had a heart.' He laughs too.

'I deserve that and a lot more. I can't apologise enough Meadow. I also owe you a huge thank you.'

'What for?' I ask but really, he owes me a million of them for the jobs he's asked me to do, and like the good little secretary, I went ahead and did them without any complaints.

'For my suits. I love the way you coordinate them and my shirts. You place them just right, so they stay nicely pressed.'

'You have nice suits they should be kept in order, so they stay neat and tidy. We can't have you wandering in and out of meetings not looking like the sharp-suited man you are. Your reputation would be in tatters.'

'Ha, ha, thank you.'

'You're welcome. So that little speech about falling for someone making you weak and clouding your judgment—it seemed you knew what you were talking about.' It sounded like he'd been hurt at some point in his life. I'd like to know more about him and what makes him tick. Whatever happened to him in his past has made an impact on his future to date. I know this firsthand as I've seen how many women, he's had one-night stands with—no long-term relationship, and from what he's just divulged about being attracted to me.

'Yes, I've had firsthand experience as have many people, but I promised myself that I wouldn't put myself in that situation again.'

'Tell me about it. I want to know what made you the man you are today.' He sighs heavily and moves closer to me, taking my hand in his.

We both sit side by side, heads resting together and our feet up on the coffee table.

'The day I came out of the army...'

'Wait. I didn't know you were in the army.' I sit up so I can look at him.

'Yes. I signed up for three years. I came out a few months after my twenty-first birthday.'

'Wow! Your brothers never mentioned it. What made you join up?'

'I wanted the experience. I was looking for a trade and I thought what better way than the armed forces. It was an easy choice. We'd struggled after my dad's death so it was one less mouth to feed and I could send money home to my mum as well as save up towards my future. I'd always planned to set up my own security business since I found out my uncle had swindled my mum out of my dad's share of the security firm, they had run between them.' I'm shocked again; I didn't know this either but why would I? Connor and Henry don't have to tell me everything.

'You're not the only one to have an uncle who'd rip off his own.' He strokes his thumb over my knuckles and shifts in his seat getting comfortable. 'I'll tell you about him some other time.'

'Can't wait. If you need a hand sorting him out then I'm your girl,' I jest, knocking him with my elbow and then I settle back against the settee.

'Oh, I wouldn't worry, he's dead.'

'Oh well, the offer was there.'

'Indeed, it was.' He kisses the side of my head, his lips soft and welcoming, may I add. 'Thank you,' he then whispers, his breath warm against my head.

'You're welcome, anytime.' I struggle to get the words out due to the heat building between us. It's hard to focus and maintain any kind of restraint when he's this close, especially when his lips are touching me.

I'm given a reprieve when he sits back against the settee. I pick up my glass, taking a quick drink just to cover up the blush that is creeping up my neck and hopefully, the alcohol will calm me down. It does the trick, so I turn to him and listen keenly.

'As I was saying, the day I came out of the army, I'd arranged with some of the lads to go on a night out. I'd already been accepted into the police force—I'd applied beforehand knowing I wasn't going to sign up for another stint with the army. I was waiting to go away on my basic training and needed to let off some steam before I went. To cut a long story short, on the night out I met Julie. We hit it off and we ended up dating. She knew I was going away for a while and was happy to wait for me. Through my training and the first year I was in the police, we became close. I loved her or so I thought, and she told me she loved me. She lived in a small flat which was great because after coming out of the army I'd moved back in with my mum and brothers. There was barely enough room for all of us so taking Julie home was a big fat no. I stayed a lot at hers. I told her all about my plans to open my own business one day and she encouraged me to do so. I don't know how I didn't see what was going on right in front of me. But they do say love is blind.'

'So, you were serious about her then?' I need to ask because I find it difficult to believe he was serious about a woman.

'Not at first, no. We both slept about but after a while yes, we became serious.' He shrugs his shoulders like it's no big deal. To be fair I suppose it isn't.

'Chris, one of the lads from my old unit was on leave and he came to visit. We had a few nights out, Julie coming with us. They got along well so when he dragged her up to dance, I never gave it a thought to be more than friendship. It's what we all did just for a bit of fun, flirting with our mate's girlfriends. Only it wasn't a bit of fun on their part anyway.' Ah, now I get it.

'Sometime after, she started to feel sick on and off. I had

wondered before she came out and told me she was pregnant if she was. God, It seems like another lifetime ago now.'

'Were you happy about the pregnancy?'

'I should have been. I'd never thought about having children. We were only young, and I had so many things I wanted to do.'

'How old were you?'

'I was twenty-three at the time and Julie was twenty-five. To answer your other question yes, I was happy about it once I'd gotten over the shock. We made plans for me to move in with her before the baby was born. Or I thought we'd made plans, turned out it was just me making the plans.' He speaks so casually about something in his life that I know he's going to tell me didn't end well for him. But then I guess he's had a lot of years to get over it. Or has he gotten over it? I suppose not because from what he's telling me he seemed to be a decent guy, and this was probably a turning point for him.

'I'd noticed a change in her. How she was reacting to me. Our sex life was nonexistent by the time she was six months gone. I put it down to her pregnancy and hormones at first but that all changed when I noticed another change in her. She was becoming secretive, sly almost. This was about the same time I'd noticed my bank account had taken a hit significantly.'

'How so?'

'I'd been saving every penny I could each month since joining the army and continued to do so when I joined the police force. Callum, Mason, and I had spoken about buying a run-down house, doing it up, and selling it. Both of them had left school and were working in the building trade so we all had money to put in the pot. Mum had been able to land a job working for Ray a few years before and I no longer needed to help her out.'

'Is that how she met him? Ray, I mean.'

'Yes. She played hard to get for a while. I think she was scared of what my reaction would be.'

'Was it just you?'

'I think so. Connor and Henry were always going to be fine, and I think Callum and Mason were, but it was different for me. I'd seen how hurt she was when my dad died. We all struggled. From the age of fourteen, I had to man up and help take care of my brothers. I even babysat the neighbours' kids to get some extra money into the house as well as stocking shelves in the local shop at the weekend. I'd do anything as long as it was legal to support my mum.'

'Your mum must be proud of you?'

'I think she is.' He turns to me, a soft smile on his face.

'You're a good son and brother, I'm sure your dad would be proud of you too.'

'I'm sure my brothers think I'm an arsehole just like you do.' He throws that cheeky wink at me, and I blush. 'But yeah, my dad would be proud of me,' he says chuckling, noticing how his flirty ways affect me. 'Anyway, where was I? Julie was six months gone and money was evaporating from my bank account. I'd given her my bank card to buy things we needed for the baby and the flat. I know things come at a price but I'm not stupid, so I questioned her on it. I didn't want to upset her; I knew her hormones were all over the place, but something wasn't right. We got into an argument and that's when it all came out. The baby wasn't mine.' My shocked reaction, even though I had an idea this was coming, stops him from what he was saying. I squeeze his hand gently and he continues. 'Turns out it was Chris' and he'd been sleeping with her every time he came home from leave. She'd told him about the baby, and he asked her to go out to Germany to be with him. That's where he was based. Of course, they needed money to do this and thought they'd help themselves to mine.'

'The bastards. What was she going to do with all the baby paraphernalia, ship it over?'

'She hadn't bought anything except baby clothes. She told me she had but said it would all be delivered nearer the time of the birth, so I was none the wiser.'

'Crafty. So, what happened, once she confessed?'

'I packed the few things that I had at her flat, I'd not moved in properly and I went home. But not before I threatened her with the police if the money she'd taken wasn't in my account by the following morning.'

'And was it?'

'It was minus her flight money. I let her have that. What riled me up the most was why didn't they come clean straight away. They'd been sleeping together behind my back for over a year. If she or Chris had come to me and told me they'd fallen for each other— yeah, I'd have been pissed about it. Upset, but it wouldn't have hurt so much. I'd have probably wished them all the best but with the way they went about it, well it just angered me, I swore I'd never let it happen again.'

'So that's why you just use women for sex?'

'I don't just use women for sex.' He sounds offended. "If I'm invited to a social event where I need a plus one, I know of many women who'd like to accompany me. If sex is offered and I'm interested, then why not? I'm only human, Meadow. What I never wanted from any of them though was a relationship.'

'So that is why you were awful to me. Because you'd fallen for someone who'd hurt you and you didn't trust that it wouldn't happen again.'

'In a nutshell, yes. But if I sat and thought about it, I don't think I ever loved her.' He sits up and turns his body to face me, taking hold of both of my hands. His blue eyes show so much emotion. 'I'm sorry for putting you in the middle of it when some of them wanted more. I shouldn't have let you do that.' He does sound sincere. 'But what I'm truly sorry for is not being man enough to tell you how I felt and in turn making your life difficult within the company. Can you forgive me?'

Can I forgive him? Does he deserve my forgiveness? To be fair he's not the first to be taken for a ride in matters of the heart and he certainly won't be the last. Treating me the way he has, isn't just going to go away overnight. I might be reacting to him differently now but that's only because he's been paying me so much attention. Making my body come alive with his seductive words, his kisses, and his touch. He put things on hold and brought in staff to help me out. He's changed since that night he brought me here. Showed me he can be a decent man and that he does have a heart. For a while, I thought he might have had a different dad from his brothers because of their personalities. Now I can see they all have the same traits. It was just Kane who hid his caring nature behind a scowling mask and a vicious tongue. Now the mask has lifted, and the venom has been replaced with words of desire, the little crush I tried to hide is bubbling to the surface. It's true I've always found Kane attractive and maybe had a little crush on him but chose to bury it deep and keep it hidden due to his conduct. Looks like Callum and Mason hit the nail on the head when they suggested that Kane and I had a love-hate relationship. I'm not saying I love him or that he loves me, but we clearly do have something going on.

He's made it clear he wants me but what do I know about relationships—I've never been in one. Not a serious one anyway. I'd need to forgive him if I was to give him what he wanted. Who am I kidding—it's what I want too.

'I can see you're giving it some serious consideration,' Kane's amused voice cuts through the air, bringing me back to the here and now.

'I am.'

'And have you come to a decision?" It's not hard to forgive him. Being able to forget about it is the hardest part but if he stays true to his words then I think that will reduce over time.

'I think so. You're forgiven but don't think for one minute you're off the hook. No more Mr Grumpy or I'll kick your arse.'

'I don't doubt for one minute that you won't put me in my place if I revert to my old ways.'

'You bet I will.'

'I'm glad we were able to sort things out.' He smiles at me.

'Me too.'

We sit quietly for a moment lost in our thoughts. Then I nearly jump out of my skin, when he startles me with his next question.

'What was that all about last night?'

'Huh? Do you mean me being scared of thunder and lightning?' I know exactly what he means but I was hoping he'd forgotten about my slip of the tongue. No such bloody luck.

'Your comment about me looking like Clark Kent with my glasses on.' Could this get any more embarrassing? I sink into the settee, hoping it will swallow me up.

'Why are you blushing?' he asks with that sexy smirk on his face. Arsehole.

'Oh, I didn't realise I was. It must be the wine.' Liar, liar pants on fire the little devil on my shoulder sings.

'Liar,' his voice is low and husky, taunting me.

'Okay, okay.' I sit up straight, shaking my head at him and folding my arms across my chest. 'I might have a little crush on Christopher Reeves and find him extremely hot as Clark Kent.'

'The glasses?' I nod my head. 'And you think I look like him with mine on.' He loves this. Making me squirm in my seat.

'No. Well, I didn't until Henry mentioned it when we were watching Superman the other night. He said you looked like him. I'd never seen you with your glasses on until last night.'

'But you agree with him?'

'I might…'

'Wait here.' He says grinning like the cat who got the cream as he rises in one swift movement from the settee. And even though I know that he's making his way to the bedroom to retrieve those damn glasses from his bedside table, I do as he says. I must be raving mad.

'What do you think?' He's back in no time at all, standing there with his hands on hips and those thick black glasses making him look even sexier than he is. If that's even possible.

'Mmmm,' I muse, tapping my finger on my lip. Might as well play him at his own game.

'Do you have a red and blue suit on under that shirt with a big S on the front?'

'I might have. Care to take a look.' He strides purposely towards me, a sexy swagger going on as he opens two buttons of his shirt seductively and my ovaries do a little happy dance. It's not like I haven't seen him without a shirt on, I have but my lady parts are having a field day with the way he is walking towards me with a purpose.

He puts his hand out for me to take and I'm too lost in that cheeky smile to care that I'm reaching out to take it.

He helps me to my feet, pulling me into his firm body. All I can focus on are his lips. Unknowingly I'm moving forward, standing on my tiptoes as he leans down. Our lips meet. It's not the first time, only now it's me wanting to claim him. Desire runs high, surging through my bloodstream, heating my body to the core. I can't believe how he makes my whole being come alive and it's not just those sexy glasses causing it. It's him. My boss. Mr Kane Summer. The feel of his broad shoulders under my hands, his manly scent, and the way his mouth makes my body tingle from head to foot. I should stop this. I need to stop this before we go too far. We've too much going on to embark on anything physical. I've too much going on. I'm not myself. Haven't been for a while now.

Reluctantly I pull away, knowing I need time to think about what this one kiss might mean for us.

'Now was that the glasses or just me that brought that on?' His blue eyes sparkle with mischief as his lips turn up. He's got me and he knows it. Talk about being put on the spot.

I turn from him and reach down, picking up the glass from the table. There's not much wine left in it, but I need some Dutch courage.

'As much as I should, I can't lie to you,' I say, placing the empty glass back on the table.

'What do you mean?'

'Yes, I'm attracted to you even without the glasses. But I'm not sure this'—I point between us— 'is a good idea.'

'Why not? We're both consenting adults who are attracted to each other. I don't see the problem.'

'The problem is I have too much going on at the moment to even think about you and me. Shit, you know what I mean Kane. I'm not in a great place at the moment—but that doesn't mean I don't want this.' Staring up at him, I hope he understands. Crickey I'm not sure I understand.

He takes my hands in his and brings them to his lips.

'I get it, Meadow I really do. But whatever you have going on, I'm right there with you. You know that don't you? And I'll wait for however long it takes for you.' He bends down brushing his lips across mine. I want him to claim me. Turn this tender kiss into one full of passion but I know that would be wrong. I step back from him, keeping my hands on his chest.

'Thank you for understanding.' I gaze up into those gorgeous blue eyes of his. 'I think I should go to bed now.' Those painkillers I had earlier added with a couple of glasses of wine and a heart-to-heart well it's worn me out. Plus, if I stay in his company any longer then I'm likely to embarrass myself and give in to what we both want. Even if I am tired, he's hard to resist.

'Ok,' he chuckles. 'Come on, I'll walk you to your room.' And he does. Keeping hold of my hand he leads the way.

'So, I'll see you in the morning,' I tell him as I put my hand on the door handle.

'You will.' He lets go of the hand he is holding and kisses the top of my head. 'Goodnight Meadow.'

'Night Kane,' I say, smiling as I open the door. He turns his back on me and then calls out over his shoulder.

'You know where I am if—if it thunders.' Yeah, if it thunders. What he means is if I change my mind about taking things further.

As much as my body wants to take things further, I'm sticking to my guns. We need to take it easy until I have my life sorted out. But if it thunders, I'll be there in a shot.

CHAPTER 14

MEADOW

'Come and sit down Meadow.' Mason taps the seat at the head of the table and then sits down at the one next to it. Callum, Connor, and Henry are already seated. 'Kane's just taking a call, he won't be a moment.' Henry passes a cup of coffee across the table to me, and as I reach for it, I pick up on the atmosphere in the room. Worry.

'Is everything okay?' I ask looking between them all while picking up the cup. They all have that same worried look going on.

'We've come across some information regarding your uncle.'

'What is it?'

'Let's wait for Kane to come back in then we'll discuss what we've found out.'

'Okay.' I sit down and take a drink of my coffee. It's my first one this morning and I'm grateful for it.

I had a restless night thinking about Kane and what he'd said last night as well as that hot kiss. A hot kiss that I reciprocated. My mind was running a million miles an hour and didn't settle until the birds were tweeting. Due to this, I then slept in. Knowing Kane was going to work this morning I quickly showered and dressed then came into the kitchen, hoping I hadn't missed him. That's when I heard voices coming from the dining room.

'Good morning, Meadow,' Kane greets me with a smile as he saunters into the room. I smile back at him remembering how that mouth felt against mine last night. I shake off the thought, knowing his brothers are here and have something serious to tell me. Jake the security officer from downstairs strolls in behind him. He says good morning to everybody then sits down helping himself to a coffee. Kane stands at the far side of the table, one of his hands rubbing against his mouth, he looks troubled.

Protecting Her

'Right let's get started. Meadow, you know Jake?'

'Yes, of course, I know Jake,' I answer, looking confused at him.

'Sorry, it's been a long day already and it's not even dinner time.'

'What's happened? Everyone seems'—I look around the table at everyone— 'worried.'

'Last night I couldn't sleep.' He picks up his cup, his eyes meeting mine. I wasn't the only one then. 'So, I got up and went downstairs for a catch-up with Jake. Did you know he was in the police force Meadow?'

'Yes, I knew.' I turn to Jake. 'We chat all the time, don't we?' Most of the time it's when I'm up at the crack of dawn and come into work at stupid o'clock. With no one else around we sit and have coffee together. He told me all about his wife dying and then him retiring from the police force. He mentioned he wasn't coping well without his wife and being at home all the time was driving him crazy. So, when he bumped into Kane, and he offered him a job he jumped at the chance.

'We do.' He gives me a sweet smile.

'Anyway, we got talking and I happened to mention your uncle. Turns out Jake was one of the arresting officers and remembers the case well and your uncle.'

'You do?' He nods his head slowly.

'Yes. I didn't know he was related to you Meadow. Not that it makes any difference. You're nothing like him, kiddo.'

'Thank you, that's good to know.'

'Do you want to tell her what you know, Jake?'

'You go ahead, and I'll jump right in if I'm needed.'

'Right, we figured out that Uncle John is a gambler.' Everyone agrees with him. 'Well, his gambling issues go way back well before he was locked up. In fact, in his statement, he did apologise and said he'd only done it so he could pay off the people he owed money to. That his gambling addiction had landed him in quite a bit of trouble with some not-so-very-nice people and if he didn't pay them off then his life would be in danger.'

'Who were these people? Did he pay them off?' I ask, wondering who the hell he'd got mixed up with.

'No, he didn't pay them off, well not fully anyway. John got caught before he could finish paying the half-million pounds, he still owed to Jimmy McKay.'

'Half a million. How the hell did he owe them that much? And who is this— Jimmy McKay?'

'He owns a couple of casinos around town and he's not a very nice man. Your uncle liked to live the high life. He'd flash the cash around to gain attention from the ladies, have them hanging off his arm, and lavish them with gifts. He lived in a penthouse in the middle of the city centre, he also owned a half-a-million-pound detached house and a few cars. He had lots of assets.'

'I didn't know this. I was only young when John was around and didn't take much interest. How did John get involved with this man?'

'He didn't. Jimmy's father was in charge when he first started gambling. The debts were huge, but your uncle always paid him on time and because he got along with old man McKay if he was ever late with his repayments then it wasn't a big deal. He'd give him more time knowing he could rely on men like John to come back. He made a lot of money out of John over the years and not just him.'

'The McKay's were well known for loaning money with a high percentage payback rate. They were also known for allowing a certain type of clientele to build up a tab at the casinos they run and again adding interest.' Jake adds.

'And what happens if they couldn't pay at all?' I turn to Jake. He seems to know this family well and my uncle.

'Well usually they'd give them extra time but, in some cases, it had been known for them to come down heavy on the person who owed them. The family was known to the police. We'd had a few people come to us scared to death of what they were going to do to them and on a few occasions, we were told that they'd put pressure on family members. If you get my meaning?'

'What do you mean put pressure on family members? Did they hurt them?'

'I don't want to go into too much detail Meadow, but a few were hospitalized.' I blow out a breath. This just gets worse.

'Couldn't the police stop them? Arrest them or something?'

'We could have if there was any evidence but, in all cases, they had covered up their tracks, so they got away with it.' His eyes widen and he gives me a sad smile.

'So, my uncle owed them money and because of this, he got himself involved in swindling elderly people to pay them back. He was caught doing this and made to pay the money back, I presume?'

'Most definitely. I think it was all paid back. Your uncle's assets were frozen. The judge ordered that any property he owned be seized and sold then added to whatever he had in the bank to pay them back.'

'And he had some property for them to seize.'

'Yes,' he answers. My mind races back to my teenage years trying to remember where John lived. I come up with zilch. Nothing. I can't even remember what he did for a living.

'You said he had paid some of the money back to this McKay family. So, does he still owe them? I mean half a million, that's some serious money. From what you've said I doubt these people would let that amount of money just slip away.'

'Yes, he still owes them.' Kane comes and stands at the side of me, placing his hand on my shoulder. He gives it a gentle squeeze as he pulls up a chair and sits in between Mason and me then he takes hold of my hand. I don't look at the twins. Nervous about what they will think. I'm sure there's some rule about not getting involved with a friend's older brother or is that just directed at a man getting involved with his best friend's sister? I focus my eyes on Callum whose mouth lifts at the corner as he throws me a cheeky wink. This settles my nerves a little but the questioning stare I feel radiating from my two best friends still leaves me cautious. I'm going to have some explaining to do as soon as we have finished up here.

'As we have said Meadow, Jimmy and his men are not people to mess with. In the past, John got away with paying late to Jimmy's father and paid little interest on what he owed him. Regardless of how much Jimmy complained to his father that he was showing weakness, John got away with it. Whereas others probably got their kneecaps broken and more.' I blow out a long breath. If I didn't think this was serious before then I do now.

'This all came to a head when Mr McKay was rushed into hospital with a bleed on his brain. Straight away, Jimmy took over the business, covering for his father and he cleaned house. Anyone who owed the family money was sent a message to pay up within the week.'

'Well, it wasn't exactly a message,' Jake adds. 'It was a threat.'

'A threat that people took seriously—except John,' Kane continues. 'He thought he was safe with having such a good relationship with the old man but that didn't mean shit to Jimmy. He hated John and because of this, he made it his duty to ruin him.' This is a lot to take in and a headache starts above my eyes. I don't mention it to Kane because I want to hear what else they have found out, so I grip tightly onto Kane's hand and listen carefully.

'John was unable to pay the tab that he had run up at the casino and because he was an addict, he needed the rush of gambling like drug addicts need their next fix. This was the only place he could go. Jimmy had put the word out to other establishments not to let him in and because Jimmy gets what he wants your uncle was blacklisted from all casinos in town. He had no choice but to hand over his penthouse as collateral for what he owed.

Within six months John ended up losing the penthouse and his cars. The McKay's didn't know about the house he owned but they took pretty much everything else from him to repay his debt.

During this time, Mr McKay died so Jimmy was free to run the business any way he wanted. The two younger brothers weren't interested and left him to it.'

'So how did he end up getting involved with the two men who were ripping off old people?'

'He met them in the casino. They'd all worked in the insurance business, and they were all gambling addicts. One of them came up with the idea to help get them out of shit with Jimmy. They all needed the money.'

'They were desperate at this point,' Jake says. 'They had lost everything. Your uncle had sold his house and downsized. He was staying at a friend's house so he could rent it out, but it wasn't enough. His addiction had got him in so much debt with Jimmy that he couldn't see any way out of it.'

'And he told all this in his statement to the police?" I ask. He nods his head. 'And the police believed him and these two other men and didn't do anything to stop Jimmy McKay?' Even though my uncle had an addiction that landed him in trouble, I still can't feel any emotions toward him. Not after what he did to those old people, but I do think the police should have put a stop to this Jimmy character. He sounds like a bloody gangster.

'Whether they were believed or not, they did commit an offence and were found guilty. And like I said before Jimmy McKay had been rolled in by the police on many occasions, but he always had an alibi for any violent attacks that he'd been associated with, and we never found any evidence to place him there. When he was asked about any money John owed him from running up a tab and the amount of interest that he'd added, he told us he didn't run such a tab and that it was his father who had lent him money out of kindness and since his father was no longer here to ask for it back it was his job to do so. Jimmy McKay comes across as a very shrewd businessman.' Kane makes a noise of disgust.

'Do you know him?' I turn to Kane.

'I know his brother, Michael. I went to school with him. Jimmy was two years older than us; he was a bully back then. He sold cigs and alcohol for double the price and because teenagers couldn't get it any other way, they'd pay it. He ran a tab back then as well and if it wasn't paid when he said then he and his goons would beat up the kids who owed him. Michael was nothing like him.'

'Anyway, we never found anything illegal to tie him to,' Jake finishes.

'So how does my uncle still owe him money? He's only just come out of prison.'

'He owed him from before he went inside. Any money he had left was used to pay the people he had ripped off. With added interest, he still owes almost half a million.'

'How do you know this?'

'Once Jake had told me what he remembered about John and Jimmy, I telephoned Michael. I haven't spoken with him in a long time but we're still friends. He doesn't get along with his brother. I'd go as far as to say that he hates him. He has his reasons and so does the youngest brother Carl. Michael might not have much to do with the running of the casinos, but he keeps a very close eye on his brother and how he runs things. That's who I was on the phone with when you came in. I'd spoken to him earlier and he told me he'd phone me back. It only took him an hour to find out how much John still owed.'

'Wow, no wonder John was so desperate to get his hands on some money. How he thought he'd find such an amount in the house, I'll never know.'

'How much is your house worth, Meadow?' Connor asks. Other than Kane, Jake, and me it's the first time one of the brothers has spoken.

'If I was to guess I'd say about three hundred thousand. Do you think he's after selling it to pay off his debt?'

'When he went inside, he owed a quarter of a million. His debt has risen some since. Yes, I'd say he is desperate to sell it and get what he can to pay him off.' Kane says.

'Meadow knowing what we know about Jimmy and what your uncle owes him, we all'—he looks around the room— 'we all agree that you might be in danger not just from your uncle but from Jimmy McKay as well.' My stomach tightens into a knot and my hands begin to shake.

'Why?' I ask but I needn't have bothered. I'm the only family member John has and if Jimmy knows this, he might think getting to me will get his money from my uncle. There's no chance of that. My uncle doesn't give a crap about anybody but himself.

'Why?' Kane echoes my question. 'Because he has until the weekend to come up with the money and if he doesn't then Jimmy's going to come looking. If he finds out he has a niece—well, I don't want to say what he might do.' Kane almost growls the last part out. His expression looks murderous.

I squeeze his hand, trying to reassure him and calm him down. 'I'm here—he doesn't know I exist, right? —he can't get to me here.'

'No, he can't.' There's a chorus from all the brothers and Jake too. Kane stays quiet. Too quiet.

'Can I speak with Meadow alone?' He looks at his brothers, his eyes pleading for them to give him some alone time with me. They all nod their head and stand up. They leave the room and Jake follows.

When they have all left the room Kane turns my chair so I'm facing him and pulls his closer to me. 'Meadow, I need you to listen to me.' He places his forehead on mine and takes hold of my hands. 'I can't stress how serious this is. You can't leave this apartment until all this is over. Not even with one of us.' He sounds so fraught and so sad. It makes my heart ache for him. I know he cares. This whole situation shows me how much he does.

'I know,' I tell him, lifting my head from his.

'Then promise me you won't do anything stupid.' I don't think I've ever heard him sound so serious about anything and this is Mr Grumpy we're talking about.

Placing my hand on his chest and my lips on the side of his

mouth. 'I promise I won't do anything stupid again—well not until this whole ordeal is over.' I smile against his lips trying to lighten the mood. It works because he smiles back as he places his hand on the back of my head then leads us into a passionate kiss, taking away any worry and fears.

'Can we come in?' The sound of Connor's voice breaks us apart and I sit up quickly, smoothing my hair back.

'Yes,' Kane tells him as he rises from his chair. 'I need some water; would you like some?'

'Please.'

'Anybody else want a bottle?'

There's a round of yes and no's then once he's out of hearing distance the twins pounce.

'What the hell is going on with you two?' Henry's face is a picture of I can't believe it.

'Keep your nose out,' Callum intervenes before I have time to open my mouth.

'Hey, Meadow is our friend and Kane is—well he's our older brother.' It's Connor's turn to voice his concern. I'm not even sure if it is a concern because both brothers look amused.

'Kane and I—oh, I don't know.' What do I say to them? 'There's something there between us but I'm not sure I can explain it at the moment. Plus, he'll be back any minute so can we talk about this later?' I know he won't want whatever is going on between us a topic of conversation. 'Now is not the time.'

'Yeah, we get that but the first chance you get then…' Connor stops speaking when Kane enters the room.

'Is everything okay?' His eyes glance around the room.

'Yeah, I was just telling Meadow we can now collect her things from the flat.' My eyes widen in surprise. That's a bit of good news. There's not much there because I didn't take much with me but at least I'll have a few more of my possessions.

'Do you still have Meadow's keys that she gave you the other day?'

'I do.' Connor answers. 'I'll call round this afternoon.'

'I'll come with you,' Kane says as he untwists the top of the bottle of water and passes it to me.

'We'll bring everything back here and if the landlord is around, I'll hand him the keys back because you won't be going back there.'

He looks at me as if he expects me to argue with him. Any normal day I would have, but not today. I don't ever want to step into that flea-ridden pit again.

Chapter 15

Meadow

As I survey my handiwork, a smile tugs at my lips. Happy with myself I pick up one of the delicious treats that I've been making all afternoon and take a bite. It's my first attempt at coconut macaroons and raspberry jam flapjack with a double chocolate drizzle and they look absolutely gorgeous and smell divine even if I do say so myself.

I haven't stepped out of Kane's penthouse for two days, not even to go down to the office to stretch my legs. Since learning about my uncle's serious gambling addiction and the trouble he is in, which in turn could land on my doorstep if this Jimmy McKay guy realises that he has a niece, well it scared the living daylights out of me. I was even hoping there might have been some light thrown on the art dealer and my uncle. Had he managed to get his hands on the pictures he was supposed to have displayed in her gallery? My thoughts were if he sold them, he might have enough money to keep this man at bay for a while. I even contemplated sending him a message telling him I knew everything and to sell the house. It's worth a few hundred thousand, I'm sure. However, my guardian angel thought otherwise. Kane reminded me that the house belonged to my

grandparents. A house they had brought up their children in and then me. He also reminded me that my grandad had kicked Uncle John out for reasons unknown at the moment, but our bets are on the despicable thing he did. After listening to him I agreed. Whatever money John owes has nothing to do with me. The trouble he has landed himself in again has nothing to do with me even if it could come and smack me in the face if I don't hide out of the way. Weighing this up, I decided to listen to Kane. Hopefully, my uncle will find the money and pay this guy back.

I'm just about to take a bite of a flapjack when I hear the front door open. The sound of two male voices tells me Kane and Callum are here. I place the flapjack back down and take the clingfilm in my hands ready to cover up two of the trays.

'It smells delicious in here; what are you treating us to today?' Callum's eyes sparkle with delight. 'Wow, these look good.' His hand reaches out to grab a coconut macaroon. I don't stop in because those are the ones I'd made for Kane and his brothers.

'Why have you made so many?' Kane asks as he picks up one too.

'You have that big meeting in the morning, so I thought I'd give you a helping hand and treat your guests to a sugar rush.' I remember writing the date and time in his diary a few weeks ago. A new company is looking for security staff for their building site. It's a two-year contract or until the building is finished that is. They've heard nothing but good things about Summer Knights Security, so they asked for a meeting with Kane and his brothers.

Kane looks surprised. He had probably forgotten that I was the one who set up the meeting.

'I don't know how you have remembered that with everything you have going on.'

'It's my job,' I say then stop myself. 'Or was.'

'It still is once everything is back to normal, you know this.'

'Thank you,' I say with a smile. I needed to check that he hadn't changed his mind. 'Anyway, these two trays are for tomorrow.' I pick one up and clingfilm it. 'The others you can eat.'

'Thanks,' Callum says around a mouthful of macaroon. 'I'll take mine to go just in case the others call around.' He's right to do so because if Mason, Connor, or Henry do come over then they will devour the lot.

'Don't you have something to ask Meadow?' Callum says, leaning against the worktop, his lips twitching with amusement.

'Oh, yes, I do.' Kane crosses his arms over his chest, his tone serious but there's a softness in his eyes. 'I had a lovely email today from Mrs Chadwick, the chair of All Saints Church Hall, thanking me for my contribution of one thousand pounds to the Christmas fund. With the offer of a cup of tea with her and the elderly ladies from the committee next time I'm in the area.' He tilts his head, his eyes narrowing on me and if I'm not mistaken, he's trying hard not to smile behind the hand that has just covered his mouth. 'Care to explain.' I bite my lip to stop myself from laughing. I know exactly what he's talking about. The company does give to many charities in the area and sponsors a few under tens football clubs. Kane and his brothers are always willing to help out where they can so when I was approached by the elderly lady, I didn't see a problem.

'Mrs Chadwick regularly goes in the sandwich shop across the street, and I happened to be in there one day when she was talking to the owner. She was hoping he'd support their good cause.'

'Which is?' he asks.

'The money will help to buy hampers for the one-parent families at Christmas and also pay for a Christmas dinner for the homeless. They are good causes so when Billy the owner of the sandwich shop offered her two hundred and fifty pounds and then pointed her my way—he knows who I am and that I work for you—well I had to up the ante, didn't I? Summer Knights is a lot bigger company and I'm sure our revenue is considerably higher than the sandwich shop. So, I told her I'd speak to you and get back to her. When I got back to the office you had that face on—unapproachable—so I went to Mason and he agreed that I could send them a check.' I shrug my shoulders. It's no big deal, Summer Knights Security is worth a mint, I could have given more and it wouldn't hurt the company.

'And what about the girls under tens football team? I had a nice letter signed by all the players, thanking me for sponsoring them and two tickets to their next game.'

'Now, funny thing was, I bumped into Mrs Chadwick again....'

'In the sandwich shop, no doubt.'

'Yes, how did you guess.'

'Just a hunch.'

'Anyway, she mentioned that the coach who runs the boy's football club was setting up a girls club and they were raising money to help pay for the kit. I knew you wouldn't mind so I told her we'd sponsor them. The day I was going to mention it to you, your whole body language screamed, I'd be getting a big fat no if I asked you anything so I went to Mason again.'

'I'd never say no to a good cause, Meadow, you know that.'

'I know, but sometimes it was easier to go to Callum or Mason if I wanted anything. I knew you'd support them. You'd already sponsored the boys' team, but you looked like you'd had a really bad day, so I left you alone.'

'I'm sorry, I made you feel like you couldn't come to me.' He pulls me towards him, taking me in his arms. I relish the warmth of his body and his strong arms around me. I've missed him today. 'I know in the past, I've given you many reasons to stay clear of me but from now on no matter what Meadow, never feel as if you can't ask me anything.' He breathes into my hair.

I pull away and look up at him, loving how his blue eyes see me. 'In future, I will kick your arse if I ever feel like you are slipping back to your old ways.'

'I'm sure you will.' He leans down, his lips touching mine. It's just a brush and I want more. Or I did until I heard someone cough. Callum. I forgot he was there.

'I'll just take these and leave you to it.' There's a smile on his face as he lifts the tray from the worktop.

'Hang on a minute,' Kane says, letting go of me. 'Can you drop some to Jake on your way down?' He takes a plate from the cupboard and adds a few macaroons. 'You don't mind, do you?' he turns to me.

'No, not at all. Here,' I add a few pieces of flapjack. Kane has a real soft spot for Jake, I do too. He's a lovely man who doesn't have anyone. When I was working, I always stopped at the desk for a chat with him on my way in. He was just getting ready to go home and would often have a coffee with me before he left. He's given us some valuable information and I'm extremely grateful to him.

Kane wraps the plate in clingfilm and hands it to Callum. He kisses me on the cheek and Kane follows him out to the door.

Half an hour later Callum has gone home with a tub full of goodies for himself and a plate for Jake and I'm just finishing cleaning up the kitchen.

'How are you feeling?' Kane comes to stand next to me, holding out a glass of wine. It's a bit early for me, we haven't even eaten yet, but I take it anyway.

'Apart from being bored, I'm not bad. My foot feels a lot better.'

'You seem a little tense.' Well, I thought I was doing okay all things considered but maybe I'm wrong. 'How about you have a soak in the jacuzzi, take your wine with you, and I'll order a takeout for when you are ready to get out.' Now that sounds like the absolute bomb. I've been dying to get in that tub but haven't got a clue how to turn the bloody thing on. And yeah, I might be a bit tense.

No sooner does Kane tell me it's ready, I'm in there like a shot, shoving him out of the door. There's a few candles lit, and he's left me a glass of wine on the side. Once I'm undressed, I sink into the tub covering myself in the scented bubbles. The stream of water flowing out of the jets hits the right spot and I'm soon closing my eyes relaxing as the not-too-hot water soothes the stress away. The smell of lavender and chamomile lulls me and before I have a chance to drink any wine my eyelids are closing.

'Meadow.' I hear Kane calling my name and I open my eyes and sit up quickly. I must have nodded off. It can't have been for long because the water is still warm.

'Sorry, I thought you'd fallen asleep in here,' he says standing in the doorway, his eyes straining not to look at my bare breasts. We might have kissed and had a cuddle. I've even slept in his bed, but I was covered up. I save us both from embarrassment and cover them with my arm.

'I think I did dose off,' I tell him, trying to reach for the towel so I can cover my top half.

'Here, let me.' He grabs the towel as he averts his eyes then passes it to me. Such a gentleman. Who'd have guessed?

"Thanks."

Once I'm covered, he sits down on the side of the bath. 'Feeling better.'

'Much, thank you. This is a dream. If I had one, I'd be in it every night.'

'Feel free to use it whenever you want.' He leans over me and lifts the glass of wine from the ledge where he had left it. 'I might join you.' His words whisper across my cheek, the huskiness in his tone, causing all kinds of tingles. 'But not tonight. Get dry and I'll order something to eat. What do you fancy?' he asks as he hands me the wine, his sexy eyes meeting mine and a knowing look on his face. He did that on purpose. I want to say, you because I'm feeling overwhelmed by his presence. His sexy smile, broad shoulders, and how his shirt sleeves are rolled up, displaying strong forearms are playing havoc with my libido.

And don't get me started on his manly scent. I feel as if I'm having a Kane Summer overload. I'm sure he notices the struggle

I'm having because he gives me that flirty smile and throws a cheeky wink at me when he rises from the side of the tub. My mouth becomes dry, and I feel my face heat up.

'Shall I order Indian or Chinese?' he asks, leaning on the bathroom door. I cough into my hand then swallow trying to gain some moisture.

'Err, any is fine by me.' He gives me a slow nod of his head then strolls out of the door, closing it behind him and leaving me with a quandary.

I know he wants me and it's clear I want him. Can I hold out until all this is over or do I throw caution to the wind and go for it? I don't know what will happen between us once this whole ordeal is over. Will I be able to go back to my home, my job, and my boring life? If I take things further with Kane, will it jeopardise my job if things don't work out? So much to think about.

I decide to leave it for now and get dry before I wrinkle up like a prune then I slip on a pair of short pjs and my dressing gown. I make my way into the dining room where I find Kane setting out the plates.

*

'Have you heard anything from Sam or Antony about my uncle?' I ask as we make our way into the living room. We sat in the dining room to eat and have just finished clearing things away. I didn't pig out as much as I did the other night when his brothers were here. Still overcome by the way my body was reacting to him, I struggled to get anything down me, so I just picked at it. Plus, I can sometimes put Connor and Henry to shame with the amount I can eat, and I was trying to be ladylike.

'Sam rang me earlier, your uncle only left the house once today,' he says, sitting down. He leans over the arm of the settee and sits the bottle of wine and two glasses on the side table then he pats the seat between his legs for me to sit down. I stand there for a moment unsure whether this is a good idea or not but when he puts his hand out for me to take, I give in to my urges. His long legs and muscular thighs are spread wide, so I snuggle between them and press my back against his chest. 'He said, he went out for groceries and then came straight home. He hasn't been anywhere since.'

'Do you think McKay will come looking for him?' He leans back and reaches over the arm of the settee to where the wine and glasses are sitting on a side table. He pours us both a glass and hands one to me.

'I do. I'm not sure how long it will take them to find him, I don't know if Jimmy knows where your uncle is living but I'm sure it won't take him long to find out.'

'It's sad really.' I take a sip of fruity wine. 'If he had come to me and asked for help instead of bulldozing his way in then bullying and frightening me, I'd have helped him.' Kane's arms wrap around me, and he places a soft kiss on my neck as he listens. It makes me tingle with desire. I want to turn in his strong arms and place my lips on his, but I stop myself and continue with what I am saying. 'If I hadn't known about what he'd done and his stint in prison, I'd have helped him out. He's my only family member and that counts for something in my book. Now, I just want to hit him around the head for what he's done to those people, and for getting himself into a predicament that might land me into trouble with some jumped-up gangster.'

'That jumped-up gangster will not get anywhere near you.' He takes my wine from me and places it on the table. 'You're too soft, Meadow. You owe that man nothing.'

'I know but you'd have done the same thing for your family.'

'You're right, I would. For my mum and brothers, I'd do anything. My dad's brother is a different matter altogether. If I'd been a violent man then I'd have ripped his head off for what he did to my mum after my dad died. Instead, I swore I'd make him pay for leaving us with nothing.'

'What did you do?' He did mention his uncle to me but didn't elaborate on what happened.

'What did I do? I kept a close eye on him right up to the day he went bankrupt.' He nods his head slowly, a triumphant look on his face.

'While I was in the police force, Mason and Callum had started working and we were all saving in the hopes we could get on the property ladder. Do them up and sell them on. If you know what you're doing, then it can bring the money in. We aimed to raise enough capital so we could buy a building and set up a business together. We always knew we wanted our own security company. And luck has it, we did exceptionally well. I didn't have the time to do much of the building work in the properties that we bought but Callum and Mason did, and they knew lots of guys who'd help out at the weekend. Our turnaround was good, we were making a decent profit on all of the properties and when this place came on the market, we had enough to buy it outright.'

'Did it need a lot of work to get it looking the way it does?' It's a beautiful building and I know they didn't do the work themselves.

'Yes and no. We hired an interior designer and then brought in the relevant contractors. With the houses we bought it was easier to get them ready for sale, but this was too big a project and needed people who knew what they were doing. It did take longer than we anticipated but, in the end, we were extremely happy with the result.' His smile is magnificent, and why wouldn't it be? He set the ball rolling years ago to get to where he and his brothers are now. This building was the heart of their growing empire. However, he still hasn't told me about his uncle.

'You've all done a brilliant job at getting where you are today but where does your uncle come in on this?'

'Like I said, I kept an extremely close eye on him and how he ran the company that was originally set up by my dad. When everything was coming into place with Summer Knights Security, I set up meetings with companies who had put out tenders. Did a lot of wining and dining, if needed…'

'So did you use this?' I cut in, running my hand up and down his body. It's not a secret that Kane has in the past used what God gave him to get ahead, I think Callum and Mason might have as well. His raised eyebrows have me laughing out loud which causes him to shake his head at me.

'To be truthful on the odd occasion, it might have helped,' he says, wrapping his arms tighter around me. I snuggle into his chest. 'But a lot of my meetings were with men, and I don't think this'—he waves his hand over his body and sends me a flirty wink— 'would be what they wanted. What they did want was a CEO with a shrewd business sense, one who could show that their company was top notch.'

'Oh, I don't know, I bet there's many a man out there that would like to know what's hiding under here,' I flirt, pulling at his t-shirt, uncovering a part of his firm stomach and when I pull at the short hairs around his belly button, he lets out a growl. One minute, I'm sat on his knee, legs stretched out on the settee and the next I'm pinned underneath him watching him wide-eyed as he pushes my top up. His mouth kisses my stomach and I let out a giggle when he runs his tongue over my belly button.

'You're playing with fire, honey,' he says looking up at me with fire in his eyes then he goes on to tickle me again with his tongue. I'm ticklish in the most sensitive areas and one sensitive area is hooting with desire. A desire that only Kane Summer can arouse. When his wicked tongue circles my belly button again and then travels to my waistline, I squeal loudly, my body bucking at the sensation. I feel him laugh against my skin. Evil bugger. He knows what he's doing. The vibration causes me to buck again but with his body pressed firmly against mine and his hands holding me still, I have no other choice than to let that naughty mouth of his do its thing.

After a minute or two I can't take any more and squeal out loudly, 'I'm going to wet myself.' Amused at my predicament he chuckles and lets me up then slaps my arse when I take off at record speed to the toilet.

While I'm there I try to compose myself. I'm hot and I do mean hot. My core is trembling, my face flush. If I go back in looking like this then he'll know in an instant just how much he can turn me on with just his lips and tongue. I run my fingers through my hair, wet my face with cold water then dab it dry with a towel and once my breathing is in order, I make my way back to the living room.

He sits there with a huge grin on his face, holding out my wine for me to take and patting the space between his legs for me to sit down. I roll my eyes at him, take the wine then get comfy between his legs. 'You, ok?' he asks as he wraps his arms around me and kisses my shoulder. My body reacts and trembles. I'm still affected by him and his lips. However, I know how to pay him back.

'Peachy,' I smile as I wiggle my hips, grinding my arse against him. Instantly I feel him harden.

'You wicked woman.' He leans back to adjust himself and I must admit I'm seriously in love with that husky voice.

'Payback is a bitch, isn't it?' Turning I look over my shoulder, a smug smile on my face. And from the way his eyes are ablaze, I know my little bit of mischief has affected him.

It's evident we are both ready for this, but we need to slow things down a little if I want to hear the end of his story.

'Are you going to finish telling me what happened with your uncle?'

'I could think of better things we could be doing.' He wiggles his eyebrows at me. I'm tempted but we're adults we can wait a little while longer. I don't think he has much more to tell me.

'I want to hear what happened to him." He nods his head as I place my hands on his chest and proceeds with his story.

'Our company went through the tendering process like any other would do and because we are good at what we do we gained a hell of a lot of new contracts. Once we were up and running, I did some digging around and found out which companies used my uncle then when the time was right, I undercut his quote and ended up with all but one of his. Six months later, the last one came to us, and his company went under. He was bankrupt and I didn't lose a wink of sleep knowing I'd helped with that. A year later, he was dead.' He shrugs his shoulders not caring one iota about his dad's brother. And why should he care? The man didn't give two hoots when his only brother died and he ripped off Kane's mum, leaving her and her sons destitute.

'Anyway, let's forget about it all for tonight and just enjoy some alone time.' His uncle is now forgotten. I incline my head to look at him and he leans down and brushes his lips across mine. The sensation is intense and builds spectacularly when our tongues entwine, and his hands caress my body. This is what I want. What I need to take my mind off what is going on in my life. I'm not going to think about the consequences this might lead to because his lips are causing too much pleasure. And to be truthful I don't care.

Chapter 16

Meadow

'Oh, Meadow, I'm so glad you've come down,' Kaylee beams, jumping up out of her seat to greet me, eyes full of excitement. 'I asked Kane if you were coming down today, and he said you were having a lay-in.'

Kane wasn't home when I rose this morning. I was a little disappointed not to see him. The night we shared was—what can I say—it was the best. I've never had a man make me feel the way he did, and from the noises he made and how his body reacted to mine, I'd like to think he felt the same. Last night meant something to me, although I know it shouldn't. Kane isn't used to relationships, I of all people know that. I've seen the state some of the women have been in when they've tried to get another date with him, only to be told a big fat no. Then again, it's a long time since I was in a relationship. so maybe we've both got a lot to learn. When I woke up and realised that he wasn't there I felt as if I'd been used. It hurt thinking he could dismiss what we had shared and just take off to work without a word.

After I had pulled myself together and stopped feeling sorry for myself, I showered and dressed then made my way into the kitchen. That is when I found his note. He'd woken late and because he had a meeting this morning, he had to hurry out plus he said I looked too snug to wake up. My mood lifted especially since he'd left a kiss at the bottom of the note.

In his haste, he'd forgotten to take the flapjack and macaroons with him so after I'd made myself a coffee, I thought I'd bring them down.

'You need to see what I've found, Meadow,' Kaylee says breaking me from my thoughts at the same time Mason walks in.

'Meadow you are a star.' He kisses me on the cheek as he takes the trays from me. 'Maybe don't keep him up so late when he's got an early meeting.' He grins at me with that cheeky glint in his eyes. They all have the same look. It's cute really.

'Hey,' I slap his arm. 'I didn't make him late. Anyway, the Harrisons aren't due for another twenty minutes.'

'I know but we were having a family meeting and he forgot these.' He looks down at the trays in his hands.

'Don't eat them all, I made them to sweeten up Mr Harrison.' He rolls his eyes and tuts at me as he turns towards Kane's office door.

'The cheek of her. Maybe make more next time.' He chuckles to himself as he enters the office, the door closing behind him.

'The cheek of him,' I say out loud, laughing as I turn to Kaylee. 'So, tell me what's got you all smiles this morning besides Mason.' I think she has the hots for him.

'Oh, isn't he just a girl's dream, they all are, excluding Kane Summer, I know you and him have a thing going on,' she lowers her voice, her eyes shooting around the office just to make sure no one can hear her. I haven't got the foggiest idea how she knows about me and Kane, I thought we'd been careful. 'Not that he isn't hot because he is, oh you know what I mean. Anyway, if I was going to get all goo, goo eyed about any of them then it'd be Connor.' She wiggles her eyebrows. 'He's the sexiest man I have ever met.' Connor does get a lot of attention from the ladies; he's just got something about him that they love, and he is a handsome bugger. I've known him so long; I must be immune to his charms. Not his older brother though. 'Let's forget about him for the moment.' She moves around her desk—or my desk should I say—and sits down. 'Come round this side Meadow, I can't wait to show you this.' Her eyes are like saucers. 'Look.'

'What am I looking at?'

'Watch.' And I do watch. I watch as she places her hand inside the bottom drawer, taps on something then the panel at the side falls open. 'Presto! You know I'm interested in this type of desk, so I've been in my element playing around with it for the last few days. This morning while I was looking for some staples, I came across this tiny little button. I don't know how I even found it because it's so tiny. However, I did, and when I pressed it, this happened. I've been bursting to tell someone. I didn't mention it to any of them,' she tilts her head towards Kane's office door. 'I don't want them thinking I have nothing better to do. I need this job.'

'Hey, don't worry, you're doing a great job.'

"Thank you. Anyway, this fell open." She points under the desk and to the panel on the right.

'Wow, unbelievable. I've been looking for other compartments for years and never found any more than the ones I found with my grandad. Is there anything in there?' She gives me a slow nod of her head.

'Get on the floor and take a look.' She gets down on her knees and I follow her.

I can see what looks like plastic tubes with a strap, probably six or seven of them.

'What are they?'

'Well, I don't know for sure because I haven't looked inside them but they're poster tubes so I'm thinking posters.' She turns her head to me, shrugging her shoulders. 'Here.' She passes them out and I place them on top of the desk. This is exciting. I've never found anything hidden in here. It has me wondering who put them in here and what is actually inside them.

'There's more,' she says as she passes me the last tube and then crawls out from under the desk to the other side. This time she eagerly opens the bottom drawer on the left side and does the same as she did with the bottom drawer on the right. And just like the right-side panel, the left falls open.

'Wow, I can't believe this.'

'Believe it, Meadow. Look.' This time she pulls out two A4-size envelopes.

'This one doesn't have anything written on it,' she says handing it to me. 'But this one,' she holds the other up. 'Has your name on it.' I take them from her intrigued and a little puzzled at what they could be. I quickly stand, my fingers itching to tear them open. I scan the writing. Three words. To Meadow Walters. My grandad wrote this. It's his writing. The way he puts a swirly curl on the beginning of the M for Meadow and does the same with the W for my surname, it's easy to tell he wrote it.

I pick up the letter opener from the desk and delicately open the one that has my name on it. Then I take out the letter inside.

A tear rolls down my face. Not with sadness but because I knew my grandad wouldn't let me down. It's the deeds to the house, signed over to me along with his will. I quickly place it back into the envelope and then wipe at my tears. I open the other envelope and I'm shocked to find three photos. I pull them out and what I see shocks me even more. The photos are old. Probably taken using an expensive camera. From the haircuts and the clothes of the two men who look to be caught in a compromising position, I'd say these photos are over forty years old. I don't know who they are, but I bet my grandad took them. Why? I don't know. I slip them back into the envelope, suddenly needing to be alone before I see what might be in the plastic tubes.

'I'm going to take these upstairs before the Harrisons turn up.'

'Of course. Is everything okay?'

'Yes. It was my grandad's desk, and these are some personal possessions belonging to him.' I don't want to say anymore because I don't know who the men in the photos are and I haven't looked in the tubes yet. 'Thank you for finding them, Kaylee. If there is anything I can do for you, just ask.' I hug her then pick up the tubes throwing the straps over my shoulder, Kaylee helps me.

'I mean it Kaylee anything at all don't hesitate to come to me.' I like Kaylee. When I came down the other day to apologise for my outburst when I thought Kane had employed someone permanently to replace me, we got along really well. Since then, I've joined her a few times and had a cup of coffee.

'You know there is one thing.'

'What is it?'

'I need a permanent job. The landlord is doubling the rent and the childcare costs I have to pay out are extortionate.'

'I didn't know you had a child,' I cut in, surprised she didn't mention it the other day.

'Yes, I have a son.' She reaches for her phone and brings up a picture of him. 'This is my Olly. Oliver, he's three.' The little boy with mousy blond hair and huge blue eyes is being held in his mother's arms. His adorable smile would melt anybody's heart and the way his mother is smiling back at him, it's easy to see he is loved.

'He's a cute kid. He has your eyes and your hair colour.'

'Thank you. He's everything to me. Being a lone parent can be tough. I have to pay for childcare so I can come out to work. The agency pay isn't bad but with the increase in everything, I could do with something permanent and more money.' I feel for her. It must be tough doing it all herself.

'Don't you have any family who could help you? What about his dad?'

'No family and his dad was a one-night stand.' She gives me a tight smile, her face heating up. 'I know you'll be coming back to work soon but if there's a position going anywhere within the company will you put a word in for me with the boss man.'

'Leave it with me,' I place my hand on her arm, really feeling her struggle. If I had a child, I'd want to give him or her everything. 'If there isn't a job, believe me, we'll create one.'

'Oh, I believe you,' she chuckles. 'You go do what you need to do. I'm glad I was able to find those.'

'Thanks, Kaylee, we'll chat later.' With that, I turn and make my way back to Kane's penthouse.

*

I park my car under the same tree as I did the other night when I came here. I don't want to be seen by Sam or Antony or whoever might be on duty today and have them alert Kane as to where I am. From what I've found today in the envelopes and the poster tubes, I want to speak to my uncle alone. He owes me some answers.

Switching off the engine, I climb out of the car, and lock it up. I make my way through the alley and then towards the back of my house. I don't creep about like I did last time. I push open the gate, taking the back door key from my pocket then once I'm at the door I unlock it and enter.

I'm surprised to see the mess that greeted me the other night has now been cleaned up. All the drawers are back in the kitchen units. The pots and pans are all washed and put away and the worktops and sink are sparkling clean. This is unbelievable. He must have brought in a cleaner because I can't see him doing it himself.

A noise grabs my attention and when I turn towards the kitchen door my uncle is standing there, leaning against it. 'You're back.' He sounds surprised.

'Yes. We need to talk.'

'Okay. But can I say one thing first?' He moves further into the kitchen, standing by the sink. I nod my head at him. 'I'm Sorry.' He runs a hand through his hair, his eyes, meeting mine. 'I, I shouldn't have…'

'I know John.' I put my hand up stopping him from carrying on. 'I know everything.' I move to the fridge and open the door, looking for milk. I could do with a stiff drink, but coffee will do for now. I lift out the milk and take a sniff of it. It's fresh. In fact, the fridge is packed full of fresh groceries, again I'm surprised. I'm even more surprised that my uncle looks clean and smart. The tatty beard has gone, it makes him look younger than he did. His clothes look freshly laundered and pressed.

'What do you mean, you know everything?'

'I know about your criminal activities and your stint in prison.' He lowers his eyes to the floor, obviously embarrassed. 'I know about your gambling addiction and the people you surrounded yourself with before you were put away. And I know all about Jimmy McKay.'

He tucks his hands into his front pockets and slowly nods his head. 'Why doesn't it surprise me that you know all this? Who told you?'

'I have my sources.'

'Meadow you've got to understand that I was desperate.'

'Stop.' I hold up my hand and let out a sigh. I want to be able to understand, I really do but for the life of me, I'm struggling. I switch on the kettle and take two cups out of the cupboard, holding one up. 'Do you want one?'

'Why not?' I make us both a drink and then suggest we sit down. I want the truth from him, the whole truth, and I want questions answered.

Over the next hour, Uncle John tells me about how he got into gambling. How in the beginning he could take it or leave it. Then without him even realising it, he became dependent on it. He needed the rush of winning like he needed to breathe—only he didn't always win but that didn't matter anymore to him. He was hooked, and he'd do anything to be in the card game.

He told me all about Mr McKay, Jimmy's dad. How he took a shine to Uncle John and would let him build up a tab, keeping the interest rate low—which I knew already. Then he told me about Jimmy, who had a grudge against him for being favoured by his father over his eldest son, as well as hating him for sleeping with his girlfriend.

'I honestly didn't know that Michelle was with Jimmy. I'd never seen him around with her.'

'Okay,' I say just to pacify him. I don't really care about Michelle.

'When Mr McKay was rushed into hospital, Jimmy stepped into his shoes and that's when things went tits up.' I almost laugh at my uncle's phrase about things getting bad. 'He wanted me to pay my debt and because I couldn't pay it all, he added interest. And it wasn't the same as what his father would have charged. Within two months the amount I owed had quadrupled and I couldn't pay it.'

John continues his story, including how he had to sell his apartment in the city centre and then his cars. When he gets to the part about the two men, he met in the casino who offered him a way to get Jimmy off his back, I listen with interest. I want to know how he was easily manipulated into ripping off people's life savings.

'What I did was wrong Meadow, I know that, and I'll never forgive myself for what I put those people through. I am genuinely sorry. I know it doesn't make any difference, but I was under the impression that it was companies we were swindling. If I'd known beforehand—before it was too late then I would not have gotten involved.' He rests his elbows on the table and buries his face in his hands. 'It was too late by the time I found out. If I'd tried to back out there would have been consequences. These people would have broken my kneecaps, if not more.'

'So you went along with it, got caught, and were sent to jail. Your other house was seized and any money you had to pay back the people you had conned.' He nods his head. I know all of this, and I know Jimmy is still gunning for him, wanting the money he still owes him. What I want to know is what was the argument he had with my grandad about.

'Before you went away, to prison I mean, you came to see Grandad.'

'I did.'

'What was the argument about?' It might have been a long time ago, but he must remember it.

'My dad had bailed me out many times. I've been a gambling addict for a long time. I'd even been to Gamblers Anonymous a few times but at the time it hadn't worked. When he found out what I'd done, that I was going to court and probably looking at several years behind bars, he flipped. He was ashamed of me.'

'Well of course, he would have been, like any parent. You can't blame him for that.'

'I know. I don't blame him for kicking me out and not wanting anything to do with me. I'd shamed him. I'd let myself down and I'd let both my mother and father down.' He actually does look remorseful.

'So, if you were sorry for everything, you'd done then why did you come back here with a will that clearly isn't worth the paper it's written? Furthermore, why treat me the way you did?'

'Again, I was desperate. A few months back, Jimmy got a message to me. He hadn't forgotten about what I owed him. I'd never been able to pay him back fully and while I was away—in prison, the debt mounted up considerably. I'm sorry Meadow but the only way I could see getting myself out of this mess was to take this house from you.' He looks around at the home we both grew up in, probably remembering the happy times we shared here. 'My cellmate concocted the plan; it seemed an easy way out.'

'A coward's way out.'

'It was,' he agrees.

'I found what you were looking for and I found the original will. Tell me about the photos. I know that's what you've been looking for while you've been here, and I know you've met with an art dealer and some journalists from the local paper.'

'Who are you, Meadow Walters?' He widens his eyes at me.

'I know people who know people,' I tell him, shrugging my shoulders.

'You know, you're a lot like your grandad. You remind me of him.' He smiles as he says it. 'I've known for many years that he had signed everything over to you. In the event of his death before Mum's, he wanted to make sure I didn't get my hands on anything. I don't blame him. I didn't deserve anything. If something had happened to him first and he hadn't put things in place for you, well he knew fine well your grandma would have given into me. He was right to do what he did. And it was a dick move of me to try and take it from you. You were always a good kid Meadow. You'd lost your mum at a young age.'

'She was your sister and I know you were close when you were younger.'

'We were. We were all close once.' A tear slips down his cheek and he quickly wipes it away. I look away so he doesn't feel embarrassed.

'So, tell me about the photos I found.'

'Your grandad was an excellent photographer. How he captured the light and the shadows against the object was—well he could have made a career out of it,' he says proudly. 'Before your mum and I was born he worked as a freelance photographer. He got work where he could and for a short while, he worked for the local paper. That is how those photos of the two men came about. Stories were going around that a certain member of parliament from our area was being unfaithful to his wife. Your grandad saw this as an opportunity to make a few quid. Only the photos never went to press due to the editor of the paper being arrested for false allegations over something else. From what I was told the paper was shut down and Dad put the photos away under lock and key. For what? I don't know.'

'And the man in the photos was being unfaithful with another man and back in those days it would've been the end of his career—and his family.'

'Yes. He would have lost his constituency without a shadow of a doubt.'

'But the photos never saw daylight.'

'No.'

'And why did you want them?'

'The MP in the photo is old now but he's still alive and kicking and I'm sure his family would have paid a tidy little sum for them. I'd also been in touch with a journalist. I'd have given them to the highest bidder.'

'And now?'

'And now?' He rises from his seat and makes his way over to the kettle. He switches it on and then turns to me. 'You can set fire to them for all I care. I'm desperate, I know but hurting more people for my own selfish gains—well I can't do it again.'

'That's good. If you can see the wrong, you were doing then that must be good.'

'Oh, it is but it won't keep the wolves at bay.'

'Jimmy, you mean?' He nods his head then takes my cup. He

washes it out along with his own then sets about making us both another drink.

'What about the posters?' When Kaylee handed the posters to me, I didn't look at them. I waited until I went upstairs. I never would have believed what was in them if I hadn't seen it with my own eyes. Seven photos of my grandma. Beautiful black and white prints of her as a young woman in various stages of pregnancy. The first one was her naked, the camera capturing the beauty of her smooth skin, her long hair covering one side of her breasts while the other side was free to view. Her hands were placed delicately on the small swell of her stomach where my mum was growing within. The second photo was taken probably in her second trimester. Again, exhibiting the beauty of a woman who was comfortable in her own skin. The third was taken during what I assume was childbirth. The swollen stomach was in contraction, the pain evident on her face. Another photo showed relief and unconditional love for the small child that had been placed on her chest. The last three photos included my grandfather. One with his hands placed lovingly on his wife's stomach. Another with his hand on the baby's back as he bent down and kissed her head. Then the last one was of him, in his boxers laid out on the bed at the side of my grandma, kissing her cheek as my mum was curled up, content and asleep. Grandad must have set his camera up to capture the last few with him or had someone take them. However, he did it, he got the desired effect. A young loving family who were content to show the beauty of love.

'I don't know if you were aware that your grandparents were an extremely passionate couple. They weren't afraid to show it either.'

'I've seen the pictures—the ones that were around the house, I mean, and I've looked at the prints that were hidden in the desk.'

'They're beautiful photos and I know Mum and Dad did have the idea of trying to get them into a gallery. I'm not sure why they didn't.'

'Did you know where they were kept?'

'Yes. I'd seen Dad looking at them years ago. He didn't know I'd seen him hide them inside the desk. When he told me I'd never get my hands on this place, and he'd signed everything over to you—I knew you didn't know about it. He never would've subjected you to what I'd done. Well, it didn't take a genius to work out where he would've put his will as well, which is why I was so pissed when I thought the desk had been sold. I'd set everything up with Miss Simpson. We had a deal—None of that matters now. I'll be going to see Jimmy tomorrow. Better to go to him than have him come looking for me.'

'Do you think he knows where you are?'

'I'm not sure. If he's done his homework, then he will.'

'Will he hurt you?'

'Oh, yeah. He'll want to make an example of me. It doesn't matter how long you've owed him money he'll want to show others that he doesn't forget.'

'Would the sale of the house and the money you'd have got for the prints have been enough to pay him off?' I don't mention the pictures of the old MP and the money John might have got through blackmail or selling them to that journalist because I don't agree with that and as soon as I get back to Kane's I'll be burning them.

'No. The house would cover some of it. I'd have had to wait to see if the pictures sold. If they sold at all.' He runs a hand through his hair and then takes a sip from his cup.

I'm just about to tell him that I could loan him some money. It won't be anything like the amount he owes Jimmy, but it might keep the wolves at bay so to speak. The money might have been what my grandad left me; the money he told John he'd never get his hands on. But my grandad left it to me, and he knew fine well what a soft touch I was. I'd never see anyone get hurt, no matter how much they'd hurt me. I don't get to say it though, because we both turn towards the back door when we hear heavy footsteps approaching.

'It's fine,' I try to assure John when he jumps from his seat and comes to stand in front of me. I'm shocked. My uncle has gone from a despicable human being, one whom only the other week was pushing me around, snarling and being aggressive towards me, to one in the last hour I've been able to have a civil conversation with and now his putting himself in harm's way. 'It will be Kane.' I move to the side of him ready to greet the man who is sure to be scowling because he thinks I've put myself in danger. To be fair it could have gone either way.

The noise of the door, flying off its hinges causes me to jump, and when three men, two of them dressed like the Blues Brothers with only one of them wearing dark sunglasses, the third man is a lot smaller to their burly stature but the look in his eyes just as frightening, come to stand in its way, my heart gallops in my chest.

'Get behind me,' John orders, grabbing hold of my arm and placing himself in front of me.

'Stay where you are,' Glasses orders as he moves into the kitchen.

'Well, who do we have here?' The smaller of the three men asks, a sinister look on his face. 'This must be your lovely niece, John.' He wanders around, looking me up and down.

'Leave her alone, she has nothing to do with this.'

'Are you giving me orders?' His voice is raised and intimidating.

'No. How did you find me?' John asks, changing the subject.

'I have my ways.'

'Why are you here? I have another thirty-six hours.'

'Do you have my money, John?' If I wasn't sure who this man was then I do now. He's not how I pictured him to be. He's not much taller than me and doesn't have much weight to throw around but he is aggressive. Probably got little man syndrome. If he didn't have the two goons with him, I'd take a pop at him. I laugh to myself. Well, I thought it was to myself.

'Something funny, Miss?' He gets in my face. His breath too close for comfort and the smell of his cologne overpowering and not in a good way. It practically chokes me.

'No. Nothing just nerves.' I cough out my answer. He scowls at me then steps back and looks at my uncle.

'Well?' He wants an answer to the question he asked him. My uncle shakes his head.

'So, this is what's going to happen.' He throws his arm around my shoulder, squeezing me tightly and engulfing me in that irritating stench. 'I'm going to take your niece as collateral…'

'Excuse me?' Throwing his arm off my shoulder I step out of his way. Glasses and the other goon, which I'm trying to come up with a name for, move in precision, flanking either side of me. My brow furrows at them. I should be scared of these meatheads and the wannabe gangsters but I'm not. Does that make me crazy, because he's definitely made a name for himself? Or am I just sick of being pushed around in my own home? 'You do know that kidnapping is a criminal offence?'

'And that's a problem, why?' Jimmy tilts his head, his confidence bordering on arrogance.

'Leave her alone, she has nothing to do with this,' my uncle intervenes before I have time to say anything.

'On the contrary my friend, she has everything to do with this. I've waited a long time for the money you owe me, and your time is up.' He stands in front of John, placing his hands on my uncle's shoulders. John's eyes meet mine and he looks scared. Maybe I've judged the wannabe gangster wrong, and he is someone I should be wary of. Of course, he is. Kane and Jake know him well. They warned me to stay in the apartment because of him. My uncle knows him well too. If he looks scared, then I should take notice and not rile him up. 'Get me my money and you'll get her back safe and sound. You have thirty-six hours.' His eyes meet Glasses, and he inclines his head towards the door.

Swiftly I'm practically lifted off my feet as Jimmy's goon, grabs me by the scruff of the neck and forces me out of the door. I kick and scream but it's a waste of time because he covers my mouth with his large sweaty hand, his strength overpowering my feeble attempt to get free. 'Put her in the car and show him what will happen to her if I don't get my money in the time stated.' Jimmy barges past us, striding off ahead, and as I'm dragged across the garden, I hear the telltale signs of furniture being broken as well as grunts of pain coming from my uncle.

Three blacked-out BMWs line the street. Where are the neighbours when you need one? If Jimmy and his men had come through the front either Sam or Antony would have seen them but because they came in the same way I did, they have gone unnoticed.

'You know my uncle won't give a damn about what you do to me,' I say as I try to dig my feet into the ground as Glasses opens the back door of one of the cars and pushes me forward.

'If that's the case then you've just signed your own death warrant.' My eyes widen in shock, and I feel as if I want to throw up. Death warrant. Is he messing with me? Just trying to scare me? Well, he's doing a fine job. 'I wouldn't tell Jimmy that. Keep him sweet, and you might just get through this.' This time he smiles, well if you can call it a smile. It was more of a smirk. Oh, he thinks he's funny, well I don't.

He climbs in the car after me and closes the door. Jimmy must have got in one of the others. I settle into my plush surroundings and rest my head against the window, not sure of where I am going and unsure of what will happen next.

Tracey Gerrard

Why the hell didn't I listen to Kane?

Chapter 17

Kane

I open the door for Andrew Harrison and his eldest son who is also called Andrew and we make our way out into the reception area, three of my brothers follow behind. The meeting went on longer than I would've liked but Andrew Senior was impressed with our setup and had lots of questions. By the time we had finished, we had come to an agreement, and contracts were signed, which I was expecting. Callum and Mason had already put it together, knowing this was a done deal.

'Thank you for your time, Kane,' he says as I gesture toward the next set of doors for them to leave. 'I'll look forward to working with you—and please give my thanks to Meadow for the macaroons, they were delightful.' Oh, I'll thank her. Maybe I should buy her some flowers as a thank you and as soon as all this shit is sorted out, take her somewhere special.

Meadow sealed this deal. For whatever reason this old man took a shine to her. They had long conversations over the telephone and once she'd sent him the figures for the amount of manpower he wanted, he then asked for a meeting with me and my brothers. He felt it would bond us if we could all meet and to be fair, I did like the old man and his son. Just like my youngest brother, his youngest son couldn't make the meeting. Connor is on duty today, I'm unsure where Andrews's son was but he did send his apologies.

'Well, it was good to meet you all and we'll definitely have to meet up for a drink one day.'

'We'll hold you to that.' Callum shakes his hand.

By the time they leave, I'm eager to see Meadow. Waking with her wrapped around me snuggled into my chest, well I could have stayed like that all day. The night we shared had meant everything to me. Sharing my bed with Meadow felt natural just like it did the night she needed comforting. Only last night was more. Making love to her for the first time was—well let's just say it has never felt that way for me before. I didn't want it to end and neither did she, so it was the early hours before we finally drifted off to sleep.

Leaving her this morning fast asleep, didn't sit well with me. I wanted to wake her so I could give her a good morning kiss and tell her I was going to work but she looked too content to wake. The smile she had on her face; I'd like to think I'd put it there. Taken away all the pent-up stress from the last week or so, leaving her feeling relaxed and fulfilled.

'You did? What was in there?' I'm brought out of my musing by Mason's questions.

'Two envelopes and six or seven plastic poster tubes,' Kaylee answers him.

'What's this?'

'Kaylee found some hidden compartments in Meadow's desk.' He bends down and starts fiddling with the drawers.

'Does Meadow know?'

'Yes. I told her when you were all in the office, she's taken them all upstairs.'

My brothers and I all glance at each other. I'm sure they are thinking the same as me. Could these things be what her uncle has been looking for?

'Did you see what was inside them?'

'The envelope with her name on had an official letter in it and there were some photos in the other one, but I didn't see who it was. She took the tubes upstairs to look at.' She looks between us. 'I don't know what was in them.'

'Well let's go see.' Callum jumps to his feet from where he is sitting, his face excited as he races to the door. 'This could have some bearing on all this shit.'

We all exit the office and make our way to the lift, on the way up to the penthouse I call Meadow. It goes straight to voicemail, so I call her again and I get the same response. Something isn't right. For the last few days when I have called her, she's answered almost straight away. An uneasy feeling sits in the pit of my stomach.

I'm the first to enter the dining room. 'Meadow,' I call out, making my way to the dining room table. There are photos of various sizes laid out as well as a couple of envelopes.

'What is all this?' Henry asks, picking up one of the pictures.

'Take a look, while I see if I can find Meadow.' I take off in search of her, but I have a feeling she is nowhere in the house.

'Kane, do you know who this might be?' Callum shoves a picture of two men with their mouths locked together under my nose as I race back into the room.

'She's not here.' I snatch the photo from his hand and throw it on the floor. 'We need to find her. She can't be out there alone.'

'Calm down,' Callum says, picking the photo back up. 'We'll find her.'

'Here.' Mason hands me a piece of paper and I let out an agitated breath as I read it.

I'm sorry, Kane, for putting myself in danger again but I needed to speak to Uncle John and find out what all this means. Although I can probably work most of it out for myself. XXX

'She's gone to the house.' I run my hand through my hair. 'Shit. I told her not to leave this place,' I say, sounding probably more like her dad than her lover. I dial Sam's number and he picks up straight away.

'Boss.'

'Where are you?'

'Outside the house. Where else would I be? This guy is becoming a recluse…'

'Has Meadow turned up there?'

'No. I'd have called you.'

'Go to the back of the house. She uses the back door.'

'Shit, Ok, stay on the line.' I can hear him exit the car and his feet pounding the pavement.

'Do you know who this is Kane?' Callum shows me the picture of the two men again.

'I have no idea. What else is there?'

'The original will, which leaves everything to Meadow. And the couple with the baby in those photos, Henry thinks are Meadow's grandparents when they were young.'

'Are you sure?'

'Yeah. I've been to Meadow's many times and seen family pics of them when they were younger,' Henry confirms as he rifles through the prints one at a time.

'Kane, we have a problem,' Sam's voice sounds urgent as he

comes through on the loudspeaker.

'What is it?'

'The back door is busted open. Uncle John has taken a beating, he's breathing but unconscious. Kane, there is no sign of Meadow, but she's been here her bag is on the kitchen table.'

'Shit!' I lose it. My phone takes the brunt of it as I fire it at the wall. It smashes into pieces. The next thing to fly across the room is one of the dining room chairs. It too bounces off the wall and then crashes to the floor, taking with it one of the paintings that were hanging there. This can't be happening. The poor girl will be scared out of her wits. I know who's got her. Why didn't she listen to me? I explicitly told her not to leave the building. She promised she wouldn't do anything stupid.

'Kane, stop.' Callum grabs me by my shoulders, holding me firmly in a tight grip.

'Let go of me, I need to go find her.' My hands ball into fists. I will kill the person who has her.

'And we will help you with that, but you've got to think strategically. Going in all guns blazing will only get someone hurt.' I know he's right. Jimmy McKay is a revolting, nasty little man. He's even hostile to his brothers. He has no close friends due to how unpredictable his mood swings can be. Women give him a wide birth. Again, this is due to him getting physical and not in the sexual sense. Most of them find him vile. The men who work for him are not opposed to knocking a woman around if he gives the order. As much as I want to rip apart his casino, McKay too, I need to listen to my brother.

'Are we good?' He searches my face. I blow out a breath and even though I'm churning inside, I show him I'm calm enough to form a plan to get Meadow back.

'Yes.'

'Good. Now let's get over to Meadows.'

By the time we all get over to Meadow's home, Antony has joined Sam, and they are both checking John over. He's sat up in the chair sporting a nice cut to his left eye and a few bruises on his face. Sam is holding an icepack against the man's ribs. Although he's battered and bruised, he is talking.

'I was just about to ring an ambulance for him when he came round,' Sam tells us as Antony applies a plaster across the wound.

'Where's Meadow?' John sits forward in his seat, his stare probing.

'Who are you?'

'It doesn't matter who I am what does matter is where your niece is.'

'You could be anybody.'

'My name is Kane Summer. I'm your niece's boss and…'

'She mentioned you,' he says before I get a chance to tell him I'm her boyfriend. Am I, her boyfriend? We've not put a label on what we are, and the boyfriend does sound so immature.

'You need to tell us what you know so we can find her and quick.'

'McKay has her. Jimmy McKay.'

'Shit!'

'Do you know him?' I nod my head. 'I don't know how he found me.'

'I do.' Henry holds up his phone. 'Connor just sent a message. Mr Horn has been attacked, he's in hospital.'

'You mean the cellmate?'

'Yes. He has just been rushed in.'

'Is Connor at the hospital?'

'No. He was on another call when he heard it over the radio.'

'That's how they found me.' John shifts in his chair and grimaces with the pain his ribs are causing him. Good, he deserves to be in pain. 'They must have beat it out of him.'

'They would've found you somehow,' Sam says, handing him a glass of water and what I assume are painkillers.

'I don't care about you or Horn. But I do care about Meadow, and we need to find her.'

'The casino would be our best bet,' Mason intervenes.

'No,' John coughs out as he sits up straight. He winces and places his hand on the left side of his ribcage.

'What do you mean no?' I'm getting seriously pissed off. We can't hang about. God only knows what this man could do to Meadow. He's unpredictable and has serious issues with John and I don't think it's all about the money. Meadow will be scared to death. She comes across as gutsy when realistically she's delicate and easily breakable. Being amongst McKay and his men will—well I don't want to think about how frightened she will be.

'It's the last Thursday of the month, right?' We all nod our heads in answer. 'Jimmy has a card game set up at his house on the last Thursday of each month. It's a big thing and a big game. Lots of wealthy people. The type that wouldn't want to be associated with casinos but enjoys a game where they can relax without being posted online. He also has a basement.'

'Do you think that's where he will have taken Meadow?'

'I do. He'll want everything set up perfectly for tonight. McKay doesn't trust anyone; he likes to oversee everything himself.'

'You know where he lives?' I'm raging inside. From a young age, I always trod on the right side of the law. I always knew I was one of the good guys, just like I always knew, I'd join the armed forces and the police. Since starting my own business I've never stepped out of line, always kept my business and my personal affairs clean and in order. At this moment, I'm ready to break all my own rules to get my woman back safe and sound.

'Yes.'

'Then what are we waiting for?'

'Kane, don't you think we should call the police?' Henry asks a concerned look on his face.

'Once we know for sure where she is and I've got her safe and sound, I'll bring in my contacts to tear him to shreds.' And I don't mean just him. Whatever he has his name to, will come under scrutiny and be ripped from him. From what I gather, his father was a decent sort, a fair man and I know his brothers are. I'm sure they will be only too happy to see him fall.

'What do you mean?' Sam gives me a sideways glance.

'I don't expect him to be alone or to let us just walk in there to get her back so I'm going to do what I do best, and I will be going in armed.' I look at Sam and he knows I'm right. He nods his head and then leaves the room. I've known him and Antony for a long time. They have both served in the armed forces and worked in the close protection service since coming out of the army. I have at least ten members of staff that lone themselves out for jobs like this and I know Sam will be contacting them now. He'll be sending a code to see who is up for a little surveillance and extraction.

'Jesus.' Callum sucks in a breath and shakes his head. 'You don't know if anyone will be tooled up Kane let alone if Meadow is there. You can't just assume that. Think about what you are about to do.'

'I have and I'm doing this.' I look at my brothers. They look shell-shocked. I never spoke much about my time in the armed services. Even though it was some time ago and I was only young, I excelled in my field and met many good men while serving some I still stay in contact with. In the police, again, I made my mark.

'We're on,' Sam says as he enters the room. 'We have four ready to go when you give the word, so I've told them the address and to make their way here as soon as possible. Three are out of the country and I'm still waiting for the others to get back to me.'

'What are you talking about? Who are these people?' Callum asks as he looks between Sam and me.

'They are on the payroll, Callum. This is the kind of work they do best.'

When I set up this company, I didn't just want security staff that would work doors, festivals, retail, or any other venue that would warrant some sort of protection. I wanted to expand. Setting up alarm systems and CCTV in commercial outlets, schools, and various other premises. I also took on some staff who were trained in close protection. These men are highly trained and hold a specialist license as well as a gun license. They come from an army background and have served the country well over the years when they were in the forces. Doing jobs that some wouldn't have the guts to do. I trust them to be in and out in record time, and with limited damage.

Callum stays quiet, knowing fine well I'm not going to budge on this. Using the police is not an option, it'd take too long for them to act. Needing a warrant to gain access will just waste time. Time, we haven't got.

'Including ourselves we have seven men—'

'You have ten if you include us,' Henry interrupts.

'You three will stay here and keep him company.' I'm being serious. I know my brothers can handle themselves in a pub brawl or up against a street thug. I haven't sat idle all these years and let them become soft. With our father dying when we were all young and only having our mum to bring us up, I stepped in and made sure they were all able to take care of themselves and each other. To be truthful, I didn't need to do much. They were all capable boys and now grown are strong and reliant men. Our dad would be proud of them.

'I don't think so, Kane,' Henry chimes in. I knew it'd be him who'd challenge me, and I know if Connor was here, he'd do the same—although I think he might be all for roping in the police, rather than going in ourselves. He knows we'll be breaking the law, carrying weapons. It doesn't matter whether I have a gun license or not, taking it with me with intent to use would land me in the slammer, along with the others. Henry and Connor are good friends of Meadow too, they've known her a long time and treat her like a sister. Well, she's mine now to take care of, and we're going to do this my way.

'No way lad,' Sam gets in before me. Henry scowls, not liking being called a lad or told no.

'Listen to me. I can't do my job if I'm worrying about you three. If anything happened to any of you, I wouldn't forgive myself. I have to keep you safe too, I promised Mum and myself when Dad died that I'd take care of you all. Sending you out there not knowing who or what we are up against—I wouldn't be keeping my promise, would I? Plus, Mum would murder me if she ever found out.' I let out a chuckle and wink at Callum. He understands, as does Mason. Henry might be a grown man and can do what the hell he likes, but he's not trained for this. I need them all to stay here.

'He's right.' Callum comes to stand at my side. 'As much as I want to go, we need to let them do their thing. They don't need to be worrying about us.' Mason is the first to agree, even if he isn't happy about it. Henry comes around to my way of thinking soon afterwards.

'So, what can you tell us about McKay's and this card game? We need to know where he lives and as much as you can tell us about his staff,' I turn to John, once we're all in agreement.

Chapter 18

Meadow

I pace the small, boxed room that Glasses shoved me into and wonder if Kane has noticed yet that I left his penthouse. He's going to be furious with me. He told me it wasn't safe to leave his place alone or even with somebody with me. I promised him I wouldn't but what choice did I have? I needed to speak with my uncle. I needed answers. I ended up getting more than I bargained for.

I didn't expect Uncle John to be so forthcoming with his answers to my questions. As he bared his past of all his wrongdoings, and the reasons behind them I saw a different man than the one he proclaimed to be a few weeks back. He was softer just like I remembered him from years ago. He even proved that he did have a backbone when McKay and his men showed up as he tried to protect me from them. I know I shouldn't worry about whether he's okay because I've got a dilemma of my own at the moment, but I can't help myself. I do seriously hope that he is okay after the beating Hands dished out. I've named McKay's other goon Hands due to their size. He could use them for mining diamonds.

The sound of voices has me making my way to the door. Placing my ear on the wood, I try to make out who it is out there. I get nothing apart from the sound of heavy footsteps retreating from the door.

The silence is deafening. The walls of the room close in on me and make it look even smaller than it already is. I take a few deep breaths trying to combat the panic that is consuming me. It helps but I know it won't stay at bay for long. Being abducted is frightening. I might come across as strong—and self-confident, but at this moment in time, I'm scared witless.

Not long after we set off, Glasses placed a blindfold on me. I tried to stop him. Kicking at him and screaming for him to let go of me but I soon complied when he backhanded me. Wallop right across the cheekbone and even though it hurt enough to bring tears to my eyes the worst part was seeing the conceited look on his face. He enjoyed seeing me in pain and retreating into myself. I place my hand on my cheekbone and wince at the touch. These people are not to be messed with. They have no morals. I can safely say I expect McKay to stand by his word to my uncle if he doesn't come up with the money, he owes him. The thoughts in my mind darken. Seeing one of my fingers placed in a box and sent to my uncle delivered in a package or photos of me beaten to a pulp and sent through the post. I shake my head, giving myself a pep talk. This is not a bloody movie. It might not be, but it sure feels like one.

Sliding down the door until my behind comes in contact with the cold concrete floor, I stare up at the narrow window. It's too high up for me to see out of and far too small to try and climb through even if there was something for me to stand on—which there isn't. The room is empty. Not a thing but the floor space and dampness. I must be in the cellar. Although I couldn't see anything when they brought me here, it didn't need a detective to tell me this house is huge. When they dragged me out of the car, the sound of gravel crunched under my feet then after a few meters the ground became hard and smooth. We seemed to be walking for a while, so I assumed they were taking me around to the back entrance. Once inside, I sensed there was just me and the monster who smacked me in the face. He led me by my upper arm along corridors, around bends and through doors then down a flight of steps to the room I'm in now. Not once did I hear anybody else's footsteps apart from our own.

I cross my arms over my knees then lay my forehead on top. I'm tired, hungry and I need the toilet. I doubt anyone would hear me if I knocked on the door. I reside to the fact that I'm going to be here for some time, so I close my eyes in the hopes I can fall asleep and when I wake up, I'll be in Kane's bed, safe in his arms and this will have all been a bad dream.

I must have drifted off for a while because when I lift my head, I can see through the tiny gap in the window that the sun has moved. Clearly, it wasn't a dream as I'm still sitting on the floor of the cold damp cellar, and like always when I come around after a sleep I need to pee.

There's nothing in here to use as a toilet. I could always use the corner of the room—nobody would see me. I decide that option is out because let's face it there could be hidden cameras somewhere in the walls or ceiling. I'm getting desperate now so I stand and walk around the room in the hopes it will wear off. It doesn't. Pounding on the door is the only answer to my problem. Whether someone answers my call will have to be determined.

Using the side of my clenched fist I pound hard on the door. 'Hello. Hello, is there anybody there?' Nobody answers me. I hit it harder and then holler. 'I need the toilet, can someone let me out?' Still, there's no reply. This is stupid. Who leaves someone in a room with no means of a toilet? I beat at the door over and over again. Giving it up due to my hands becoming sore, I kick at it instead. Using the soles of my feet, I lay boot after boot rage now getting the better of me. My anger soon stops and is replaced with shock when I hear a key in the door. Bloody hell, somebody heard me. In seconds the handle moves, and the door comes flying open.

'About bloody time,' I rant, standing with my hands on my hips.

'You are one cocky little madam,' Glasses mumbles. 'And a pain in my arse.'

'Hey, I didn't ask to be brought here. You could have left me where I was, and I'd have been just fine. Now I'm desperate for the toilet, so if you could just lead the way—otherwise there'll be a puddle at your feet.' I look up at him and I see the snarl on his face. He doesn't like me very much, probably because I stand up for myself. However, I need to be careful around him because he isn't averse to dishing out backhanders. 'Please,' I add just to pacify him.

'Come this way.' He grabs hold of my arm and marches off, dragging me with him. 'Do not give me a reason to show you some manners,' he chunters as we make our way through the house. 'I have enough on my plate today and I don't need a spoilt little cow causing me more shit.' He's going to show me manners. The big baboon wouldn't know etiquette if it jumped up and hit him in the face. I bite my tongue, knowing it's for the best. Ripping into him will only land me in more trouble plus if we don't get to the toilet sharpish then I will wet myself.

'How far is it?' I ask as we get to the top of the stairs.

'Just down the hall,' he grunts as we pass by what looks like a library. There are a few more doors that are all closed and coming from somewhere—I'm not sure where—I hear hushed voices. Whispers. We pass an elaborate room. I can't see much but with the double doors slightly ajar I catch sight of the plush furniture, long drapes, and a crystal chandelier. Even the corridor we are walking down has high ceilings and the décor on the walls looks like an interior designer's handy work.

'Here.' He stops outside a door and opens it for me. 'Don't be long.' I'm told as he manhandles me inside.

'Any chance of a drink and a sandwich when I'm finished?' I try my look. The furrow in his brow tells me not to push it.

Closing the door behind me, I quickly turn the lock and then make my way over to the loo. As I sit there doing my business, I survey my surroundings. I don't think this is the main bathroom—it's too small for a house this size and it doesn't have a bath—but it is of decent size. White marble flooring and tiles throughout, matching sink and pedestal with white oak cabinets.

When I'm finished, I wash my hands and face then wince when I catch my cheekbone. With being so wound up I'd almost forgotten about that. Glancing in the mirror, the red and purple bruise stands out and so do my tired eyes. I use the Egyptian cotton towel and gently dab my face dry. Then gaze at my reflection in the mirror again. I look to have aged in just a few hours.

I need to do something to try and get out of here. I can't rely on my uncle. God only knows what state he's been left in plus I know he doesn't have the money he owes McKay. If Kane's finished his meeting and gone up to the penthouse, he will have seen my note. Will he have gone over to my house, knowing that's where I'd gone? Most definitely. But there's always the chance he is still in the meeting. Mr Harrison does like to chat. I can't rely on ifs and buts to get me out of here.

I don't have much time to search my surroundings for something that I could use to help me get out of here, Glasses will be knocking on the door any minute. I don't even have a plan.

In the cabinet is a small can of men's deodorant. I'm determined to use it as a weapon. I've seen the movies. I'm not averse to squirting it in Glasses' eyes. 'Shit.' I curse. How the hell can I spray it in his eyes when he's wearing glasses? Doesn't matter, the mist will still stop him if I spray enough. Hopefully, he'll inhale enough to stop him in his tracks, coughing. I also find a pair of tweezers. They may come in handy. I tuck them in the waistband of my jeans.

Taking I quick look in the mirror, I say to myself I can do this. I need to get out of this house or to a telephone so I can call Kane. I wouldn't be able to tell him where I was because I don't know where I am. The blindfold made sure of that. It wasn't taken off me until I was thrown in the cellar but at least he'd know who had me.

'I can do this,' I say again as I make my way to the door. I've unfastened two top buttons on my blouse, showing the swell of my breasts. That should get his attention—well according to my friend it does. She's quite shameless really, especially when she's going clubbing. Then while he's enchanted with my boobs, I'll use the spray, I have hidden up my sleeve with my finger on the nozzle ready to disarm him. A hard stomp on his instep then a quick jab to his nuts and I'm off running. Where to, I haven't a clue. I don't give myself time to doubt my plan before I open the door. True to plan, Glasses eyes lower taking in the swell of my breasts. Just as he sucks in a breath I strike with the spray. I get the desired effect I wanted. He coughs loudly and before he has time to right himself, I stand on his foot and at the same time I grab his balls and squeeze. He lets out a strangled noise and that's my cue to shift. I hightail it as fast as I can, moving like a zebra trying to outrun a lion. I'm determined.

It's not long before I hear heavy footsteps closing in on me. 'You little bitch,' Glasses rages behind me. Boy, he's not happy. I quicken my speed unsure of where I am or where I'm going as I twist and turn, making my way swiftly through the house. My pursuer has a lot more weight than me and it shows as the gap between us lengthens. I round a corner and come to an abrupt halt, there's a closed door in front of me. Fumbling with the door handle I'm surprised when it opens. It's a dining room. Like the wind, I blow through making my way to the opposite side of the room where there's another door. I yank it open and pay no mind to the staff who are cooking something up in the kitchen. It smells delicious whatever it is they are making but I don't have time to stop and sample the delights. The two men in chef whites eye me suspiciously but ignore me when I shoot past them, knocking over a stack of plates. They make one hell of a clatter which I'm sure will alert my abductor to where I am. I crash through another door, praying I'm coming to a door that leads me to the garden. As if the Lord heard my prayers I fly out into the fresh air. However, I don't have long to enjoy my freedom when someone grips tightly onto my hair. 'And where do you think you're going?'

'Let go of me,' I scream and thrash at him. I'm breathless. Tired out. He's too strong and that overpowering stink of McKay's aftershave is choking me. He tightens his hold on me. Twisting my hair around his fist as his other arm wraps around my waist.

'I don't think so.' He only just manages to get the words out when someone appears at the side of us.

'Let her go McKay before this gets messier than it already is.' I can't see the man who's giving the orders, but I'd know Sam's voice anywhere. Oh, thank God, I let out a breath. If Sam is here, then Kane won't be far away.

'I think I'll keep her a while longer,' McKay states as he turns us so I'm facing Sam and McKay is behind me. I'm stunned to see him dressed all in black. Black combat pants, boots, t-shirt, and jacket. What stuns me most is the gun in his hand. McKay edges back taking me with him, and I feel something sharp nick at my neck. 'Put the gun away or I'll slit her throat.' My legs buckle and my head feels woozy. I going to pass out, I think.

'No, you won't. You might be a lot of things but a killer you're not.' Sam's words should make me feel better, but they don't. There's always a first time for everything. 'Give it up Jimmy. Most of your men are incapacitated, you're on your own man.'

Before he has time to respond the door behind us bursts open and Glasses comes barreling out. McKay sniggers and shakes his head. 'Get rid of this piece of shit,' he orders then drags me through the door backwards by my hair.

I'm practically horizontal, my feet struggling to keep up with the speed he is going. My heels slip and slide as I'm pulled along the wooded flooring. I feel my hair tear from my scalp, and I cry out. I fall onto my back, but I'm yanked back up and dragged a few more feet. The men who are cooking lower their heads, ignoring what their boss is doing, and my screams for them to help me.

I kick out my legs and grab hold of his hands while digging my fingernails into his skin, hoping he will let me go. He lets out a sinister laugh and tightens his grip. My attempt to get free is futile. Tears are streaming down my face. The pain radiating from my scalp is unbearable.

He yanks open the door, pulling me through with him; the sound of a gun going off in the distance turns my stomach, leaving acid in my mouth. I slump to the floor no longer able to go on. He lets go of my hair and I turn on all fours, my head spinning as I cough the lining of my stomach up.

Through the fuzzy noise in my brain, I hear voices. One voice stands out as it booms like thunder. Kane. Through my clouded vision, I see McKay being tackled. Two bodies fly through the air landing with a hard smack against the floor. They roll around, grabbing at each other, fist flying. Kane is the first to jump to his feet, a red welp on the side of his face. He strikes McKay around the head with a kick so hard, he must be seeing stars. Then lands another kick to his stomach when he bends to stand up. McKay goes down again. I watch Kane jump on him and deliver punch after punch to the man who gave orders to have me kidnapped and thrown in a cellar. The one who threatened to slit my throat and pulled so hard on my hair it ripped from my scalp. I feel no sympathy for him. Kane could kill him for all I care. Slit his throat and I wouldn't bat an eyelid. But I do care for Kane and killing McKay could land him in prison.

'Meadow.' Antony drops to his knees in front of me, obstructing my view. He takes something from his pocket and places it on my cheek. A cool pack, I think. I take it from him and place it on the back of my head. That's what hurts the most. Over the next few minutes, it could be longer more men appear, Sam being one of them which I'm grateful for. I've grown to like him and Antony. They're good guys. Antony fusses around me like an old mother hen. He even takes out some painkillers from his pocket and hands me a bottle of water to swallow them down with.

'Enough, Kane!' Someone commands and that's when I realise Kane was still beating the living daylights out of McKay. I don't recall seeing this man who is built like a brick wall, shaven head and tattoos down his neck but the order he's just given stops Kane in his tracks. This authority figure must have some sway with Kane because I've never known him to take orders from anyone before. I can only assume he's served with him either in the army or the police force.

Kane staggers backwards, his breathing heavy as he leaves Jimmy McKay motionless on the floor. He turns to me, his face red with rage but it soon softens when our eyes meet. He's by my side in an instant, crouching and wrapping me in his arms.

'Meadow.' He doesn't say anything else, just breathes into my hair as he holds me tight, then peppers kisses on my face. I've never felt safer than when I'm with him. I should have listened to his advice and never left the apartment. I'm so stupid sometimes. That's my problem, I never listen to sound advice. I always think I know best.

A commotion by the door has me lifting my head, I see a few more men joining the party. The first one is sharply dressed in a made-to-measure suit, with neatly cropped hair and clean shaven. Probably in his late fifties, the other three men are all in fine thread too. Their attire is a far cry from what Kane and the men who have come to rescue me are wearing. Kane, Sam, Antony, and the rest are all dressed in black combats, boots, and t-shirts. Earpieces and mics, black beanies on their heads. The way they moved in and took control of the situation to rescue me—well I reckon it's not their first time at something like this.

Sam is the first to speak. 'I suggest you make your way home Judge, the police will be here shortly, and I don't think being associated with that piece of shit'—he nods his head towards McKay who is now moving and groaning— 'will do your reputation any good. And the rest of you should follow. Go home. There will be no card game tonight.' The men mumble between themselves but quickly get with the program and disappear through the door that they came through. I look around dazed and confused. What the hell was happening here? What card game? And where were these men when I ran through the house screaming like a banshee?

'Where else are you hurt Meadow?' Kane asks as he gently strokes his thumb over the bruise on my cheek.

'Just the back of my head, I think.'

'Have you bumped it?' He moves so he can take a look and I hear him suck in his breath and curse.

'No. That arsehole dragged me by my hair.' I nod my head to where McKay is still sprawled out, Antony and Sam are now keeping guard over him.

'We'll get you checked out at the hospital, Meadow. Why the hell didn't you listen to me?' He sounds agitated as he cuddles me into his chest, his expression pained. An internal struggle seems to be going on inside him.

'I'm sorry, I didn't think...'

'I know, I know,' he soothes as he breathes into my hair, peppering kisses. 'It's over now but please don't ever put yourself in danger again. I don't think I could take it again.' He doesn't think he could take it; he should have been in my shoes. But I understand what he means because if he'd been in danger then I'd feel the same.

'You lot should go too before the cavalry turns up. You're all carrying, I don't want any of you getting arrested,' Kane advises, as he keeps me snuggled into his chest. I hold on tight to him not wanting him to ever let me go.

'I'll stay.' The big guy offers as he moves toward McKay. 'His men are all tied up in the kitchen. The police will know you weren't alone in this, there's too many of them.' Kane nods his head in agreement.

'Do you have your story straight?' Sam asks, looking between them both.

'Yes,' Kane answers. 'Now go the lot of you. I'll meet you back at the office once I've had Meadow checked out at the hospital.'

'Okay, let's roll everyone.' He claps his hands together and in no time at all Sam, Antony, and the other men disappear into the night.

Kane stands with me in his arms and sits us both down on a chair.

'Meadow, when the police ask questions stick to what you know. Do not even try to decipher what just happened and who was here. Do you understand?'

'I couldn't if I tried.' It's true. Everything that's happened since I went to speak to my uncle seems like a bad dream. Being kidnapped, smacked about by a big bruiser, and thrown in a cellar. Coming up with a plan to try and escape and putting it into action. Being chased through the house by a man who'd hurt me in any way he saw fit, only to be caught by a crackpot who was even worse, happy to drag me about by the hair. It makes me feel sick just thinking about it. The throbbing in my head increases. It feels like the cast of River Dance is in there, and it makes me feel dizzy. I sit up, needing some air.

'Where are you going?' Kane asks. Not wanting to let go of me, he keeps hold of my hand. I push off his knee and stagger when I stand.

'I need some fresh air.' I only just manage to get the sentence out when everything turns black.

Chapter 19

Meadow

Three weeks have passed since I was abducted and not a day goes by that I don't thank Kane and his friends for rescuing me. Things could have turned out differently, so much worse than a bruise to my face, a sore head, where my hair was pulled out, and cuts on my wrists due to the cable ties. According to what I was told, the hatred toward my uncle went deeper than just an owner of a casino trying to reclaim debts owed to him. It goes back to when my uncle slept with Jimmy McKay's girlfriend. Well, she wasn't a girlfriend—more of an acquaintance that he bedded from time to time. When he found Michelle—I think her name was— and John together, he took it as a betrayal and was out for blood, even though he'd pushed her away in the past. Flaunting other women under her nose and told her she'd never be more than a woman who'd warmed his bed. The green-eyed monster reared its ugly head and he set about ruining them both.

Michelle moved away, sick of his games, but John thought he knew better and stayed. He knew McKay had it in for him but never thought he'd sink so low and ruin his livelihood. It was easy for Jimmy to play games with John, to force him into a corner. Recalling debts owed to him or his father, knowing the interest he'd added was extortionate, which put the debt up considerably, forcing my uncle to sell his property to help pay some of it back. This should have been a wake-up call for John only, it wasn't. His gambling addiction kept him in McKay's pocket and landed him in more trouble with the crazy man. If that wasn't bad enough, he then got himself involved with a couple of criminals.

Their inexcusable act of fraud landed them all in court with a guilty sentence hanging over their heads. They all went to prison for their crimes with John still owing money to the despicable man Jimmy McKay.

I can't excuse my uncle's conduct. However, he had paid back the money he stole, served his time for the crime he committed, and even though he did make my life a living hell when he turned up at my home, he did come up trumps when needed. Kane isn't as forgiving as me. In his words, it is due to your uncle's activities that you were kidnapped in the first place and then subjected to the abuse of two men. To be fair he is right but that doesn't matter anymore because John moved out of my home a week after the kidnapping. He's moved up to Scotland. John explained how he'd been in contact with an old school friend who had moved to Ayr years ago and as luck had it this friend offered him a job in his pub. Of course, he jumped at the chance to have a fresh start, packed his bag and left within the week. He apologised profusely for what he put me through, I accepted it and wished him well—after all, he is my only blood relative—but Kane just snarled at him. I don't think he and his brothers will ever forgive my uncle.

Jimmy and his two henchmen were arrested and remanded in custody on not just one charge but four. Abduction, illegal gambling, assault, and demanding money with menace. They had no proof that my uncle owed them any money at all but whether he did or not the way they tried to obtain it landed them in a whole heap of trouble.

Since then, Michael, Jimmy's brother has taken over running the casino. He cleaned house, terminating some of Jimmy's loyal employees and replacing them with a new team. He spoke to Kane and told him that the money John had owed was now written off. As far as he was concerned the amount of interest he had paid to Jimmy before he was sent to prison was enough to cover what he originally owed Michael's father. However, he did ban him from the casino, stating it was in his best interest, which was a good thing in my book. All in all, things have turned out well.

I haven't returned to work yet, but I will. It's not that I don't want to return to my job as Kane's assistant, I do but it will be weird. I always enjoyed working for Summer Knights Security, it was Kane who made things difficult. Now things have changed between us, it will be strange working for him. Kane hasn't pushed me to go back to work. I think he wants me to rest up for a little while longer and I agreed I would. Then there's the living situation.

Kane let me stay here because I had nowhere else to go. He felt sorry for me, I think. I could go home now my uncle has left but at the moment I'm having the whole house redecorated and a few home improvements done. New bathroom and doors, that sort of thing. It's well overdue.

I don't know what Kane wants. Does he want me to return home now? Will he want our relationship to be strictly business now everything is sorted? We never put a label on what we were. He did tell me he'd been attracted to me from day one and because he had been burnt once in a relationship, he was then reluctant to enter into another. There's also the fact that he was my boss and my two best friends' elder brother so that put paid to him acting on his feelings and the reason why he had behaved like an arsehole. He seemed sincere when he told me but I'm still skeptical about what will happen when I do eventually move back home and go back to work.

We haven't spent much time together over the last week or so due to him having so much work on. He's been out early in the morning and hasn't been returning home until after seven in the evening. The first week he never left my side. Tending to my needs. He was so affectionate and warm; it blew my mind. Being held in his arms every night was something I could get used to. However, the following week, he was up early and out of the door before I got up. When he returned home, we'd eat together, then he'd go to his home office to work some more, and I'd fall asleep on the sofa watching TV. I'd wake up through the night in his bed with him snuggled into my back and his arm around my waist. He'd carried me to bed. His bed. I don't know what to think anymore. Maybe it's just me. Kane's a busy man. He'd put so much on hold while he was helping me. Passed lots of work onto his brothers. I should be grateful for what he has done, and I should probably speak to him about where we go from here.

I'm brought out of my musing when my phone alerts me to a Facetime call. I answer it straight away when I see Louise's name displayed. At last, she's calling me back. She hasn't returned any of my calls or messages over the last couple of weeks, I was getting worried about her.

'Where the hell have you been? And why haven't you returned my calls?'

'Well, hello to you too Mother,' she grins at me, amusement in her eyes. 'I haven't called because we were camping in the back of beyond with no signal for the last ten days, we've only just got back to civilization. Thank God. It's good to have all the comforts of a nice hotel.'

'Sorry, I didn't know. You never said you were going camping the last time you called.'

'It was a spur-of-the-moment thing. One of those being with nature kind of trips. You know, building fires, sleeping in tents, and no showers. Can you imagine that—me not being able to shower and do my hair? I've had it tied up the whole time. We only got to the hotel last night, so I've been having a pamper day.'

'Sounds about right. I can't believe you went camping, doesn't sound like you at all.' She hates roughing it and she's scared to death of bugs.

'I know. It was Brandon's idea. I've been spoilt since we set off from England, so I thought I better let him have his own way. It wasn't all bad. We went horse riding, canoeing, and rock climbing. I've never done anything like that before, it was fun. I even lit a fire with a flint, rock, and a bit of hay.'

'Oh wow, look at you getting all outdoorsy.'

'It won't be a regular occurrence. Once was enough, I'm glad to be back in the land of the living and Wi-Fi.'

'So where are you now?'

'Greece. It's beautiful. What more could one ask for than sun, sea, and sand? We're going out on a yacht tonight.'

'That sounds lovely.' I'm genuinely happy for her even if a little part of me wishes I was there.

'It will be. A Champagne reception then a bite to eat and cocktails and I get to dress up. I can't think of anything better. So, tell me what you've been up to since we last spoke. Are you still having trouble with your uncle? More importantly are you still at Kane's?' She's wearing that mischievous smile as she wiggles her eyebrows.

'Yes, I'm still at Kane's—for now.'

'What do you mean for now?'

'I'm not sure where to start.'

'The beginning is usually a good place.'

'Well, you know how and why I ended up at Kane's.'

'You did mention it, yes, but I think you left a few things out due to Connor and Henry being in on our last call. Why don't you start from that night.' And I do.

I spent the next hour explaining everything to her, not missing out on any of it. She doesn't judge me for sleeping with Kane. Just comments, I don't blame you, who wouldn't want to sleep with him, he's hotter than hell. But when I get to the kidnapping part, she becomes alarmed.

'Why the hell did you go there alone when you'd been told how dangerous this Jimmy thingamabob was? I can't believe you'd put yourself in danger like that.'

'I know. It was stupid of me. I just wanted to speak to my uncle about everything I had learned about him and about the things that were found inside the secret compartments of my desk.'

'I get that Meadow, but you could have waited for Kane or Henry and Connor to go with you.'

'I was too impatient. I needed answers.'

'So, tell me what happened once they'd thrown you in the cellar? I swear to God if I ever meet these men, I'll cut off their dicks and serve it to them with their balls as a side dish.' I can see she's upset and out for vengeance. I'd have been the same if I were her, and I can't help but laugh.

'It's not funny Meadow, you could've been badly hurt or killed.'

'I'm sorry, I know it's not funny but I'm fine now and they're all locked up. I can't see them getting out soon.' I go on to finish the story.

'Geez, how are you feeling now?' She asks once I'm finished.

'I'm good.'

'I can't believe Kane broke the law to rescue you. He must really care. Who knew the big bad boss had a heart.' I chuckle at her comment about Kane. He does have a big heart and he did break the law, which is something he'd never do unless the people he cares about are in trouble or danger. Carrying a gun with intent, even with a license, is a definite infringement of the law. Breaking and entering, no matter the reason is another. He could have called the police, which he did, but only to call in a favour from an ex-colleague.

'How are things now with you both?' Louise breaks into my thoughts.

'I don't know. My house will be finished in a couple of weeks, so I'll be going back home once it's done, if not before. Then I will need to return to work. I don't know if we're a couple in a relationship or if what we shared was just while I was here.'

'You need to speak with him. Lay your cards on the table.'

'I know but he's so busy at the moment. I don't want to come across as needy. I'm not bothered about a label on our relationship. I'm happy to go home and just date if you see what I mean.'

'I do,' she says then startles me when she jumps up all excited. 'Oh, I have an idea.' She grins as she runs her hand through her hair.

'You do.' I smile at her.

'Come here.'

'What?'

'Come to Greece. We're going to be here for two weeks, maybe more. It will do you good to have a bit of sun and sea air. We can hang out together and it will give you and Kane time apart to think about what you both really want. I mean you've had a lot on Meadow. So much has happened in such a short space of time. You need time to think. While you're away it will give Kane time to miss you. If he genuinely cares for you, then he'll be there when you get back and you can talk to him with a clear head.'

'I don't know, Louise,' I say but deep in my gut I know she's right. I need a holiday. Too much has happened all at once. A week or two in the sun to recharge my batteries does sound good but I've got so much to sort out. I've got a painter and decorator as well as a joiner and plumber at my house. Plus, I'll need to go back to work soon.

'Come on Meadow. Brandon's going to be working from his laptop for the next week or so, we'll have a blast. Sunbathing, going on walks, and taking in the sites. Plenty of cocktails by the poolside. What more could you ask for?'

'It does sound good,' I tell her as I try to figure out a few things. 'Give me an hour or two, I have a couple of things to sort out.'

'Okay, so you're coming?' She asks, her face lights up with excitement.

'Fingers crossed.'

'Woohoo! Go do what you need to do, and I'll check the flights.'

Once she hangs up, I call the workmen, asking how long it will be before they are finished. I'm told a couple of weeks, so I arranged for them to drop the keys in at the office when they are finished and send them their full payment by bank transfer. I trust these men they were recommended by Callum.

By the time Kane arrives home from work, I'm buzzing. He's earlier than he has been all week and I'm wondering why. However, whatever the reason, he has that beautiful smile on his face which is a good sign because I have something to tell him. My flight is booked for tomorrow afternoon, and all the little jobs I need to do are done which leaves me with one huge one. Telling Kane.

I bite the bullet straight away. 'I have news,' I say, smiling as he places his briefcase on the kitchen island and then strides across the kitchen toward me. I'll never tire of that swagger he has going on. Dressed in a dark blue suit, his muscular arms defined by the cut of it, his light blue tie pulled loosely at the knot, he oozes power. Masculinity at its best. My knees weaken and those butterflies that appear in my stomach whenever he is around start somersaulting like an Olympian gymnast.

'Well, it must be good news because you look fit to burst.' My excitement must show for him to pick up on it. I am excited but I'm also feeling a little down. I'm going to miss him like crazy while I'm away. He's shown me another side of him that I didn't know existed. He can be so loving, thoughtful, and giving. I don't think he realises how grateful I am for what he has done for me. He went from being my overbearing, twat of a boss to my protector overnight. Opening his home to me, using his men and connections to uncover the truth about my uncle. My problem became his and he'd do anything to fix it. In the weeks that followed he became my lover. I know it's going to hurt, leaving him for a few weeks, because we have so much to talk about—to sort out—but I have to go. I need this time away, and to be truthful I think Kane needs it too. So much has happened in such a short space of time— he has a ton of work that he needs to catch up on because of me— and I think time apart will give us both a breathing space to think about what we want.

He takes me in his arms, his lips lightly brushing across mine. 'So, tell me, my little ray of sunshine,'—oh I love it when he refers to me as his sunshine— 'What are you all excited about?' I almost buckle when he steps back, his hands moving to my hips and those electric blues gaze into mine. I don't. I know there's no time like the present.

'I'm going to Greece.'

Chapter 20

Kane

'I'm going to Greece.' Four words have my heart rate slowing down. It's always raised when I'm around Meadow and the uplifted mood that I'd been in ever since I packed up for the evening with the hopes that we could spend some time together, deflates. What the hell does she mean she's going to Greece? Is she planning on moving out there—I wouldn't blame her after what she's gone through—or just going for a holiday? I'm almost too afraid to ask.

I know she's gone through so much since her uncle turned up but for the best part of it, I've been there for her. Showing her how much I care about her. Nothing was too much. Then three weeks ago when it all came to a head, I took the week off work and stayed at home. I wanted to look after her—I needed her to know I'd always be there by her side, no matter what life threw at us. If it meant taking time away from work, then so be it.

After the first week, she made it quite clear that she was absolutely fine in the apartment on her own and practically threw me out of the door. So, I returned to work and Meadow got on with having her house re-decorated as well as a few other jobs. It should have been fine, only I'd underestimated how much work I had on which meant the last two weeks had been hectic. Meeting after meeting and being snowed under with paperwork had me leaving early morning and not returning until late into the evening. I hated not having breakfast with Meadow, but I wasn't going to wake her at five in the morning. Yeah, we ate together in the evening but then I went straight to my home office to work through more paperwork. By the time I had finished, Meadow was fast asleep either in bed or on the settee. Many nights I carried her to bed, and she didn't even flinch. I'd have loved nothing more than to make love to her, but I wasn't about to wake her up plus I was wrecked with the hours I was keeping at work.

Today that all came to a head. I'd caught up on everything and managed to reassign a few meetings over to my brothers. Knowing work would be a lot more manageable, I finished early and booked a table at a little Italian restaurant down the road. I knew Meadow and I needed to talk. Our relationship had come together unconventionally. Before all the hassle with her uncle, we barely had any kind of relationship even though she worked for me.

I thought it would be nice to go out on a proper date and talk about what we both wanted. She had mentioned wanting to return to work, but I didn't want her overdoing things. She'd been kidnapped and attacked—she needed to rest. Then she decided to have her home done up, so I told her not to worry about work until she had everything sorted out. I also wanted to know where we stood on the living together front. Meadow has been sleeping in my bed for the last three weeks plus the times before then. Was she planning on going home? I hoped not.

I know the time I've spent away from her over the last couple of weeks will have had her wondering where we stood on things. Now I think about it, she probably thought I was avoiding her. I wasn't. I even had the idea to take her away for a few days, a week maybe. Now that's all been thrown under the bus. Now I want to know, why Greece? Who's she going with and for how long?

I know I can't stop her. I'd never try and dictate what she should and shouldn't be doing. Some time away might be what she needs. Sea air and all that. Yeah, it'll do her good. God, I'll miss her. She's been under my feet, and in my home, taking up my space for almost two months now. Sharing my bed, the lingering flowery scent of her perfume on my sheets and the heart-shaped cookies she has started to make me. Her smile, her kiss, and her warmth wrapped around me; how could I not miss her? It's crazy, I know but I have fallen madly in love with this woman, and I'd do anything if it meant keeping her.

*

It's been twenty days, eight hours, and thirty-five minutes since I last saw Meadow. To say I miss her terribly would be an understatement. I can't think straight and my mood around the office is bordering on psychotic. Everything in this place reminds me of her. The apartment isn't the same without her. Just like the office, I see her everywhere only she's not there. Anybody would think she'd gone for good, the way I've been behaving. To be truthful I don't know when she's coming home. She never said and I never asked.

When Meadow told me she was going to Greece, I had questions. I never got the chance to ask because she was so giddy and eager to tell me, she never shut up all evening. Once I found out she was meeting up with her friend Louise, I understood why she had to go. She needed to let her hair down and have a bit of fun.

We never got the chance to talk about us due to her needing to pack and pick up her passport from the house as well as take a trip to the shops to purchase a few bikinis and shorts. I was only too happy to run her around. I even offered to drop her off at the airport, but she'd booked a taxi when she'd booked her flight. Our goodbye consisted of a quick kiss and cuddle and nothing more. She never said how long she was going for and I didn't ask. I was so cut up about her leaving that I said goodbye to her on the morning of her flight and then left for work.

I am struggling without her. Who the hell knew she'd have such an impact on my life?

For two years, I wanted to get rid of her. Tried all sorts, hoping she'd leave, all because of the way I was struggling when she was around me. It scared the hell out of me, the feelings she evoked. I'd never felt anything like them. I'd been with plenty of women. I'd lived with a woman before, but my heart didn't beat wild in my chest every time she was near, her voice didn't sound like a choir of angels when she spoke, nor did I want to hold her in my arms and never let her go the way I do Meadow. I told myself I was stupid and that I didn't need her in my life. I hated the way I was feeling. I'd never been good with feelings so why would I want them now?

Only, I did want them, and I wanted her. Which is why when I found her in my office asleep and she relayed all the things that had happened with her uncle and the fire at the flat, my heart broke for her. She needed me and I'd do anything for her as well as put right all the times I had upset her.

'Penny for them.' I look up from my phone. I'd been scrolling through the reals of photos she had sent me. Pictures of her on the beach, laughing as she throws her head back. The column of her neck reminds me of the times I've pressed my lips against it and tasted her skin. Her sun-kissed skin gives her such a beautiful healthy glow. Not that she isn't beautiful without it.

Callum takes a seat on the other side of my desk and observes me with concerned eyes. He knows what I'm going through, but I don't think he understands it though. He's never been in love so how could he? The other three walk in and stand behind him. My brothers, caring and interfering.

'Can I help you?' I ask as I put my phone away.

'We could say the same thing.'

'What do you mean?'

'Well, you haven't stepped out of this office since Meadow went on holiday, not even for a few pints at the pub.' Callum reminds me that I've become a bit of a recluse.

'I'll remind you that I have attended many meetings out of this building.'

'Yeah, yeah.' He flicks his hand in the air. 'Don't give me that, Kane, you look like shit. None of the staff wants to come near you in fear for their lives.' I chuckle, I might not be good company at the moment but I'm certainly not bad enough to scare the employees.

'Have you called her?' Mason butts in.

'What?'

'Have you had any contact with Meadow since she went away?' I've refused to talk about her. Told my brothers to keep their noses out. I'm a grown man I don't need them interfering even though I know they mean well.

'Yes.' It's only partly a lie.

'What a few messages here and there. I meant have you spoken to her, asked her when she's planning on coming home.'

'No, I haven't spoken to her. Meadow is a grown woman who has gone away to spend some time with a friend. She doesn't need me pestering her.' I haven't called her because I don't want to come across as needy.

'Kane,' Callum sighs heavily, his expression tells me I'm a jerk. 'Just because she's away on holiday, spending time with Louise doesn't mean you can't talk to her. Ask how she is. Is she having a good time and what she's doing?' That's why I haven't called her. It scares me to death that she's met someone while she's been out there. There'll be lots of hot-blooded men vying for her attention. She's a beautiful woman. How could they not be? Even if she doesn't want to be bothered, all it takes is one too many cocktails and…

'Stop. I can see that little cogwheel going around. You can trust Meadow. She is one of the good guys.' Henry and Connor agree with him.

'She cares for you Kane, don't let your insecurities come between you. We've,' Connor points between him and Henry. 'We've known her a long time and she'd rather cut off her own arm than hurt someone.' I already know this. Look at her with that gigantic spider. She was scared shitless of it but rather than let it wander around the office, in fear of one of us standing on it, she collected it in a glass. Most people would have squashed the bloody thing. Then look at how forgiving she was with her uncle. I'm lucky to have such a caring woman in my life.

'I'm surprised she hasn't phoned you,' Henry comments as he folds his arms across his chest, his brow furrowing.

'I didn't really give her a good sendoff, did I?'

'What do you mean?'

'Oh, I don't know,' I answer, frustrated with the way I am feeling. 'I need a drink, let's get out of here.' Pushing back my chair, I pick up my phone and then make my way toward the door, ignoring the raised eyebrows that my brothers are giving me. I'm not about to tell them that on the morning she was leaving I just hugged her, told her to have a nice time then left for work. All because I was pissed off that the plans, I had in mind were derailed due to her going to Greece.

'A drink does sound good and a bite to eat then you can answer Henry's question,' Callum says as he turns out the lights and we all head out of the office.

*

Turns out all I needed was to unwind with my brothers and a good talking to, to make me see sense. After they all gave their opinions on why I should be calling Meadow and forget about the way I reacted to her news as she probably has, I came home feeling a bit more optimistic.

Henry seemed to think that she'd be returning soon anyway, because Louise and her boyfriend were supposed to be heading off to Turkey, and he knew Meadow wouldn't want to tag along. Apparently, she'd holidayed there with her grandparents when she was a teenager and got a bad case of food poisoning. She swore she'd never go back.

Knowing Meadow, Mason thought she hadn't called me because she thought I'd be busy, and by texting and sending photos she kept me in the loop. This was her way of letting me know she was okay as well as letting me know she was thinking about me. He added that she might be wondering the same thing as I was—Where do we stand?

Maybe he's right. Maybe they're all right, and I need to get my head out of my arse and do something about it.

I left them in the pub and came home. I needed to think about what I'd say to her, and how I'd approach the subject of when she'd be home, without her feeling pressured. Most of all, I needed to hear her voice. As long as I spoke to her, that was all that mattered.

It's eight o'clock here which means it's ten in the evening over there. Would she be out or at the hotel? I didn't care as long as I spoke to her.

Instead of just calling her number, I video-call her on Messenger so I can see her beautiful face. On the third ring, she answers.

'Kane.' Her voice is music to my ears, even if she does sound tired.

'Hey, how are you, sweetheart?' I keep my voice soft and caring.

'I've felt better.' She moves the phone and that's when I can make out that she's lying in bed. The light from the bedside lamp illuminates her face and I'm shocked to see how pale she looks—a huge transformation from the healthy glow she has in the photos she sent me. Her eyes look dark and heavy.

'What's wrong?'

'I have a stomach bug.' Her voice is low and croaky. She tries to sit up, then as if she hasn't the energy to complete the simple task, she sinks back into the bed, with her head resting on the pillows.

'When did it start? Has Louise been taking care of you?'

'I woke up feeling like crap yesterday morning and then spent the rest of the day and today with my head down the toilet.'

'Have you been able to drink anything?' I ask concerned that she will dehydrate.

'Just sips of water.'

'Ask Louise to go and get you something from the chemist to put the salts back in your body?' She looks as weak as a kitten. Her eyes close then flutter back open.

'Hmmm, she's not here.' Her eyes flicker shut again.

'Stay awake Meadow. What do you mean she's not here?'

'Turkey,' she yawns out her answer. 'They went to Turkey the night before last' Shit, she shouldn't be alone. I can't believe they have left her on her own.

'Meadow, when were you last sick?'

'Don't know. What time is it?' She opens her eyes and pulls the white sheet from her shoulder.

'It's ten o'clock where you are. Do you have a bottle of water close by?'

'Yeah, I have water and a bucket, down there.' She points to the floor.

'Can you remember when you last ate anything and when you were last sick?' I ask again.

'Mmmm, I think I last ate the day before yesterday, and I was sick a few hours ago.' She tries to sit up again but it's too much of a struggle and she ends up flopping back down like a rag doll. 'I need to sleep, Kane.'

'Okay, sweetheart. You rest up and I'll call you in the morning but promise me if you feel any worse then you call me or Callum.' I've added Callum because there is no way I'm leaving her there on her own. So, if she can't reach me when I'm up in the sky then she can contact Callum and he'll know what to do. The hotel must have a doctor that you can contact in an emergency. I don't want to call them now just in case she just has a twenty-four- or forty-eight-hour bug. Hopefully, I can get the next flight out and be at the hotel where she is staying before midday tomorrow.

'Night Kane,' she whispers, and I just manage to say night before she's gone.

Chapter 21

Meadow

My eyes snap open and I quickly sit up breathless, taking in my surroundings. For a brief moment, I'm a little disorientated. The dream I'd just had seemed so real. I was in Kane's arms, in his penthouse suite, pressed up against his chest and he was kissing me so passionately my legs had turned to jelly. His manly scent and hard body had felt like home, and I had missed home so much. Using his strong hands, he had lifted me, so my legs were wrapped around his waist and as he led us to the bedroom his erection pushed against my core. He'd stripped me naked, ever so slowly while we were in the living room and his mouth had devoured parts of me that had been aching for his attention. During that time, I had rid him of his shirt and trousers, leaving him just in his boxers. We'd reached the bedroom door, both of us hot and panting, the desire for each other ready to explode. When he kicked the door open, that's when things turned weird. Fireworks were zooming around the room, zapping from wall to wall. Crackling and popping with bright colours. Vibrant and alive with so much energy, so much heat, it actually seemed fitting for how we both felt at that moment. However, that's where it ended because I woke up.

My breathing levels out and I'm reminded of where I am. The closed vertical blinds, bedroom furnishings, and the smell of vomit also remind me of how ill I have been over the last couple of days.

Throwing the sheets off me, I gingerly climb out of bed. I feel better than I did but still have a nauseating headache. The smell from the bucket I had to use due to not having the time or energy to make it into the bathroom hits me and my gag reflex prompts me to get a move on before it's too late.

Once I'm in the bathroom, the smell fades and I'm able to go about my business without retching. I swill my face and brush my teeth, knowing I should jump in the shower, but I want to clean up the mess first. Although I slept all through the night and I do feel better than I did, I don't want to be sick again. Whatever had brought that bout of sickness on I can do without going through it again.

It takes me less time than it should—seeing I'd been laid up in bed for two days—to disinfect the floor and the bucket, shower, and dig into my suitcase to find a dress to wear. My case has been packed for the last three days as I should have been on a flight out of here the morning after Louise and Brandon flew over to Turkey. Their flight was twelve hours before mine, and I was the one who was supposed to check us out of the hotel, only that didn't happen due to being ill. I did manage to telephone the desk and let them know. They seemed concerned, said they'd extend my stay and asked if I needed anything. All I wanted was to be left alone, so I told them no. I managed to send Louise a message, letting her know I was still at the hotel and why. She called me once she had received the message and said she'd come back. I played it down on how I was feeling because I didn't want her fussing around me. There was nothing she could do. I had water, not that I could drink much of it without it coming back up, but it was there, and I just wanted to sleep.

Still feeling weak and washed out, I open the blinds and the balcony door then step outside needing some fresh air not just for myself but to circulate the room.

It's past dinner time and the guests are all sitting around the pool, taking in the sun—it's not the height of the season but it's still warm—and sipping cocktails while some are soaking in the clear water. It's a lovely hotel and a great place to visit. I've had a great time and time to think and now it's time to get back to normality.

My stomach is still feeling a bit queasy, so I go inside and straight to the fridge to get a bottle of water. The bedroom smells better than it did, which I'm pleased about. I wouldn't want to leave the suite a mess. Everything is as it should be.

I search for my phone, which I find hidden under the pillows of the bed. I need to contact the airline and try and get a flight back to England. Scrolling through my contacts for the airline's number I recognize an incoming call from last night and that's when it hit me, Kane had called me. Did I speak to him last night? I must have done.

Now I think about it, I do remember him calling me. The conversation is blurry due to me being slightly out of it.

I'd done nothing but think about him the whole time I was here, but we hadn't spoken. He seemed off the morning I was leaving, wasn't his usual self. I know he'd been working long hours and our time together had been at a minimum—that's one of the reasons I came out here, to give us some space from each other—but that morning he looked as if he had something to say then thought against it. He gave me a quick kiss, hugged me, and told me to enjoy myself then took off for work.

I've messaged him and he messaged me back. Nothing lengthy, just short and to the point. I've also sent him photos. There've been times when I wanted to hear his voice, and many times I'd get his number up, and then decide against it. If he wanted to speak to me, he'd have called, so I concluded that he was either too busy with work or our relationship—a short relationship at that—was coming to an end. We might not have been together long, but I thought he cared for me—no—I know he cared for me, and if truth be told I was falling for him.

I don't want to think about going back to my old boring life. I loved being at Kane's. With Kane. As hectic as my life was when we were together just him and me it felt right.

Deciding I don't have time to dwell on how things will turn out for us, I'll find out soon enough when I get back to England, I dial the airline. But I'm stopped from clicking the call button when there's a loud knock at the door.

Placing my phone on the bed, I make my way out into the hallway and to the front door. When I open it, my heart jumps with delight. I expected it to be room service wanting to deliver towels and such like but instead, it's the man of the hour, Kane.

'Are you going to let me in, and should you be out of bed?' There's that beautiful smile on his face but there's an edge to his tone.

'Yes, come in.' I step to one side to let him pass. 'What are you doing here?' It comes out all wrong and I kick myself for sounding so blunt. 'Sorry, I didn't mean it to sound the way it did.'

He doesn't speak, just takes hold of my hand and pulls me into his firm body. Home. It feels like home and instead of my stomach turning over because of something I'd eaten it does summersaults due to excitement.

My face is pressed against his chest and that smell that I've grown accustomed to has me inhaling. Kane must feel the same because I feel him breathe me in as his face buries into my hair. I'm so glad I had a shower.

'How are you feeling?'

'Better than I did,' I speak into his chest. He pulls away but doesn't let go of me. I never want him to let go of me. His hands hold onto my hips as he looks down at me.

'You look pale.' One hand comes up and tucks a loose piece of hair behind my ear. That touch alone has me melting like an ice pop on a summer's day. 'You should be still in bed.' His eyes hold mine. They're intense but also hold something that tells me he does still care. Of course, he does, he wouldn't be here if he didn't care.

'Honestly, I feel so much better.' He raises an eyebrow at me. 'Well, I feel better than I have over the last few days. I haven't been sick since yesterday.'

'That's good.' He brushes his lips across mine then steps back and takes hold of my hand. I follow him as he looks around the suite and once, he finds the bedroom, he leads us into it. He motions for me to sit down on the bed.

'Have you had anything to drink or eat today?'

'Just water.'

'Do you think you could manage some tea and toast?'

'I could give it a go but I'm not sure it will stay down.' You'd expect some men to grimace at the thought of someone being sick, but Kane just takes it all in his stride.

'I'll order room service and we'll see how you go.'

'Okay. I can't believe you've come here.'

'Why wouldn't I? Do you remember our conversation last night?' He asks before I have time to answer his first question.

'Vaguely. I was quite out of it. I've only just remembered that we spoke, but I can't remember a word of what was said.'

'You did look and sound out of it.' Crap I must have looked a sight.

'I bet it wasn't pretty,' I laugh, hoping he'll be kind and take into consideration I wasn't well. He sits on the bed at my side, I turn to look at him. He takes hold of my hand and I watch spellbound as he runs the tip of his tongue over his bottom lip. His blue eyes twinkle and that flirty smile that I love so much appears, even the cute dimples make an appearance.

'Meadow, you're always beautiful to me, and no matter what you always will be. If I'd known you weren't well, I'd have been here sooner.' He leans forward placing his forehead on mine. 'You should have called me.'

'I wasn't sure how things stood with us. It wasn't like you gave me a good send-off.'

'I'm sorry about how I behaved. I have no excuse'—he moves his head away from mine, placing his hand on my cheek and I lean into it— 'other than I'm an idiot. We hadn't spent much time together for a few weeks with all the work I had on, and you seemed to be pulling away from me. I'd managed to get work sorted and some time off and was hoping to get some alone time. Just you and me. So, when you told me you were coming here, I felt... well it doesn't matter what I felt. I should have been happy for you. I knew the time away would do you good.'

'It doesn't matter,' I cut in. 'You're here now.'

'Yes, I am.' He leans in, his lips brushing across mine. I'm so glad I brushed my teeth. It's just a light brush and then he pulls back. 'I should order that tea and toast,' he says, his eyes saying so much more. I can tell he feels the same as me. Even though I've had a lovely time here, I've missed him so much. Who'd have thought I'd miss my boss, Mr Grumpy? In all honesty, since he brought me to stay at his home—even before his revelation about how much he'd been attracted to me and how he'd had to fight his feelings for me—he's been loving and caring. Everything he has done for me—I don't think I'd have gotten through it without him.

My eyes follow his every movement as he moves around the bed to get to the phone. God, he's so hot. Every movement he makes is precise, confident, and sexy. I listen to his voice as he orders my tea and toast and my body reacts. It's husky with an edge to it and I imagine him whispering words of desire against my skin.

I steal my eyes away and blush when he puts the phone down, one eyebrow lifting, and that grin appears when he catches me staring.

He moves around the bed and crouches down in front of me, placing his hands on my thighs. The heat from him is like a furnace, the electricity from his touch provokes a need in me that I've never felt before.

'Meadow,' he says my name, and I shake off the feeling of dragging him into my bed. Not a wise thing to do at the moment. Maybe if the sheets were fresh. 'It's clear we have both missed each other and the time we shared meant something to us both. You're all I have thought about. I don't want to go back to the life we had before all the crap with your uncle and I don't think you do either.' He tilts his head, his eyes questioning. He's waiting for me to agree with him. He is right, I don't either. I want us to make a go of it. If truth be told, I think I'm falling in love with him. No, that's wrong. I have fallen in love with him. Geez, I'm in love with my boss. How the hell did that happen? Callum and Mason were absolutely right. Hit the nail right on the head with the love/hate thing between Kane and me. And now due to him showing how caring he can be, showing just what I mean to him, I have fallen head over heels for Mr Kane Summer. The realisation of how far we have come in such a short space of time, especially since it was only a few months back that I was telling him to stick his job up his arse. I let out a giggle when I think about it and Kane raises an eyebrow at me.

'Sorry,' I smile at him. 'Yes, I want that too.'

'Good, then why don't we stay here for a few days? Just you and me.' His eyes observe me then he takes in the plush room. It really is a gorgeous hotel suite and even though less than half an hour ago I wanted to go home now he's here I want to stay. With him, I want to stay.

'I'd like that, but I'm not sure I'll be much fun today.'

'Don't worry, you'll be fine. How about you eat your toast, then we'll see how you feel about going for a little walk.'

'I'll need to sort out my flight.'

'What do you mean?'

'I was supposed to fly home the day I was taken poorly. I was able to extend my stay here, but I didn't contact the airline.'

"You was?" He sounds surprised and looks it too. 'Okay. How long do you want to stay?'

'I'm not sure.'

'Does Sunday sound good?' Three extra days. Just Kane and me. It sounds amazing.

'Yes, that sounds lovely.'

'Right, once you have eaten, we'll check in with the reception desk just to see if we're all right to stay here until then. Then I'll get us on the same flight home.'

'Sounds perfect.' Leaning forward I place my lips on his, initiating a kiss. I feel I need to let him know that I'm all in and how happy I am that he travelled here when he saw that I was ill.

Our lips touch and I place my hands on his firm chest. His hands cup my face and in no time at all Kane leads us into a kiss so powerful my heart flutters, and my legs become weak. I moan against his lips unable to hold in how I'm feeling. I feel him smile and I follow enjoying our passionate moment knowing we'll have many of these to come.

A knock at the door puts a stop to our trice and reluctantly we pull apart. Kane's eyes look ablaze, glowing with desire.

'I'll get the door,' he coughs into his hand then adjusts his erection. I watch him saunter off to get the door and I can't help but smile.

Chapter 22

Kane

I struggle to drag my eyes away from Meadow as she stands in front of the mirror and runs the brush through her long silky hair. I watch her place the brush on the bathroom counter then continue to stare at her as she tries to fasten the button on the back of her skirt.

We've been back from Greece a few weeks now and she's stayed here every night since. Waking up to her every morning and watching her dress has become one of my favourite pastimes. Another is after work, stripping her out of the clothes she placed on her sexy body that morning and showering together. However, my all-time favourite is having her snuggle against me every night. Feeling her soft skin against mine as we make love, I'll never tire of it.

Her eyes catch mine through the mirror and she blushes when she sees mine smoldering with heat. Jesus, I'm a lost cause. I can't get enough of this woman. It was only half an hour ago that we were tangled up in the sheets our bodies entwined.

I push off the door frame and step up behind her. My arms circle her waist as my lips brush against her bare shoulder. 'Why don't we play hooky and stay in bed all day?' I suggest, my voice low and seductive. It's something we've done a few times over the last couple of weeks. My brothers find it amusing because in the past neither of us was ever late for work.

'Mmmm, sounds wonderful'—she turns in my arms, placing her hands on my chest— 'but not today. You have a meeting with Mrs Jones the business manager of All Saints Primary School and I have a doctor's appointment.'

'Don't remind me. Are you sure you don't want me to come along with you and I'll send Callum in my place?' Mrs Jones is a force to be reckoned with and I have a nine o'clock appointment with her over the electronic gates that our company fitted two months ago. They keep getting stuck. A few times during the day delivery drivers have been trapped in the grounds because the sensor, which should pick up the vehicle as it approaches and open the gate, has failed. This also happened to the staff when they had finished work. They weren't happy. Engineers have been out many times, but the same thing keeps happening. The company that supplies the sensors to us has also been out and has yet to get back to me on their findings. It doesn't take a rocket scientist to know that there is something wrong with the components they are using for the sensors. And now the business manager wants a meeting so we can come up with an agreement as to what to do about them.

'No, it's you who they wanted the meeting with and I'm only going to see the nurse for a smear test—I'm good on my own.'

'I suppose you're right.' She moves out of my arms and complains about the button on her skirt popping open. I help her out, fastening it securely and when she turns around, she brushes her lips against mine.

'Thank you,' she smiles then sashays out of the bathroom and into the bedroom before I have a chance to grab hold of her which would make us both late for our appointments.

'What time will you be back from the doctor?'

'Around ten.'

'Okay, I'll see you at the office. I should be back for eleven, we can go to lunch and then take the afternoon off.' I'm not asking this time.

'You know, you'll be getting me into trouble with the boss.' Meadow widens her eyes at me and then gives me that sexy smile of hers.

'Oh, you'll be getting into trouble with the boss all right.' I wiggle my eyebrows at her, causing her to chuckle and roll her eyes at me.

'That's my favourite kind of trouble.' She steps into my space and runs her hands over my shoulders. I lean in for a kiss, she obliges without moaning about her lipstick getting smudged. When she pulls away, she wipes at my lips with a tissue, removing any telltale signs of her lipstick.

We both leave the penthouse together and travel down to the office before we part ways.

*

I blow out a breath and sit down, placing my elbows on my desk. 'Why are we dealing with these idiots?'

'I take your meeting with Miss Trunchbull didn't go well?' Callum asks as he leans against the office door, folding his arms across his chest, Mason pulls up a chair and sits opposite me.

'The meeting went as well as can be expected and Miss Trunchbull turned out to be Miss Honey. It was the CEO of the Academy Trust who stuck his oar in and told me that under no terms would we get the contract for the other schools if we didn't change our suppliers—and fit the gates with new sensors instead of trying to fix them—oh, and they want a ten percent discount If we get the contract. Running my hand through my hair I pick up my phone. Nothing from Meadow. I rang her when the meeting had finished and got her voicemail. I've tried twice since and still nothing. She said she was seeing the nurse this morning but that was a few hours ago.

'I've looked at other suppliers and I'm meeting with two of them this week so that isn't a problem.' Callum breaks me out of my thoughts.

'And ten percent is doable if we get the contract for the eight schools,' Mason adds. He's the money man. Brilliant with the accounts... 'And I was thinking we need to reach out to other schools and colleges—offer a discount. There are so many that are academies now with around six, seven, or eight schools. If we offer a decent incentive, we could get a huge contract out of it. Speak to Mr Meldrew...'

'Who?' I ask confused.

'The CEO. Victor Meldrew. Never mind.' He shakes his head at me as if I'm dumb. Of course, I know who Victor Meldrew is, I just didn't get it at first.

'Go on,' I tell him.

'I'm just saying, if we do our homework, so to speak. Keep All Saints sweet this CEO could be our finger into the bigger pie. He puts our name about, and other schools pick up on it and not just the one Trust.'

'Sounds good. I've already agreed to the discount anyway before I left, he seemed happy with our agreement and so was Mrs Jones.'

'I'll look into other academies and do some ringing around.' Mason stands ready to get on with his search and Callum pushes himself off the door.

'I'll come with you,' he tells him.

'Have any of you heard from Meadow this morning?' They both shake their heads. 'She was supposed to be meeting me back here for lunch.'

'She's probably gone shopping,' Callum offers.

'Or for her nails doing,' Mason adds.

'Yeah, you're probably right.' I've no sooner said the last word when the door comes flying open, nearly knocking Callum off his feet, and my youngest brother Connor comes barging in looking like he could kill someone.

'What the hell is wrong…' I don't get to finish.

'What have you done?' He stands in front of my desk, smoke practically coming out of his ears.

'Me? What the hell are you on about?'

'Meadow, that's what I'm on about.'

'What about Meadow?' I jump up from my seat. 'Is she ok? Where is she?'

'She's at my house, extremely upset about something. She won't tell me what it is or who it is that has upset her. All she said amongst the waterfall of tears. Jesus, it's like Niagara Falls over there and don't get me started on the amount of tissues. All she has managed to get out is that she's made a mistake.'

'And you think it has something to do with me?'

'Who else would it be?' he says with contempt in his voice.

'Get out of my way you idiot.' Moving from my desk I push past him. 'I haven't done anything to upset her, why would I?' As far as I know, I haven't but you never know with women and their hormones.

'I swear to God Kane, if you've cheated on her, I'll castrate you myself.' I almost laugh at him, but this is anything but funny. If my woman is upset, then I need to know why and who the hell it is who's upset her. She's gone through enough these last few months. Everything has been on the up since her trip away to Greece and my visit to take care of her while she was unwell. Meadow has been happy—we have both been besotted with each other.

'I'll come with you,' Conner says as I grab my keys and phone.

'I don't think so. If Meadow is upset about something, then it is me who should be with her.'

Protecting Her

'Then why is she at my house and not here with you?' Good question. But as far as I know, I haven't done anything wrong. I treat her like a queen—I'd do anything for her. Before I have a chance to tell my brother to piss off and stop being a clever little bastard, Callum intervenes.

'Don't wind your brother up, you know he'd never hurt Meadow. I agree with him—let him go alone.'

Conner takes a step back, holding his hands up in defeat, just to let me know he'll keep out of it. But in all fairness, he's right. Why hasn't she come to me?

*

My heart stutters, my feet slowing to a stop by the door as I take in the sight before me. Meadow is laid on the settee curled up with her head on one of the cushions, a tissue in her hand, and her eyes closed. You can tell she's been crying as her nose is red and even though her eyelids are closed, I can hear her sniffle. She moves the tissue to wipe her nose and I step into the room, needing to know what has happened. 'Meadow,' I speak softly not wanting to make her jump. Her eyes open slowly, and they too look red, I also notice red blotches on her face.

'Hey, what's wrong?' I tread carefully, sitting down at the far end of the settee. I've clearly done something to upset her, I just don't know what.

Meadow sits up and blows her nose. She doesn't look at me and I can see she's reluctant to answer my question. I want to move closer to her, hold her in my arms, and tell her everything is Okay. My whole body is screaming out to take her in my arms and when she sniffles again, I make my move.

She doesn't stop me from wrapping my arms around her and I'm grateful when she buries her face into my chest, her hands gripping my shirt. She lets out a heartfelt sob, her shoulders shaking as she holds onto me for dear life. I bury my face in her hair and then place a tender kiss on the side of her head. 'Meadow, please tell me what's wrong.' She wiggles out of my hold and sits up wiping at her tears with a tissue, she then stands and turns to me. It breaks my heart to see how upset she is, especially not knowing what it is that has put her in this state.

'I need the loo. I'll be back in a minute.' Watching her turn and walk away, my thoughts are running a hundred miles an hour as to what could have happened. She'd gone to the doctor for a routine check-up and smear test. Could it have something to do with that? She's also been toying with the idea of selling her grandparents' house. Perhaps she's finally put it up for sale and it has hit her hard. I can understand her emotions would be all over the place, she was born in that house. Her memories of her mum and grandparents are all in that house. Apart from those two things, nothing else comes to mind.

I sit forward, my elbows resting on my knees and gaze at the floor when nothing else comes to mind, I rub at my face and then lift my head. I'm surprised to see Meadow sitting on the chair arm observing me. She must have tiptoed in because I didn't hear her. She's stopped sobbing and she looks as if she's swilled her face.

'How are you feeling?' I stand to go to her, but she puts her hand up to stop me. What the hell. I don't like this. I know I haven't done anything wrong, but I sit back down not wanting to push it. 'Are you going to tell me what's wrong Meadow?' I only just manage to get the words out when she speaks.

'Have you ever thought about having a family, Kane?' I'm knocked back by her question; I wasn't expecting that. I almost laugh at it.

'I don't understand Meadow, what do you mean?'

'It's straight forward question, Kane. A yes or no answer is all that is needed.' I'm still shocked at the question, but I'll play her game. Whatever it is.

'No. No, I don't think I have.'

'Liar.' There's an undercurrent of disappointment in her tone.

'I'm no liar, Meadow. I don't need to. You know about the woman I lived with years ago and apart from living together we never talked about marriage or children, it was a shock when she told me she was pregnant. You know the baby turned out to be someone else's. And there has been no one else in my life apart from you. No one of any importance anyway.' I'll be truthful, I've had a brief insight into the future and seen Meadow and I living together—we practically do now—but I haven't thought about marriage or children. I'm almost forty, do I want children at my age?

'Last year in the office,' Meadow says, bringing me out of my thoughts. 'Callum said to you that it was about time you found someone to settle down with so you could start a family, and your words were not bloody likely. The family thing isn't for me and I've plenty of brothers to carry on the family name.' Is she having a laugh? I don't remember the conversation and even if I did say it, what has that got to do with now? It's then I get with the program. Meadow has been to the doctors, she's twenty-six and she knows I'm knocking up forty maybe they've spoken about her contraception pill, she was thinking about changing it and now she's thinking she will want a family in the distant future and my age would be an issue. Not that age is an issue for men who want children later on in life, many do, it's just never appealed to me.

I make to stand because I need to be near her, touching her. 'I don't remember saying that Meadow…'

'I'm pregnant.'

I'm cut off from what I was going to say with just two words and for a brief moment I can't move or speak. Stuck stock still.

I'm pregnant, it registers again and ever so slowly I lower myself back into my seat, my legs suddenly not strong enough to carry me, a hazy fog surrounding me. My brain trying to comprehend what Meadow has just told me. This is a shock. Huge. Our relationship is still quite new to have a child. Or is it? There's that voice again. I haven't heard it for a while, not since Meadow and I got together. It tells me that I should be leaping out of my seat, but I'm rooted to it. That I should be shouting from the rooftops, telling Meadow how much I love her, and this is the best news in the world, but my mouth has suddenly become as dry as the Sahara Desert and I can't form a word let alone string a sentence together.

Silence surrounds us, giving me time to think. I love this woman with all my heart. Why wouldn't I want to go all the way with her? Do the whole family thing. If that's what she wants, then I want that too. I want to make her happy because she makes me happy. My heart beats for her and her alone.

I open my mouth to speak, and she cuts me off again with the hand thing. 'Don't you dare ask how this happened because I swear to God, I'll beat you with something.' She looks deadly serious too which causes me to smile because it is something I could see her doing.

'I wasn't going to say anything remotely like that. I was going to say—' This time I stand on strong determined legs—hell-bent on getting closer to her—and take hold of her hand. She allows me to lead her from the chair arm and onto the settee— 'I was going to say before you dropped that bombshell on me.'

'That bombshell.' She punches me in the arm. It's not hard but a warning not to refer to our child—our child bloody hell, my heart starts to pound in my chest. I'm going to be a father. I can't believe this. What kind of father would I be, I spend most of my day at work, evenings and weekends included. You'll make a smashing dad. You have a lot to give plus you are madly in love with the mother of your child. Could the little voice be right? My dad worked all the hours God sent and he still made plenty of time for his sons and our mum, while he was alive. He loved us all fiercely.

'Kane?' she throws me a questioning look when I laugh, my face breaking out into a broad grin.

'Meadow, I love you so much and I will love our little one just as much.' I take hold of her hand and then place my other on her tummy.

'But you said...'

'Whether I said that I didn't want a family or not you can't take seriously what two brothers say when they are chatting crap. Plus, things have changed now. I've changed. I want this. A family with you.'

Meadow's eyes twinkle, dancing like the stars, her smile lighting up the room. All the sadness from moments ago is now gone. She leans into me and brushes her lips against mine and without any thought my arms wrap around her, holding her tightly against my chest. Our hearts beat in time as our mouths fuse. I'm lucky to have her. Things between us could have gone so differently. I pushed her away for so long, scared to death of how she made me feel, and yet she forgave me and now she's given me a gift I didn't know I wanted. When she pulls away from me her expression tells me she has something else to say.

'What is it?' She bites her lip, worrying the hell out of it. Then she rubs her hands up and down her face and blows out a breath. 'Meadow,' I say as I gently take her hands in mine.

'It might be twins.' Her words come out quickly and yet again she has rendered me speechless. Twins. Bloody hell. Two babies. Double the feeding, changing nappies, and crying simultaneously in the middle of the night. I remember Connor and Henry like it was yesterday. The sleepless nights. Baby sick down my school shirt after I'd helped my mum wind them. I also remember how bloody cute they were. They did everything together. Sat up for the first time on the same day. Crawling and then walking with the furniture in the same week. If I remember rightly their first steps were holding hands. So bloody cute. They were also evil little buggers; I did think for a short time that we might end up calling them Ronnie and Reggie, but they turned out to be two stand-up guys and I'd like to think I had a hand in that.

Having twins is a big deal but Meadow and I are madly in love. She's it for me. If we're going to have a family, we might as well do it now while I still have my own teeth and hair. I know what I need to do.

Moving from the settee, I kneel down in front of Meadow and take her hand in mine. And the words just fall out. 'Marry me?'

Chapter 23

Meadow

'Marry me?' That is not what I was expecting to come out of Kane's mouth. If anything, I thought he might have said bloody hell. Or you're joking and do that thing where he runs his hand through his hair and then falls back in his chair. Maybe I've underestimated how Kane would respond, I could have quite easily slid off my chair and onto the floor when I found out. I think I sat there for five minutes, doing that gawping thing—mouth wide open—until it registered. I'd say it knocked me for six.

I had no idea. I'd only gone for a smear test. Marlene, the nurse who has worked at my doctor's since I was in my teens, always likes to have a bit of a natter when she sees me. Her first question was to ask how I'd been keeping and then the next was to ask if I had a man in my life yet. The last time she asked, I'd laughed and answered I can't see that happening anytime soon. This time of course I had good news, I was in a relationship and was madly in love. She told me that was lovely to hear, she was glad I'd finally found someone. Marlene then asked me questions about my contraception pill and said she could have a word with the doctor about changing it if I felt it wasn't right for me. I had been hoping to have it changed as it wasn't working for me. Of course, she asked the question if me and Kane were sexually active and then asked if I knew when my last period was and that is how we found out I was pregnant. I couldn't remember when my last period was. Was it last month? The month before? Or three months ago? I just wasn't sure. So much had happened over the last few months plus the pill I'd been taking, I only started it six months ago due to my old one causing me to bloat like a bloody puffer fish. If I remember rightly, I was told it might stop my periods so deep down it was probably why I never gave my periods a thought. As I couldn't remember, she recommended we do a pregnancy test as a precaution. I was adamant I wasn't, but I did the test anyway. A couple of minutes later, there it was.

'Meadow.' I look down at Kane, on his knees, a concerned expression on his face and that's when I remember what he just asked me and I burst out laughing.

This is Kane Summer, the CEO of Summer Knights Security, a man who's had more women hanging off his arm and warming his bed than a team of premier footballers. And he wants to get married, he's clearly crazy. Telling him I'm pregnant and then dropping the bombshell that it might be twins has obviously caused some imbalance in his brain and he's not thinking straight.

'Meadow,' he repeats my name. 'A yes or no would be good.'

'Are you crazy? You don't want to get married.'

'Twenty minutes ago, I didn't know I wanted children.' He takes hold of my hands, pulling me closer to him. 'Now I do. With you, I want it all. A baby or two.' He raises an eyebrow and that smile that has me melting for him makes an appearance.

Sitting down, I take in the man who I have fallen deeply in love with, the man that I have no doubt would do anything to make me happy and keep me safe and I know he loves me just as deeply. Knowing what I know about how he grew up taking care of his brothers to help and support his mum, it's easy to determine that he'd make a wonderful, loving dad. Our children would want for nothing, and they'd be surrounded with so much love—not just from Kane and me but from their uncles. I also know that, if we were to marry, then just like the devotion he'd have for our children, he'd be a devoted, loving husband. Saying that, I would never want him to feel marrying me was the decent thing to do. We haven't been together long. Our relationship is quite new. Finding out that I'm pregnant not with just one baby but possibly two is a shock to both of us, and I think we need—no, I know we both need—to get over the shock of becoming parents first.

Placing my hand on his cheek, I run my fingers over his stubble. I love it when he doesn't shave for a couple of days—he looks so sexy with a bit of scruff. I kneel in front of him and place one hand back on his cheek.

'You know I love you more than anything else in the world?' He smiles and those dimples make an appearance.

'I'm a lucky bastard.' He brushes his lips against mine. 'And I love you more than life itself.' His eyes hold so much love in them and when he smiles, they smile as well.

'Then we are both lucky and our baby or babies will be just as lucky to have us as parents. However, this'—I place my hand on my stomach, Kane does too, it feels warm and right— 'is a surprise to both of us and I feel we need to get our heads around the idea of becoming a mum and dad first.' I hold my breath for a moment as we both stare into each other's eyes. He doesn't speak, just kneels there stroking my belly and I fear that I've rendered him speechless again. My man isn't used to being knocked back. He usually gets everything he wants. Most people agree with whatever he says or does. I say most people, me being one that doesn't always agree with him and will put him in his place if I feel there is a need to. And lately, I've been able to get away with it.

'You don't want to get married?'

'One day but I think your proposal is due to finding out you are going to be a father…'

'I…' He tries to cut in, but I put my hand up to stop him.

'Kane, I'm not saying your feelings aren't true or that you don't want to marry me—I'll be expecting another proposal in the future—what I'm saying is, please wait until we've at least found out if we are having twins. There's so much to sort out. I'm going to freak out at some point because…'

'Hey.' Kane stands, helping me to my feet then he takes me in his arms. And I welcome it so much 'You are going to be the best mum, ever.' He cups my face, his eyes searching mine. 'You're loving and gentle. Smart, sassy, and strong. You are the strongest woman I know and we are lucky to have you. I will be with you every step of the way, Meadow. And if you do freak out at any point then so be it. I'm sure you're not the first mum to be who does and you won't be the last. As crazy as it sounds, I might freak out myself.' He lifts my chin and gives me that smile that brings out his dimples then winks at me, and I know we've got this. Yes, I might not want to get married just yet only because I do believe Kane needs time to come to terms with being a parent, I do too. And we are going to have enough to worry about without the added stress of planning a wedding.

I smile about him freaking out because I can't see that happening. 'That's better,' he announces then leans down and brushes his lips against mine. 'We've got this, Meadow.' I feel his smile against my mouth. I nod my head when he pulls away.

'Can we get out of here?' He looks around Connor's flat.

'We better before Connor turns up demanding to know what is going on. I'm sure he thought I'd lost the plot when I turned up here sobbing like a little girl and wouldn't tell him what was wrong.'

'Yeah, he thought I'd upset you.'

'I'm sorry Kane, I can only imagine the stick he would've given you.'

'Don't worry about it. Honestly, it just made me realise how much my brothers care about you and how much I need to up my game to prove that I'm worthy of you.' He takes hold of my hand and leads us out of the living room, but I stop him, needing to let him know that he is well and truly worthy of my love.

'Kane, please don't ever think that you are not the man for me. You have proven ten-fold these last few months how much you care and love me.'

'Thank you, Meadow. I think I needed to hear that from you after today. In the future will you promise me something?'

'Yes, anything.'

'Come to me if anything is troubling you. Even if it is me, please discuss it with me and not one of my brothers. I know you are close to them but what we share—have shared. What we have is special and I hope to be not just your lover but your best friend too.' He does have a point. I should have gone to him, but I was so shocked and wasn't sure how he'd react to the news of me being pregnant.

'I promise,' I tell him cupping his face and stroking his stubble with my thumbs.

'Good,' he smiles against my lips then takes hold of my hand.

'You know, this means we are going to have to move in together properly.' He keeps a tight hold of my hand as he leads me out of the flat and locks the door.

'I know.'

'And it also means, I'm going to be on bended knee at least once a week.' He gives me a sideways glance as we approach his car.

'I know that also.' I roll my eyes at him. I wouldn't expect anything else from him. When he wants something, he will stop at nothing until he's got it.

'Good, then you'll know before our child is born or children you will be my wife.' He's probably right but I will still fight him on it because as much as I love the sound of being Mrs Summer, I don't want to rush it.

'Oh, one more thing,' he smiles down at me as he takes over securing my seat belt.

'And what is that, prey do tell?' He winks at me as he closes the door and rounds the car to his side. Once he is settled in his seat, he starts the engine and moves out into the road.

'Well?' God, I hate when he does that, keeps me waiting.

'We need to tell my mum that she is going to be a grandmother.'

'Shit.' I never thought of that. Yes, I've met his mother before. Years ago, when I hung around with Connor and Henry, I'd see her when I called around to their house. She always came across as a caring woman. You could tell she loved her sons very much. However, since I started working at Summer Security, she hasn't been anywhere near. Not while I've been there anyway. 'Does she know about us?' I point between Kane and me.

'Yes. Why wouldn't she?'

'Oh, I don't know, maybe because you never really mention her. I know she's still away at the moment with Ray'—I shrug my shoulders— 'I didn't know that you've spoken to her about our relationship.'

'She does call me while she's away and like any loving mum she always knows when something is going on with one of us.'

'Oh.' I don't know what else to say.

It doesn't take long before we are pulling into the underground carpark and when Kane shuts off the engine, he turns to me. 'Meadow, you know how important to me you are so of course I'm going to mention you to her.'

He takes hold of my hand and leans in placing the other on my tummy. There is a tiny bit of a bump there, which is why I'm going for an emergency scan in the next few days because I shouldn't be showing at all. Even if I fell on the first time Kane and I slept together I should only be around seven weeks...

'She's happy about us being together. Said she always liked you. She was shocked though.'

'Why?'

'She said, she always thought you and one of the twins would have ended up together.' I burst out laughing as soon as he finished the sentence. 'What's so funny?' He looks confused.

'There was never ever going to be anything between me and Connor or Henry. We've always been just friends and even thinking about it makes me want to gag and that's not because they aren't attractive men, they are. Connor and Henry are like the brothers I never had.'

'That's understandable. And it does make me feel a whole lot better.'

'Didn't like the thought that I might have had the hots for one of them when I was younger.'

'God forbid.' He shakes his head and opens the car door to get out. I haven't even unclipped my seatbelt before he's round to my side opening the door and helping me out.

'Such a gentleman.' I attempt to place my lips on his cheek, but he turns quickly, and I end up kissing his mouth. I feel him laugh against mine and in no time at all he has me pushed up against the car door, leading us into a kiss that should be illegal. His hands take hold of my hips and if we wasn't in the car park, I'd be hitching my skirt up and wrapping my legs around him. His lips move from mine onto my neck, and I angle my head to give him better access. I love it when he trails his lips along my skin, can't get enough of it, of him. His feathery light touches stop, and he pulls away and coughs into his hand.

'We'll Chrisan the car some other time,' he winks then throws his arm around my shoulder, tucking me into his side.

'Looking forward to it.' I am too. Being with Kane has opened my eyes to sex. I've never experienced such intensity as when I'm with him and don't get me started on the positions and places.

'So, you okay if we tell my family?' He says, stopping at the lift. Am I ok with everyone knowing? I'm not sure. Thinking about it, I don't think I am. I'm only a little bit pregnant and we won't know for a few days if we are having twins. I think I'd rather wait.

'Do you mind if we wait until we've had the scan?'

'I'm absolutely fine with whatever you want to do. We can wait until you're a little further on if you want.'

'That would be probably the best thing to do, but I think I'll be showing before then if we're having twins.' Which I'm certain I am because I'm struggling to fasten my clothes now.

'Huh,' he chuckles.

'What?'

'Nothing,' he smiles, shaking his head. 'I just feel excited when you say twins. Never thought I was going to be a father and now in less than nine months I might be a father to two. I feel... Crickey I can't explain how I'm feeling at the moment. But whatever it is, it's because of you and these little ones.' He places his hand on my tummy. God knows how many times he's done that since finding out. I suppose it's going to be our normal now. And I'm happy with our normal.

'You're going to be a wonderful dad?' I stand on my tiptoes and brush my lips against his.

'And you Meadow Walters soon to be Mrs Summer will be a wonderful mother.'

'I love you.'

'I know and I love you too.'

The lift arrives and, on our way up to the office, we decide to keep my pregnancy a secret for now. Kane said he'll message his mum and Ray to arrange to go over after they get back from their cruise, which is at the weekend. Even though I'm nervous about being pregnant and meeting his mum now she knows we're together and then telling everyone about the pregnancy, I'm also excited. Just like Kane, it's hard to explain the feeling. I'm sure this feeling will change once my tummy is that big, I can't see my feet which will also be huge, most probably. When I can't go five minutes without needing to pee then because I'm the size of a blue whale, I will need to call Kane to help me up from the toilet. There's also morning sickness and stretch marks— so much to go through. Saying that, I'm sure it will all be worth it. I know it will.

Chapter 24

Kane

Meadow rolls her eyes at me then huffs and puffs as I help her off the hospital bed, making sure she gets off safely. She slaps my hands away when I try to readjust her shirt but when I raise an eyebrow at her, she lets me do my thing. I'm still reeling at seeing our babies on the screen and knowing we are having what we wanted has made me the happiest man alive and I know Meadow is over the moon too.

It was twelve weeks ago when she surprised me with her pregnancy, well, I think we were both in shock with the news. Meadow falling pregnant was definitely not something I expected to hear when I raced over to Connor's to find out what was wrong with her. Needless to say, once we both got our heads around it, we were both excited and then it was a week later when she had her first scan, and we were told we were having twins. We had some time to come to terms with the fact that we might be having twins so when they confirmed it, it wasn't as much of a shock. Actually, having it confirmed left us both overjoyed with the news and I struggled with keeping the news to ourselves. Meadow wanted to wait until she was twelve weeks, which I understood. Most parents tend to wait until after the three-month mark only Meadow was showing, and it was hard to keep her bump hidden. By the time she was ten weeks, we decided we'd let my family and Meadow's best friend know. She doesn't have any family left except for that poor excuse of an uncle who turned up causing havoc and has now buggered off to Scotland. Good riddance, I say. It's due to him and his abuse that Meadow had to leave her family home and rent a first-floor flat above a shop in a very sleazy part of town, which she had to leave in the middle of the night due to a fire.

Finding her in my office asleep and hearing what had happened to her brought home just how much I did care for this woman and hiding it—fighting it was no longer an option. She needed to know, and she needed my protection. Protecting her was easy. I'd give my life to keep her safe from harm. Becoming her lover was just as easy. Once Meadow realised, I had been fighting my feelings for her and my behaviour towards her was because of this, I now count myself extremely lucky that she was able to forgive me. And even luckier that she also had feelings for me. What we have—What we share is special and I cherish every moment we have together.

I had pondered over whether I should have thanked her uncle John in some way because it was due to his behaviour that pushed Meadow and me together. Like bloody hell, I will. Not happening. Never. It was his fault that she was kidnapped, assaulted and subjected to being locked into a cellar. She might have come across as tough in their presence but that was all a show. She might have given Jimmy's men a run for their money and stood up to one of them but when we managed to get to his house and get past his goons, we found her being dragged about by McKay, she was scared to death and my body shook with anger. I'd never wanted to kill someone with my bare hands before and putting him six feet under wouldn't have been a problem. Once I took him down, making sure he wouldn't be putting his hands on her or any other woman again, I went straight to Meadow and what I saw will stay with me for a long time. Her face was bruised, her wrists marked and how she trembled in my arms, against my chest, it was clear she was going into shock.

'They we go my lovelies.' The sonographer interrupts my thoughts as she hands over the scan picture of our two babies.

'Ooh, thank you so much,' Meadow gushes, smiling as she takes the photo in her fingers. She gently runs one over the picture then places her lips on it as a tear slips down her cheek. She's extremely emotional at the moment. Her hormones running riot and finding out today the sex of our babies has heightened them.

Taking her in my arms and brushing away her tears, my eyes also fill up when I glance at our son and daughter. We are both lost causes. God only knows how we will react when the babies come.

'You are going to be wonderful parents.' Claire the sonographer breaks the moment. 'I can always tell.' She shrugs her shoulders as she goes about changing the paper sheet on the bed.

'Thank you,' we both say together, knowing she's right. We might be new to this, but our children will have everything they need. Love they will have in abundance. And not just from us.

Choosing to go with not telling my mum and brothers until as near to three months as we could, was difficult. Not just because of the baby bump that was growing significantly, Meadow and my mum had become close. And let's just say it's hard to hide anything from my mum. If she'd have been a dog, then she'd have been working for the police. She can sniff out a lie before you've even told it. Plus, they were becoming good friends.

From the first night, we went over to see Mum and Ray, they all got along like a house on fire and met up many times since for a meal, shopping and just to have coffee. My mother gushes over Meadow every time she sees her, commenting on how beautiful she is and that I better be treating her right. It was hard to keep it from a woman who every time she sees you wants to hug the hell out of you as well as hold on to Meadow's hands as she inspected her from head to toe. Her eyes smiling as if she knew something. And she did. She said she had an idea that Meadow was pregnant the first time we went to visit as a couple but wasn't sure until a few weeks later. What gave it away was the dress that Meadow had worn which outlined the bump and if that wasn't a huge giveaway then her quick trip to the bathroom after being served minted lamb cutlets did. Mum had noticed how green around the gills; Meadow had gone when she first smelt the lamb but like the trooper, my beautiful woman is and not wanting to say anything about the lamb being one of the things that brought on her sickness, she gave it a go. However, she'd only gone as far as lifting the forkful to her lips before she had to excuse herself, making a quick escape to my mum's downstairs toilet.

Meadow put it down to feeling iffy all day and my mum and Ray quickly set to making her some ginger and mint tea to settle her stomach.

My brothers didn't have a clue, which shocked me. They see Meadow every day and with her weight being noticeable, I'd have thought the twins might have said something. When we told them they were ecstatic at becoming uncles and said they thought she was just happy and contented. All loved up, Connor said. Callum excused himself as being a gentleman who was always told never to mention a woman's weight. Henry and Mason just said they hadn't noticed.

'Are we going straight to your mums?' Meadow asks after we say our goodbyes to Claire and walk out of the door. We had arranged for everyone to meet there at five o'clock so we could celebrate knowing the gender of our babies. I'm bursting to tell them however it's a little early yet, which means I get to spend some alone time with the woman that has filled my life with so much love and laughter. I thank myself lucky that she gave me a life that I didn't know I wanted.

'I thought we could nip home first, have a few hours to ourselves then shoot over.'

'Sounds good. I could do with a soak in the bath.'

'Now that does sound appealing.' I bend down brushing my lips against hers, smiling against them. We both love tub time. Relaxing in the warm suds, with Meadow pressed against my chest as I gently run my hands over her silky skin, is my idea of Heaven. I'm fortunate to have an oversized bath that can be used as a jacuzzi or a regular bath because it means we get to do a lot more than just soak in it.

'If you're lucky I might let you wash my back.' Meadow looks over her shoulder at me as she steps into the lift. Her eyes shimmer as she gives me that sexy smile. And I know we're both on the same page. An afternoon of making love to my—fingers crossed—fiancé wasn't what I expected today but I certainly won't be passing it up.

We make our way down to the ground floor, and if it wasn't for the people who had joined us in the lift then I'd have Meadow pressed up against the door.

*

'I can't believe we're going to be late.' Meadow stomps across the bedroom as she raises her arms and shimmies into the dress that she's just got out of the wardrobe. The black dress falls perfectly around her bump and curves, sitting just above her knees. 'It's your fault,' she accuses as she turns to see what I am doing. Her breath falters and her hand shoots to her chest. And this time the expression she is wearing as my heart galloping. Maybe this time she'll say yes.

When she told me she was pregnant I wanted to do the decent thing, so I got down on one knee and proposed. I don't even think it was just that she was carrying my child, I think I knew eventually I'd have asked her. However, Meadow being Meadow wasn't having anything to do with the decent thing, and said no. She understood that her becoming pregnant so early in our relationship was a shock to us both and she knew we both needed time to adjust to the shock. Whether it was a shock or not, I had made my mind up with what I wanted and Meadow becoming my wife as soon as possible is definitely something I want. I let up that evening, but I wasn't giving up. I've been relentless in my pursuit to get her to say yes. Over the last few months, I think I've asked her at least ten times. I've taken her away for romantic weekends, out for romantic meals and just popped the question in whenever I saw fit. Each time she just laughs and shakes her head at me. But I refuse to give up.

'We've got an hour to go yet so don't panic and I didn't hear you moaning—well I did but that was for a whole different thing,' I wink at her as I stay on one knee. 'Come here.' I hold out my hand for her to take. I think she's a little shocked. Maybe she thought I'd given up on the idea because I haven't popped the question for the last few weeks.

She makes her way across to me and takes hold of my hand, her eyes holding mine. Swapping one knee for the other because I'm getting a little stiff—I'm no spring chicken—I then take hold of her other one and place both our hands on her tummy.

'Meadow, what can I say that I haven't already?' I tilt my head to look at her. 'You have made me the happiest man alive. Soon to be a father of two beautiful babies. I love you with all that I am and that will never die. I will always put you and our children first…' She stops me in mid-flow, placing her finger on my lips. And what I hear has me nearly toppling over.

'Yes,' she whispers as a tear slips down her cheek.

'What?' I'm on both feet, wiping it away with my thumb.

'I said yes,' she laughs, as she wipes at her eyes.

'Are you sure?'

'Never been surer.'

'But I never got to say the three words.' Not that I haven't said them many times. She rolls her eyes at me. But I'm serious. I want to say the words and hear her say, yes.

'Ask me,' she says, knowing how much this means to me and because she has already said yes, I know it means as much to her.

'Meadow, will you marry me?' I don't muck about. You never know with her hormones she might change her mind. I hold out the ring in front of her.

'Yes, A big fat yes.' She throws herself into my arms and I encompass her, pressing her against my chest. We stay that way for a few moments. My whole being too overwhelmed to do anything other than place my face in her hair. Eventually, when we do part, I take the sparkling diamond and place it on her finger. It fits for now.

'If it gets tight, we can have a piece put in then have it taken back out when you've had the babies.'

'Thank you. It's beautiful.' She holds it up to the light, her eyes watering. "It's absolutely gorgeous. I love it.'

I cup her face in my hands and take her mouth gently. 'No, you're gorgeous, and I love you. Thank you for finally saying yes.'

'I was always going to say yes, I just needed a little time,' she says against my lips then she kisses me.

Our kiss turns powerful and intense, and if we weren't due at my mum's, I'd be taking Meadow back to bed.

'Are you happy?' I step back from her, keeping hold of her hands.

'Extremely. And you?'

'I have everything I want Meadow, I'm crazy happy.' How the hell did I get so lucky? I ask myself. Having Meadow by my side for the rest of our lives just seems surreal and we haven't even said I do yet. I am lucky to have her and in less than five months we'll have two little bundles of joy.

'We need to go.' She pulls her hands out of mine and I'm struggling with losing contact. 'Your brothers have been blowing up my phone. They're excited to know what we are having.'

'Bollocks to them. They can wait a bit longer.' I don't mean it. I know my family were as excited as we were for today. They can't wait to find out, they've even taken bets on it.

'You'd better get moving then.' I slap her arse softly and get a little squeal from her. We might be meeting my family to celebrate but I can't see me wanting to stay too long. Not when Meadow and I have a little celebrating of our own to do.

ABOUT THE AUTHOR

Tracey Gerrard is kept extremely busy with her full-time job and family life. However, she does set aside a little time for herself. This is where she gets to relax, either with a good book or sitting with her laptop, creating her next romance novel.

Other Books by Tracey Gerrard

Ain't Nobody Series:

When We Dance Book 1

When We Hurt Book 2

When We Love Book 3

Standalone or can be read alongside the *Ain't Nobody* Series

The Deeper We Fall (prequel featuring Sebastian and Izzy)

Let Me (Zach and Jennifer)

Trust In Us (Nicholas and Lucy)

Coming Soon

Saving Them, Book 2 in the *Summer Knights* Series

You can find all my books here:-

https://www.amazon.co.uk/stores/Tracey-Gerrard/author/B07Q1BWQC7

Printed in Great Britain
by Amazon